The Mad King

Edgar Rice Burroughs

PART I

I

A RUNAWAY HORSE

All Lustadt was in an uproar. The mad king had escaped. Little knots of excited men stood upon the street corners listening to each latest rumor concerning this most absorbing occurrence. Before the palace a great crowd surged to and fro, awaiting they knew not what.

For ten years no man of them had set eyes upon the face of the boy-king who had been hastened to the grim castle of Blentz upon the death of the old king, his father.

There had been murmurings then when the lad's uncle, Peter of Blentz, had announced to the people of Lutha the sudden mental affliction which had fallen upon his nephew, and more murmurings for a time after the announcement that Peter of Blentz had been appointed Regent during the lifetime of the young King Leopold, "or until God, in His infinite mercy, shall see fit to restore to us in full mental vigor our beloved monarch."

But ten years is a long time. The boy-king had become but a vague memory to the subjects who could recall him at all.

There were many, of course, in the capital city, Lustadt, who still retained a mental picture of the handsome boy who had ridden out nearly every morning from the palace gates beside the tall, martial figure of the old king, his father, for a canter across the broad plain which lies at the foot of the mountain town of Lustadt; but even these had long since given up hope that their young king would ever ascend his throne, or even that they should see him alive again.

Peter of Blentz had not proved a good or kind ruler. Taxes had doubled during his regency. Executives and judiciary, following the example of their chief, had become tyrannical and corrupt. For ten years there had been small joy in Lutha.

There had been whispered rumors off and on that the young king was dead these many years, but not even in whispers did the men of Lutha dare voice the name of him whom they believed had caused his death. For lesser things they had seen their friends and neighbors thrown into the hitherto long-unused dungeons of the royal castle.

And now came the rumor that Leopold of Lutha had escaped the Castle of Blentz and was roaming somewhere in the wild mountains or ravines upon the opposite side of the plain of Lustadt.

Peter of Blentz was filled with rage and, possibly, fear as well.

"I tell you, Coblich," he cried, addressing his dark-visaged minister of war, "there's more than coincidence in this matter. Someone has betrayed us. That he should have escaped upon the very eve of the arrival at Blentz of the new physician is most suspicious. None but you, Coblich, had knowledge of the part that Dr. Stein was destined to play in this matter," concluded Prince Peter pointedly.

Coblich looked the Regent full in the eye.

1

"Your highness wrongs not only my loyalty, but my intelligence," he said quietly, "by even so much as intimating that I have any guilty knowledge of Leopold's escape. With Leopold upon the throne of Lutha, where, think you, my prince, would old Coblich be?"

Peter smiled.

"You are right, Coblich," he said. "I know that you would not be such a fool; but whom, then, have we to thank?"

"The walls have ears, prince," replied Coblich, "and we have not always been as careful as we should in discussing the matter. Something may have come to the ears of old Von der Tann. I don't for a moment doubt but that he has his spies among the palace servants, or even the guard. You know the old fox has always made it a point to curry favor with the common soldiers. When he was minister of war he treated them better than he did his officers."

"It seems strange, Coblich, that so shrewd a man as you should have been unable to discover some irregularity in the political life of Prince Ludwig von der Tann before now," said the prince querulously. "He is the greatest menace to our peace and sovereignty. With Von der Tann out of the way there would be none powerful enough to question our right to the throne of Lutha—after poor Leopold passes away."

"You forget that Leopold has escaped," suggested Coblich, "and that there is no immediate prospect of his passing away."

"He must be retaken at once, Coblich!" cried Prince Peter of Blentz. "He is a dangerous maniac, and we must make this fact plain to the people—this and a thorough description of him. A handsome reward for his safe return to Blentz might not be out of the way, Coblich."

"It shall be done, your highness," replied Coblich. "And about Von der Tann? You have never spoken to me quite so—ah—er—pointedly before. He hunts a great deal in the Old Forest. It might be possible—in fact, it has happened, before—there are many accidents in hunting, are there not, your highness?"

"There are, Coblich," replied the prince, "and if Leopold is able he will make straight for the Tann, so that there may be two hunting together in a day or so, Coblich."

"I understand, your highness," replied the minister. "With your permission, I shall go at once and dispatch troops to search the forest for Leopold. Captain Maenck will command them."

"Good, Coblich! Maenck is a most intelligent and loyal officer. We must reward him well. A baronetcy, at least, if he handles this matter well," said Peter. "It might not be a bad plan to hint at as much to him, Coblich."

And so it happened that shortly thereafter Captain Ernst Maenck, in command of a troop of the Royal Horse Guards of Lutha, set out toward the Old Forest, which lies beyond the mountains that are visible upon the other side of the plain stretching out before Lustadt. At the same time other troopers rode in many directions along the highways and byways of Lutha, tacking placards upon trees and fence posts and beside the doors of every little rural post office.

The placard told of the escape of the mad king, offering a large reward for his safe return to Blentz.

2

It was the last paragraph especially which caused a young man, the following day in the little hamlet of Tafelberg, to whistle as he carefully read it over.

"I am glad that I am not the mad king of Lutha," he said as he paid the storekeeper for the gasoline he had just purchased and stepped into the gray roadster for whose greedy maw it was destined.

"Why, mein Herr?" asked the man.

"This notice practically gives immunity to whoever shoots down the king," replied the traveler. "Worse still, it gives such an account of the maniacal ferocity of the fugitive as to warrant anyone in shooting him on sight."

As the young man spoke the storekeeper had examined his face closely for the first time. A shrewd look came into the man's ordinarily stolid countenance. He leaned forward quite close to the other's ear.

"We of Lutha," he whispered, "love our 'mad king'—no reward could be offered that would tempt us to betray him. Even in self-protection we would not kill him, we of the mountains who remember him as a boy and loved his father and his grandfather, before him.

"But there are the scum of the low country in the army these days, who would do anything for money, and it is these that the king must guard against. I could not help but note that mein Herr spoke too perfect German for a foreigner. Were I in mein Herr's place, I should speak mostly the English, and, too, I should shave off the 'full, reddish-brown beard.'"

Whereupon the storekeeper turned hastily back into his shop, leaving Barney Custer of Beatrice, Nebraska, U.S.A., to wonder if all the inhabitants of Lutha were afflicted with a mental disorder similar to that of the unfortunate ruler.

"I don't wonder," soliloquized the young man, "that he advised me to shave off this ridiculous crop of alfalfa. Hang election bets, anyway; if things had gone half right I shouldn't have had to wear this badge of idiocy. And to think that it's got to be for a whole month longer! A year's a mighty long while at best, but a year in company with a full set of red whiskers is an eternity."

The road out of Tafelberg wound upward among tall trees toward the pass that would lead him across the next valley on his way to the Old Forest, where he hoped to find some excellent shooting. All his life Barney had promised himself that some day he should visit his mother's native land, and now that he was here he found it as wild and beautiful as she had said it would be.

Neither his mother nor his father had ever returned to the little country since the day, thirty years before, that the big American had literally stolen his bride away, escaping across the border but a scant half-hour ahead of the pursuing troop of Luthanian cavalry. Barney had often wondered why it was that neither of them would ever speak of those days, or of the early life of his mother, Victoria Rubinroth, though of the beauties of her native land Mrs. Custer never tired of talking.

Barney Custer was thinking of these things as his machine wound up the picturesque road. Just before him was a long, heavy grade, and as he took it with open muffler the chugging of his motor drowned the sound of pounding hoof beats rapidly approaching behind him.

It was not until he topped the grade that he heard anything unusual, and at the same instant a girl on horseback tore past him. The speed of the animal would have been enough to have told him that it was beyond the control of its frail rider, even without the added testimony of the broken bit that dangled beneath the tensely outstretched chin.

Foam flecked the beast's neck and shoulders. It was evident that the horse had been running for some distance, yet its speed was still that of the thoroughly frightened runaway.

The road at the point where the animal had passed Custer was cut from the hillside. At the left an embankment rose steeply to a height of ten or fifteen feet. On the right there was a drop of a hundred feet or more into a wooded ravine. Ahead, the road apparently ran quite straight and smooth for a considerable distance.

Barney Custer knew that so long as the road ran straight the girl might be safe enough, for she was evidently an excellent horsewoman; but he also knew that if there should be a sharp turn to the left ahead, the horse in his blind fright would in all probability dash headlong into the ravine below him.

There was but a single thing that the man might attempt if he were to save the girl from the almost certain death which seemed in store for her, since he knew that sooner or later the road would turn, as all mountain roads do. The chances that he must take, if he failed, could only hasten the girl's end. There was no alternative except to sit supinely by and see the fear-crazed horse carry its rider into eternity, and Barney Custer was not the sort for that role.

Scarcely had the beast come abreast of him than his foot leaped to the accelerator. Like a frightened deer the gray roadster sprang forward in pursuit. The road was narrow. Two machines could not have passed upon it. Barney took the outside that he might hold the horse away from the dangerous ravine.

At the sound of the whirring thing behind him the animal cast an affrighted glance in its direction, and with a little squeal of terror redoubled its frantic efforts to escape. The girl, too, looked back over her shoulder. Her face was very white, but her eyes were steady and brave.

Barney Custer smiled up at her in encouragement, and the girl smiled back at him.

"She's sure a game one," thought Barney.

Now she was calling to him. At first he could not catch her words above the pounding of the horse's hoofs and the noise of his motor. Presently he understood.

"Stop!" she cried. "Stop or you will be killed. The road turns to the left just ahead. You'll go into the ravine at that speed."

The front wheel of the roadster was at the horse's right flank. Barney stepped upon the accelerator a little harder. There was barely room between the horse and the edge of the road for the four wheels of the roadster, and Barney must be very careful not to touch the horse. The thought of that and what it would mean to the girl sent a cold shudder through Barney Custer's athletic frame.

4

The man cast a glance to his right. His machine drove from the left side, and he could not see the road at all over the right hand door. The sight of tree tops waving beneath him was all that was visible. Just ahead the road's edge rushed swiftly beneath the right-hand fender; the wheels on that side must have been on the very verge of the embankment.

Now he was abreast the girl. Just ahead he could see where the road disappeared around a corner of the bluff at the dangerous curve the girl had warned him against.

Custer leaned far out over the side of his car. The lunging of the horse in his stride, and the swaying of the leaping car carried him first close to the girl and then away again. With his right hand he held the car between the frantic horse and the edge of the embankment. His left hand, outstretched, was almost at the girl's waist. The turn was just before them.

"Jump!" cried Barney.

The girl fell backward from her mount, turning to grasp Custer's arm as it closed about her. At the same instant Barney closed the throttle, and threw all the weight of his body upon the foot brake.

The gray roadster swerved toward the embankment as the hind wheels skidded on the loose surface gravel. They were at the turn. The horse was just abreast the bumper. There was one chance in a thousand of making the turn were the running beast out of the way. There was still a chance if he turned ahead of them. If he did not turn—Barney hated to think of what must follow.

But it was all over in a second. The horse bolted straight ahead. Barney swerved the roadster to the turn. It caught the animal full in the side. There was a sickening lurch as the hind wheels slid over the embankment, and then the man shoved the girl from the running board to the road, and horse, man and roadster went over into the ravine.

A moment before a tall young man with a reddish-brown beard had stood at the turn of the road listening intently to the sound of the hurrying hoof beats and the purring of the racing motor car approaching from the distance. In his eyes lurked the look of the hunted. For a moment he stood in evident indecision, but just before the runaway horse and the pursuing machine came into view he slipped over the edge of the road to slink into the underbrush far down toward the bottom of the ravine.

When Barney pushed the girl from the running board she fell heavily to the road, rolling over several times, but in an instant she scrambled to her feet, hardly the worse for the tumble other than a few scratches.

Quickly she ran to the edge of the embankment, a look of immense relief coming to her soft, brown eyes as she saw her rescuer scrambling up the precipitous side of the ravine toward her.

"You are not killed?" she cried in German. "It is a miracle!"

"Not even bruised," reassured Barney. "But you? You must have had a nasty fall."

"I am not hurt at all," she replied. "But for you I should be lying dead, or terribly maimed down there at the bottom of that awful ravine at this very moment. It's awful." She drew her shoulders upward in a little shudder of horror. "But how did you escape? Even now I can scarce believe it possible."

"I'm quite sure I don't know how I did escape," said Barney, clambering over the rim of the road to her side. "That I had nothing to do with it I am positive. It was just luck. I simply dropped out onto that bush down there."

They were standing side by side, now peering down into the ravine where the car was visible, bottom side up against a tree, near the base of the declivity. The horse's head could be seen protruding from beneath the wreckage.

"I'd better go down and put him out of his misery," said Barney, "if he is not already dead."

"I think he is quite dead," said the girl. "I have not seen him move."

Just then a little puff of smoke arose from the machine, followed by a tongue of yellow flame. Barney had already started toward the horse.

"Please don't go," begged the girl. "I am sure that he is quite dead, and it wouldn't be safe for you down there now. The gasoline tank may explode any minute."

Barney stopped.

"Yes, he is dead all right," he said, "but all my belongings are down there. My guns, six-shooters and all my ammunition. And," he added ruefully, "I've heard so much about the brigands that infest these mountains."

The girl laughed.

"Those stories are really exaggerated," she said. "I was born in Lutha, and except for a few months each year have always lived here, and though I ride much I have never seen a brigand. You need not be afraid."

Barney Custer looked up at her quickly, and then he grinned. His only fear had been that he would not meet brigands, for Mr. Bernard Custer, Jr., was young and the spirit of Romance and Adventure breathed strong within him.

"Why do you smile?" asked the girl.

"At our dilemma," evaded Barney. "Have you paused to consider our situation?"

The girl smiled, too.

"It is most unconventional," she said. "On foot and alone in the mountains, far from home, and we do not even know each other's name."

"Pardon me," cried Barney, bowing low. "Permit me to introduce myself. I am," and then to the spirits of Romance and Adventure was added a third, the spirit of Deviltry, "I am the mad king of Lutha."

II

6

The effect of his words upon the girl were quite different from what he had expected. An American girl would have laughed, knowing that he but joked. This girl did not laugh. Instead her face went white, and she clutched her bosom with her two hands. Her brown eyes peered searchingly into the face of the man.

"Leopold!" she cried in a suppressed voice. "Oh, your majesty, thank God that you are free— and sane!"

Before he could prevent it the girl had seized his hand and pressed it to her lips.

Here was a pretty muddle! Barney Custer swore at himself inwardly for a boorish fool. What in the world had ever prompted him to speak those ridiculous words! And now how was he to unsay them without mortifying this beautiful girl who had just kissed his hand?

She would never forgive that—he was sure of it.

There was but one thing to do, however, and that was to make a clean breast of it. Somehow, he managed to stumble through his explanation of what had prompted him, and when he had finished he saw that the girl was smiling indulgently at him.

"It shall be Mr. Bernard Custer if you wish it so," she said; "but your majesty need fear nothing from Emma von der Tann. Your secret is as safe with me as with yourself, as the name of Von der Tann must assure you."

She looked to see the expression of relief and pleasure that her father's name should have brought to the face of Leopold of Lutha, but when he gave no indication that he had ever before heard the name she sighed and looked puzzled.

"Perhaps," she thought, "he doubts me. Or can it be possible that, after all, his poor mind is gone?"

"I wish," said Barney in a tone of entreaty, "that you would forgive and forget my foolish words, and then let me accompany you to the end of your journey."

"Whither were you bound when I became the means of wrecking your motor car?" asked the girl.

"To the Old Forest," replied Barney.

Now she was positive that she was indeed with the mad king of Lutha, but she had no fear of him, for since childhood she had heard her father scout the idea that Leopold was mad. For what other purpose would he hasten toward the Old Forest than to take refuge in her father's castle upon the banks of the Tann at the forest's verge?

"Thither was I bound also," she said, "and if you would come there quickly and in safety I can show you a short path across the mountains that my father taught me years ago. It touches the main road but once or twice, and much of the way passes through dense woods and undergrowth where an army might hide."

"Hadn't we better find the nearest town," suggested Barney, "where I can obtain some sort of conveyance to take you home?"

"It would not be safe," said the girl. "Peter of Blentz will have troops out scouring all Lutha about Blentz and the Old Forest until the king is captured."

Barney Custer shook his head despairingly.

"Won't you please believe that I am but a plain American?" he begged.

Upon the bole of a large wayside tree a fresh, new placard stared them in the face. Emma von der Tann pointed at one of the paragraphs.

"Gray eyes, brown hair, and a full reddish-brown beard," she read. "No matter who you may be," she said, "you are safer off the highways of Lutha than on them until you can find and use a razor."

"But I cannot shave until the fifth of November," said Barney.

Again the girl looked quickly into his eyes and again in her mind rose the question that had hovered there once before. Was he indeed, after all, quite sane?

"Then please come with me the safest way to my father's," she urged. "He will know what is best to do."

"He cannot make me shave," insisted Barney.

"Why do you wish not to shave?" asked the girl.

"It is a matter of my honor," he replied. "I had my choice of wearing a green wastebasket bonnet trimmed with red roses for six months, or a beard for twelve. If I shave off the beard before the fifth of November I shall be without honor in the sight of all men or else I shall have to wear the green bonnet. The beard is bad enough, but the bonnet—ugh!"

Emma von der Tann was now quite assured that the poor fellow was indeed quite demented, but she had seen no indications of violence as yet, though when that too might develop there was no telling. However, he was to her Leopold of Lutha, and her father's house had been loyal to him or his ancestors for three hundred years.

If she must sacrifice her life in the attempt, nevertheless still must she do all within her power to save her king from recapture and to lead him in safety to the castle upon the Tann.

"Come," she said; "we waste time here. Let us make haste, for the way is long. At best we cannot reach Tann by dark."

"I will do anything you wish," replied Barney, "but I shall never forgive myself for having caused you the long and tedious journey that lies before us. It would be perfectly safe to go to the nearest town and secure a rig."

Emma von der Tann had heard that it was always well to humor maniacs and she thought of it now. She would put the scheme to the test.

"The reason that I fear to have you go to the village," she said, "is that I am quite sure they would catch you and shave off your beard."

Barney started to laugh, but when he saw the deep seriousness of the girl's eyes he changed his mind. Then he recalled her rather peculiar insistence that he was a king, and it suddenly occurred to him that he had been foolish not to have guessed the truth before.

"That is so," he agreed; "I guess we had better do as you say," for he had determined that the best way to handle her would be to humor her—he had always heard that that was the proper method for handling the mentally defective. "Where is the—er—ah—sanatorium?" he blurted out at last.

"The what?" she asked. "There is no sanatorium near here, your majesty, unless you refer to the Castle of Blentz."

"Is there no asylum for the insane near by?"

"None that I know of, your majesty."

For a while they moved on in silence, each wondering what the other might do next.

Barney had evolved a plan. He would try and ascertain the location of the institution from which the girl had escaped and then as gently as possible lead her back to it. It was not safe for as beautiful a woman as she to be roaming through the forest in any such manner as this. He wondered what in the world the authorities at the asylum had been thinking of to permit her to ride out alone in the first place.

"From where did you ride today?" he blurted out suddenly.

"From Tann."

"That is where we are going now?"

"Yes, your majesty."

Barney drew a breath of relief. The way had become suddenly difficult and he took the girl's arm to help her down a rather steep place. At the bottom of the ravine there was a little brook.

"There used to be a fallen log across it here," said the girl. "How in the world am I ever to get across, your majesty?"

"If you call me that again, I shall begin to believe that I am a king," he humored her, "and then, being a king, I presume that it wouldn't be proper for me to carry you across, or would it? Never really having been a king, I do not know."

"I think," replied the girl, "that it would be eminently proper."

She had difficulty in keeping in mind the fact that this handsome, smiling young man was a dangerous maniac, though it was easy to believe that he was the king. In fact, he looked much as she had always pictured Leopold as looking. She had known him as a boy, and there were many paintings and photographs of his ancestors in her father's castle. She saw much resemblance between these and the young man.

9

The brook was very narrow, and the girl thought that it took the young man an unreasonably long time to carry her across, though she was forced to admit that she was far from uncomfortable in the strong arms that bore her so easily.

"Why, what are you doing?" she cried presently. "You are not crossing the stream at all. You are walking right up the middle of it!"

She saw his face flush, and then he turned laughing eyes upon her.

"I am looking for a safe landing," he said.

Emma von der Tann did not know whether to be frightened or amused. As her eyes met the clear, gray ones of the man she could not believe that insanity lurked behind that laughing, level gaze of her carrier. She found herself continually forgetting that the man was mad. He had turned toward the bank now, and a couple of steps carried them to the low sward that fringed the little brooklet. Here he lowered her to the ground.

"Your majesty is very strong," she said. "I should not have expected it after the years of confinement you have suffered."

"Yes," he said, realizing that he must humor her—it was difficult to remember that this lovely girl was insane. "Let me see, now just what was I in prison for? I do not seem to be able to recall it. In Nebraska, they used to hang men for horse stealing; so I am sure it must have been something else not quite so bad. Do you happen to know?"

"When the king, your father, died you were thirteen years old," the girl explained, hoping to reawaken the sleeping mind, "and then your uncle, Prince Peter of Blentz, announced that the shock of your father's death had unbalanced your mind. He shut you up in Blentz then, where you have been for ten years, and he has ruled as regent. Now, my father says, he has recently discovered a plot to take your life so that Peter may become king. But I suppose you learned of that, and because of it you escaped!"

"This Peter person is all-powerful in Lutha?" he asked.

"He controls the army," the girl replied.

"And you really believe that I am the mad king Leopold?"

"You are the king," she said in a convincing manner.

"You are a very brave young lady," he said earnestly. "If all the mad king's subjects were as loyal as you, and as brave, he would not have languished for ten years behind the walls of Blentz."

"I am a Von der Tann," she said proudly, as though that was explanation sufficient to account for any bravery or loyalty.

"Even a Von der Tann might, without dishonor, hesitate to accompany a mad man through the woods," he replied, "especially if she happened to be a very—a very—" He halted, flushing.

"A very what, your majesty?" asked the girl.

"A very young woman," he ended lamely.

Emma von der Tann knew that he had not intended saying that at all. Being a woman, she knew precisely what he had meant to say, and she discovered that she would very much have liked to hear him say it.

"Suppose," said Barney, "that Peter's soldiers run across us—what then?"

"They will take you back to Blentz, your majesty."

"And you?"

"I do not think that they will dare lay hands on me, though it is possible that Peter might do so. He hates my father even more now than he did when the old king lived."

"I wish," said Mr. Custer, "that I had gone down after my guns. Why didn't you tell me, in the first place, that I was a king, and that I might get you in trouble if you were found with me? Why, they may even take me for an emperor or a mikado—who knows? And then look at all the trouble we'd be in."

Which was Barney's way of humoring a maniac.

"And they might even shave off your beautiful beard."

Which was the girl's way.

"Do you think that you would like me better in the green wastebasket hat with the red roses?" asked Barney.

A very sad look came into the girl's eyes. It was pitiful to think that this big, handsome young man, for whose return to the throne all Lutha had prayed for ten long years, was only a silly half-wit. What might he not have accomplished for his people had this terrible misfortune not overtaken him! In every other way he seemed fitted to be the savior of his country. If she could but make him remember!

"Your majesty," she said, "do you not recall the time that your father came upon a state visit to my father's castle? You were a little boy then. He brought you with him. I was a little girl, and we played together. You would not let me call you 'highness,' but insisted that I should always call you Leopold. When I forgot you would accuse me of lese-majeste, and sentence me to—to punishment."

"What was the punishment?" asked Barney, noticing her hesitation and wishing to encourage her in the pretty turn her dementia had taken.

Again the girl hesitated; she hated to say it, but if it would help to recall the past to that poor, dimmed mind, it was her duty.

"Every time I called you 'highness' you made me give you a—a kiss," she almost whispered.

"I hope," said Barney, "that you will be guilty of lese-majeste often."

"We were little children then, your majesty," the girl reminded him.

Had he thought her of sound mind Mr. Custer might have taken advantage of his royal prerogatives on the spot, for the girl's lips were most tempting; but when he remembered the poor, weak mind, tears almost came to his eyes, and there sprang to his heart a great desire to protect and guard this unfortunate child.

"And when I was Crown Prince what were you, way back there in the beautiful days of our childhood?" asked Barney.

"Why, I was what I still am, your majesty," replied the girl. "Princess Emma von der Tann."

So the poor child, besides thinking him a king, thought herself a princess! She certainly was mad. Well, he would humor her.

"Then I should call you 'your highness,' shouldn't I?" he asked.

"You always called me Emma when we were children."

"Very well, then, you shall be Emma and I Leopold. Is it a bargain?"

"The king's will is law," she said.

They had come to a very steep hillside, up which the half-obliterated trail zigzagged toward the crest of a flat-topped hill. Barney went ahead, taking the girl's hand in his to help her, and thus they came to the top, to stand hand in hand, breathing heavily after the stiff climb.

The girl's hair had come loose about her temples and a lock was blowing over her face. Her cheeks were very red and her eyes bright. Barney thought he had never looked upon a lovelier picture. He smiled down into her eyes and she smiled back at him.

"I wished, back there a way," he said, "that that little brook had been as wide as the ocean— now I wish that this little hill had been as high as Mont Blanc."

"You like to climb?" she asked.

"I should like to climb forever—with you," he said seriously.

She looked up at him quickly. A reply was on her lips, but she never uttered it, for at that moment a ruffian in picturesque rags leaped out from behind a near-by bush, confronting them with leveled revolver. He was so close that the muzzle of the weapon almost touched Barney's face. In that the fellow made his mistake.

"You see," said Barney unexcitedly, "that I was right about the brigands after all. What do you want, my man?"

The man's eyes had suddenly gone wide. He stared with open mouth at the young fellow before him. Then a cunning look came into his eyes.

"I want you, your majesty," he said.

"Godfrey!" exclaimed Barney. "Did the whole bunch escape?"

"Quick!" growled the man. "Hold up your hands. The notice made it plain that you would be worth as much dead as alive, and I have no mind to lose you, so do not tempt me to kill you."

Barney's hands went up, but not in the way that the brigand had expected. Instead, one of them seized his weapon and shoved it aside, while with the other Custer planted a blow between his eyes and sent him reeling backward. The two men closed, fighting for possession of the gun. In the scrimmage it was exploded, but a moment later the American succeeded in wresting it from his adversary and hurled it into the ravine.

Striking at one another, the two surged backward and forward at the very edge of the hill, each searching for the other's throat. The girl stood by, watching the battle with wide, frightened eyes. If she could only do something to aid the king!

She saw a loose stone lying at a little distance from the fighters and hastened to procure it. If she could strike the brigand a single good blow on the side of the head, Leopold might easily overpower him. When she had gathered up the rock and turned back toward the two she saw that the man she thought to be the king was not much in the way of needing outside assistance. She could not but marvel at the strength and dexterity of this poor fellow who had spent almost half his life penned within the four walls of a prison. It must be, she thought, the superhuman strength with which maniacs are always credited.

Nevertheless, she hurried toward them with her weapon; but just before she reached them the brigand made a last mad effort to free himself from the fingers that had found his throat. He lunged backward, dragging the other with him. His foot struck upon the root of a tree, and together the two toppled over into the ravine.

As the girl hastened toward the spot where the two had disappeared, she was startled to see three troopers of the palace cavalry headed by an officer break through the trees at a short distance from where the battle had waged. The four men ran rapidly toward her.

"What has happened here?" shouted the officer to Emma von der Tann; and then, as he came closer: "Gott! Can it be possible that it is your highness?"

The girl paid no attention to the officer. Instead, she hurried down the steep embankment toward the underbrush into which the two men had fallen. There was no sound from below, and no movement in the bushes to indicate that a moment before two desperately battling human beings had dropped among them.

The soldiers were close upon the girl's heels, but it was she who first reached the two quiet figures that lay side by side upon the stony ground halfway down the hillside.

When the officer stopped beside her she was sitting on the ground holding the head of one of the combatants in her lap.

A little stream of blood trickled from a wound in the forehead. The officer stooped closer.

"He is dead?" he asked.

"The king is dead," replied the Princess Emma von der Tann, a little sob in her voice.

13

"The king!" exclaimed the officer; and then, as he bent lower over the white face: "Leopold!"

The girl nodded.

"We were searching for him," said the officer, "when we heard the shot." Then, arising, he removed his cap, saying in a very low voice: "The king is dead. Long live the king!"

III

AN ANGRY KING

The soldiers stood behind their officer. None of them had ever seen Leopold of Lutha—he had been but a name to them—they cared nothing for him; but in the presence of death they were awed by the majesty of the king they had never known.

The hands of Emma von der Tann were chafing the wrists of the man whose head rested in her lap.

"Leopold!" she whispered. "Leopold, come back! Mad king you may have been, but still you were king of Lutha—my father's king—my king."

The girl nearly cried out in shocked astonishment as she saw the eyes of the dead king open. But Emma von der Tann was quick-witted. She knew for what purpose the soldiers from the palace were scouring the country.

Had she not thought the king dead she would have cut out her tongue rather than reveal his identity to these soldiers of his great enemy. Now she saw that Leopold lived, and she must undo the harm she had innocently wrought. She bent lower over Barney's face, trying to hide it from the soldiers.

"Go away, please!" she called to them. "Leave me with my dead king. You are Peter's men. You do not care for Leopold, living or dead. Go back to your new king and tell him that this poor young man can never more stand between him and the throne."

The officer hesitated.

"We shall have to take the king's body with us, your highness," he said.

The officer evidently becoming suspicious, came closer, and as he did so Barney Custer sat up.

"Go away!" cried the girl, for she saw that the king was attempting to speak. "My father's people will carry Leopold of Lutha in state to the capital of his kingdom."

"What's all this row about?" he asked. "Can't you let a dead king alone if the young lady asks you to? What kind of a short sport are you, anyway? Run along, now, and tie yourself outside."

The officer smiled, a trifle maliciously perhaps.

14

"Ah," he said, "I am very glad indeed that you are not dead, your majesty."

Barney Custer turned his incredulous eyes upon the lieutenant.

"Et tu, Brute?" he cried in anguished accents, letting his head fall back into the girl's lap. He found it very comfortable there indeed.

The officer smiled and shook his head. Then he tapped his forehead meaningly.

"I did not know," he said to the girl, "that he was so bad. But come—it is some distance to Blentz, and the afternoon is already well spent. Your highness will accompany us."

"I?" cried the girl. "You certainly cannot be serious."

"And why not, your highness?" asked the officer. "We had strict orders to arrest not only the king, but any companions who may have been involved in his escape."

"I had nothing whatever to do with his escape," said the girl, "though I should have been only too glad to have aided him had the opportunity presented."

"King Peter may think differently," replied the man.

"The Regent, you mean?" the girl corrected him haughtily.

The officer shrugged his shoulders.

"Regent or King, he is ruler of Lutha nevertheless, and he would take away my commission were I to tell him that I had found a Von der Tann in company with the king and had permitted her to escape. Your blood convicts your highness."

"You are going to take me to Blentz and confine me there?" asked the girl in a very small voice and with wide incredulous eyes. "You would not dare thus to humiliate a Von der Tann?"

"I am very sorry," said the officer, "but I am a soldier, and soldiers must obey their superiors. My orders are strict. You may be thankful," he added, "that it was not Maenck who discovered you."

At the mention of the name the girl shuddered.

"In so far as it is in my power your highness and his majesty will be accorded every consideration of dignity and courtesy while under my escort. You need not entertain any fear of me," he concluded.

Barney Custer, during this, to him, remarkable dialogue, had risen to his feet, and assisted the girl in rising. Now he turned and spoke to the officer.

"This farce," he said, "has gone quite far enough. If it is a joke it is becoming a very sorry one. I am not a king. I am an American—Bernard Custer, of Beatrice, Nebraska, U.S.A. Look at me. Look at me closely. Do I look like a king?"

15

"Every inch, your majesty," replied the officer.

Barney looked at the man aghast.

"Well, I am not a king," he said at last, "and if you go to arresting me and throwing me into one of your musty old dungeons you will find that I am a whole lot more important than most kings. I'm an American citizen."

"Yes, your majesty," replied the officer, a trifle impatiently. "But we waste time in idle discussion. Will your majesty be so good as to accompany me without resistance?"

"If you will first escort this young lady to a place of safety," replied Barney.

"She will be quite safe at Blentz," said the lieutenant.

Barney turned to look at the girl, a question in his eyes. Before them stood the soldiers with drawn revolvers, and now at the summit of the hill a dozen more appeared in command of a sergeant. They were two against nearly a score, and Barney Custer was unarmed.

The girl shook her head.

"There, is no alternative, I am afraid, your majesty," she said.

Barney wheeled toward the officer.

"Very well, lieutenant," he said, "we will accompany you."

The party turned back up the hillside, leaving the dead bandit where he lay—the fellow's neck had been broken by the fall. A short distance from where the man had confronted them the two prisoners were brought to the main road where they saw still other troopers, and with them the horses of those who had gone into the forest on foot.

Barney and the girl were mounted on two of the animals, the soldiers who had ridden them clambering up behind two of their comrades. A moment later the troop set out along the road which leads to Blentz.

The prisoners rode near the center of the column, surrounded by troopers. For a time they were both silent. Barney was wondering if he had accidentally tumbled into the private grounds of Lutha's largest madhouse, or if, in reality, these people mistook him for the young king—it seemed incredible.

It had commenced slowly to dawn upon him that perhaps the girl was not crazy after all. Had not the officer addressed her as "your highness"? Now that he thought upon it he recalled that she did have quite a haughty and regal way with her at times, especially so when she had addressed the officer.

Of course she might be mad, after all, and possibly the bandit, too, but it seemed unbelievable that the officer was mad and his entire troop of cavalry should be composed of maniacs, yet they all persisted in speaking and acting as though he were indeed the mad king of Lutha and the young girl at his side a princess.

16

From pitying the girl he had come to feel a little bit in awe of her. To the best of his knowledge he had never before associated with a real princess. When he recalled that he had treated her as he would an ordinary mortal, and that he had thought her demented, and had tried to humor her mad whims, he felt very foolish indeed.

Presently he turned a sheepish glance in her direction, to find her looking at him. He saw her flush slightly as his eyes met hers.

"Can your highness ever forgive me?" he asked.

"Forgive you!" she cried in astonishment. "For what, your majesty?"

"For thinking you insane, and for getting you into this horrible predicament," he replied. "But especially for thinking you insane."

"Did you think me mad?" she asked in wide-eyed astonishment.

"When you insisted that I was a king, yes," he replied. "But now I begin to believe that it must be I who am mad, after all, or else I bear a remarkable resemblance to Leopold of Lutha."

"You do, your majesty," replied the girl.

Barney saw it was useless to attempt to convince them and so he decided to give up for the time.

"Have me king, if you will," he said, "but please do not call me 'your majesty' any more. It gets on my nerves."

"Your will is law—Leopold," replied the girl, hesitating prettily before the familiar name, "but do not forget your part of the compact."

He smiled at her. A princess wasn't half so terrible after all.

"And your will shall be my law, Emma," he said.

It was almost dark when they came to Blentz. The castle lay far up on the side of a steep hill above the town. It was an ancient pile, but had been maintained in an excellent state of repair. As Barney Custer looked up at the grim towers and mighty, buttressed walls his heart sank. It had taken the mad king ten years to make his escape from that gloomy and forbidding pile!

"Poor child," he murmured, thinking of the girl.

Before the barbican the party was halted by the guard. An officer with a lantern stepped out upon the lowered portcullis. The lieutenant who had captured them rode forward to meet him.

"A detachment of the Royal Horse Guards escorting His Majesty the King, who is returning to Blentz," he said in reply to the officer's sharp challenge.

"The king!" exclaimed the officer. "You have found him?" and he advanced with raised lantern searching for the monarch.

17

"At last," whispered Barney to the girl at his side, "I shall be vindicated. This man, at least, who is stationed at Blentz must know his king by sight."

The officer came quite close, holding his lantern until the rays fell full in Barney's face. He scrutinized the young man for a moment. There was neither humility nor respect in his manner, so that the American was sure that the fellow had discovered the imposture.

From the bottom of his heart he hoped so. Then the officer swung the lantern until its light shone upon the girl.

"And who's the wench with him?" he asked the officer who had found them.

The man was standing close beside Barney's horse, and the words were scarce out of his month when the American slipped from his saddle to the portcullis and struck the officer full in the face.

"She is the Princess von der Tann, you boor," said Barney, "and let that help you remember it in future."

The officer scrambled to his feet, white with rage. Whipping out his sword he rushed at Barney.

"You shall die for that, you half-wit," he cried.

Lieutenant Butzow, he of the Royal Horse, rushed forward to prevent the assault and Emma von der Tann sprang from her saddle and threw herself in front of Barney.

Butzow grasped the other officer's arm.

"Are you mad, Schonau?" he cried. "Would you kill the king?"

The fellow tugged to escape the grasp of Butzow. He was crazed with anger.

"Why not?" he bellowed. "You were a fool not to have done it yourself. Maenck will do it and get a baronetcy. It will mean a captaincy for me at least. Let me at him—no man can strike Karl Schonau and live."

"The king is unarmed," cried Emma von der Tann. "Would you murder him in cold blood?"

"He shall not murder him at all, your highness," said Lieutenant Butzow quietly. "Give me your sword, Lieutenant Schonau. I place you under arrest. What you have just said will not please the Regent when it is reported to him. You should keep your head better when you are angry."

"It is the truth," growled Schonau, regretting that his anger had led him into a disclosure of the plot against the king's life, but like most weak characters fearing to admit himself in error even more than he feared the consequences of his rash words.

"Do you intend taking my sword?" asked Schonau suddenly, turning toward Lieutenant Butzow standing beside him.

"We will forget the whole occurrence, lieutenant," replied Butzow, "if you will promise not to harm his majesty, or offer him or the Princess von der Tann further humiliation. Their position is sufficiently unpleasant without our adding to the degradation of it."

"Very well," grumbled Schonau. "Pass on into the courtyard."

Barney and the girl remounted and the little cavalcade moved forward through the ballium and the great gate into the court beyond.

"Did you notice," said Barney to the princess, "that even he believes me to be the king? I cannot fathom it."

Within the castle they were met by a number of servants and soldiers. An officer escorted them to the great hall, and presently a dark visaged captain of cavalry entered and approached them. Butzow saluted.

"His Majesty, the King," he announced, "has returned to Blentz. In accordance with the commands of the Regent I deliver his august person into your safe keeping, Captain Maenck."

Maenck nodded. He was looking at Barney with evident curiosity.

"Where did you find him?" he asked Butzow.

He made no pretense of according to Barney the faintest indication of the respect that is supposed to be due to those of royal blood. Barney commenced to hope that he had finally come upon one who would know that he was not king.

Butzow recounted the details of the finding of the king. As he spoke, Maenck's eyes, restless and furtive, seemed to be appraising the personal charms of the girl who stood just back of Barney.

The American did not like the appearance of the officer, but he saw that he was evidently supreme at Blentz, and he determined to appeal to him in the hope that the man might believe his story and untangle the ridiculous muddle that a chance resemblance to a fugitive monarch had thrown him and the girl into.

"Captain," said Barney, stepping closer to the officer, "there has been a mistake in identity here. I am not the king. I am an American traveling for pleasure in Lutha. The fact that I have gray eyes and wear a full reddish-brown beard is my only offense. You are doubtless familiar with the king's appearance and so you at least have already seen that I am not his majesty.

"Not being the king, there is no cause to detain me longer, and as I am not a fugitive and never have been, this young lady has been guilty of no misdemeanor or crime in being in my company. Therefore she too should be released. In the name of justice and common decency I am sure that you will liberate us both at once and furnish the Princess von der Tann, at least, with a proper escort to her home."

Maenck listened in silence until Barney had finished, a half smile upon his thick lips.

"I am commencing to believe that you are not so crazy as we have all thought," he said. "Certainly," and he let his eyes rest upon Emma von der Tann, "you are not mentally deficient in so far as your judgment of a good-looking woman is concerned. I could not have made a better selection myself.

"As for my familiarity with your appearance, you know as well as I that I have never seen you before. But that is not necessary—you conform perfectly to the printed description of you with which the kingdom is flooded. Were that not enough, the fact that you were discovered with old Von der Tann's daughter is sufficient to remove the least doubt as to your identity."

"You are governor of Blentz," cried Barney, "and yet you say that you have never seen the king?"

"Certainly," replied Maenck. "After you escaped the entire personnel of the garrison here was changed, even the old servants to a man were withdrawn and others substituted. You will have difficulty in again escaping, for those who aided you before are no longer here."

"There is no man in the castle of Blentz who has ever seen the king?" asked Barney.

"None who has seen him before tonight," replied Maenck. "But were we in doubt we have the word of the Princess Emma that you are Leopold. Did she not admit it to you, Butzow?"

"When she thought his majesty dead she admitted it," replied Butzow.

"We gain nothing by discussing the matter," said Maenck shortly. "You are Leopold of Lutha. Prince Peter says that you are mad. All that concerns me is that you do not escape again, and you may rest assured that while Ernst Maenck is governor of Blentz you shall not escape and go at large again.

"Are the royal apartments in readiness for his majesty, Dr. Stein?" he concluded, turning toward a rat-faced little man with bushy whiskers, who stood just behind him.

The query was propounded in an ironical tone, and with a manner that made no pretense of concealing the contempt of the speaker for the man he thought the king.

The eyes of the Princess Emma were blazing as she caught the scant respect in Maenck's manner. She looked quickly toward Barney to see if he intended rebuking the man for his impertinence. She saw that the king evidently intended overlooking Maenck's attitude. But Emma von der Tann was of a different mind.

She had seen Maenck several times at social functions in the capital. He had even tried to win a place in her favor, but she had always disliked him, even before the nasty stories of his past life had become common gossip, and within the year she had won his hatred by definitely indicating to him that he was persona non grata, in so far as she was concerned. Now she turned upon him, her eyes flashing with indignation.

"Do you forget, sir, that you address the king?" she cried. "That you are without honor I have heard men say, and I may truly believe it now that I have seen what manner of man you are. The most lowly-bred boor in all Lutha would not be so ungenerous as to take advantage of his king's helplessness to heap indignities upon him.

"Leopold of Lutha shall come into his own some day, and my dearest hope is that his first act may be to mete out to such as you the punishment you deserve."

20

Maenck paled in anger. His fingers twitched nervously, but he controlled his temper remarkably well, biding his time for revenge.

"Take the king to his apartments, Stein," he commanded curtly, "and you, Lieutenant Butzow, accompany them with a guard, nor leave until you see that he is safely confined. You may return here afterward for my further instructions. In the meantime I wish to examine the king's mistress."

For a moment tense silence reigned in the apartment after Maenck had delivered his wanton insult.

Emma von der Tann, her little chin high in the air, stood straight and haughty, nor was there any sign in her expression to indicate that she had heard the man's words.

Barney was the first to take cognizance of them.

"You cur!" he cried, and took a step toward Maenck. "You're going to eat that, word for word."

Maenck stepped back, his hand upon his sword. Butzow laid a hand upon Barney's arm.

"Don't, your majesty," he implored, "it will but make your position more unpleasant, nor will it add to the safety of the Princess von der Tann for you to strike him now."

Barney shook himself free from Butzow, and before either Stein or the lieutenant could prevent had sprung upon Maenck.

The latter had not been quick enough with his sword, so that Barney had struck him twice, heavily in the face before the officer was able to draw. Butzow had sprung to the king's side, and was attempting to interpose himself between Maenck and the American. In a moment more the sword of the infuriated captain would be in the king's heart. Barney turned the first thrust with his forearm.

"Stop!" cried Butzow to Maenck. "Are you mad, that you would kill the king?"

Maenck lunged again, viciously, at the unprotected body of his antagonist.

"Die, you pig of an idiot!" he screamed.

Butzow saw that the man really meant to murder Leopold. He seized Barney by the shoulder and whirled him backward. At the same instant his own sword leaped from his scabbard, and now Maenck found himself facing grim steel in the hand of a master swordsman.

The governor of Blentz drew back from the touch of that sharp point.

"What do you mean?" he cried. "This is mutiny."

"When I received my commission," replied Butzow, quietly, "I swore to protect the person of the king with my life, and while I live no man shall affront Leopold of Lutha in my presence, or threaten his safety else he accounts to me for his act. Return your sword, Captain Maenck, nor ever again draw it against the king while I be near."

Slowly Maenck sheathed his weapon. Black hatred for Butzow and the man he was protecting smoldered in his eyes.

"If he wishes peace," said Barney, "let him apologize to the princess."

"You had better apologize, captain," counseled Butzow, "for if the king should command me to do so I should have to compel you to," and the lieutenant half drew his sword once more.

There was something in Butzow's voice that warned Maenck that his subordinate would like nothing better than the king's command to run him through.

He well knew the fame of Butzow's sword arm, and having no stomach for an encounter with it he grumbled an apology.

"And don't let it occur again," warned Barney.

"Come," said Dr. Stein, "your majesty should be in your apartments, away from all excitement, if we are to effect a cure, so that you may return to your throne quickly."

Butzow formed the soldiers about the American, and the party moved silently out of the great hall, leaving Captain Maenck and Princess Emma von der Tann its only occupants.

Barney cast a troubled glance toward Maenck, and half hesitated.

"I am sorry, your majesty," said Butzow in a low voice, "but you must accompany us. In this the governor of Blentz is well within his authority, and I must obey him."

"Heaven help her!" murmured Barney.

"The governor will not dare harm her," said Butzow. "Your majesty need entertain no apprehension."

"I wouldn't trust him," replied the American. "I know his kind."

IV

BARNEY FINDS A FRIEND

After the party had left the room Maenck stood looking at the princess for several seconds. A cunning expression supplanted the anger that had shown so plainly upon his face but a moment before. The girl had moved to one side of the apartment and was pretending an interest in a large tapestry that covered the wall at that point. Maenck watched her with greedy eyes. Presently he spoke.

"Let us be friends," he said. "You shall be my guest at Blentz for a long time. I doubt if Peter will care to release you soon, for he has no love for your father—and it will be easier for both if we establish pleasant relations from the beginning. What do you say?"

"I shall not be at Blentz long," she replied, not even looking in Maenck's direction, "though while I am it shall be as a prisoner and not as a guest. It is incredible that one could believe me willing to pose as the guest of a traitor, even were he less impossible than the notorious and infamous Captain Maenck."

Maenck smiled. He was one of those who rather pride themselves upon the possession of racy reputations. He walked across the room to a bell cord which he pulled. Then he turned toward the girl again.

"I have given you an opportunity," he said, "to lighten the burdens of your captivity. I hoped that you would be sensible and accept my advances of friendship voluntarily," and he emphasized the word "voluntarily," "but—"

He shrugged his shoulders.

A servant had entered the apartment in response to Maenck's summons.

"Show the Princess von der Tann to her apartments," he commanded with a sinister tone.

The man, who was in the livery of Peter of Blentz, bowed, and with a deferential sign to the girl led the way from the room. Emma von der Tann followed her guide up a winding stairway which spiraled within a tower at the end of a long passage. On the second floor of the castle the servant led her to a large and beautifully furnished suite of three rooms—a bedroom, dressing-room and boudoir. After showing her the rooms that were to be hers the servant left her alone.

As soon as he had gone the Princess von der Tann took another turn through the suite, looking to the doors and windows to ascertain how securely she might barricade herself against unwelcome visitors.

She found that the three rooms lay in an angle of the old, moss-covered castle wall.

The bedroom and dressing-room were connected by a doorway, and each in turn had another door opening into the boudoir. The only connection with the corridor without was through a single doorway from the boudoir. This door was equipped with a massive bolt, which, when she had shot it, gave her a feeling of immense relief and security. The windows were all too high above the court on one side and the moat upon the other to cause her the slightest apprehension of danger from the outside.

The girl found the boudoir not only beautiful, but extremely comfortable and cozy. A huge log-fire blazed upon the hearth, and, though it was summer, its warmth was most welcome, for the night was chill. Across the room from the fireplace a full length oil of a former Blentz princess looked down in arrogance upon the unwilling occupant of the room. It seemed to the girl that there was an expression of annoyance upon the painted countenance that another, and an enemy of her house, should be making free with her belongings. She wondered a little, too, that this huge oil should have been hung in a lady's boudoir. It seemed singularly out of place.

"If she would but smile," thought Emma von der Tann, "she would detract less from the otherwise pleasant surroundings, but I suppose she serves her purpose in some way, whatever it may be."

There were papers, magazines and books upon the center table and more books upon a low tier of shelves on either side of the fireplace. The girl tried to amuse herself by reading, but she found her thoughts continually reverting to the unhappy situation of the king, and her eyes momentarily wandered to the cold and repellent face of the Blentz princess.

Finally she wheeled a great armchair near the fireplace, and with her back toward the portrait made a final attempt to submerge her unhappy thoughts in a current periodical.

When Barney and his escort reached the apartments that had been occupied by the king of Lutha before his escape, Butzow and the soldiers left him in company with Dr. Stein and an old servant, whom the doctor introduced as his new personal attendant.

"Your majesty will find him a very attentive and faithful servant," said Stein. "He will remain with you and administer your medicine at proper intervals."

"Medicine?" ejaculated Barney. "What in the world do I need of medicine? There is nothing the matter with me."

Stein smiled indulgently.

"Ah, your majesty," he said, "if you could but realize the sad affliction that clouds your life! You may never sit upon your throne until the last trace of this sinister mental disorder is eradicated, so take your medicine voluntarily, or otherwise Joseph will be compelled to administer it by force. Remember, sire, that only through this treatment will you be able to leave Blentz."

After Stein had left the room Joseph bolted the door behind him. Then he came to where Barney stood in the center of the apartment, and dropping to his knees took the young man's hand in his and kissed it.

"God has been good indeed, your majesty," he whispered. "It was He who made it possible for old Joseph to deceive them and find his way to your side."

"Who are you, my man?" asked Barney.

"I am from Tann," whispered the old man, in a very low voice. "His highness, the prince, found the means to obtain service for me with the new retinue that has replaced the old which permitted your majesty's escape. There was another from Tann among the former servants here.

"It was through his efforts that you escaped before, you will recall. I have seen Fritz and learned from him the way, so that if your majesty does not recall it it will make no difference, for I know it well, having been over it three times already since I came here, to be sure that when the time came that they should recapture you I might lead you out quickly before they could slay you."

"You really think that they intend murdering me?"

"There is no doubt about it, your majesty," replied the old man. "This very bottle"—Joseph touched the phial which Stein had left upon the table—"contains the means whereby, through my hands, you were to be slowly poisoned."

"Do you know what it is?"

"Bichloride of mercury, your majesty. One dose would have been sufficient, and after a few days—perhaps a week—you would have died in great agony."

Barney shuddered.

"But I am not the king, Joseph," said the young man, "so even had they succeeded in killing me it would have profited them nothing."

Joseph shook his head sadly.

"Your majesty will pardon the presumption of one who loves him," he said, "if he makes so bold as to suggest that your majesty must not again deny that he is king. That only tends to corroborate the contention of Prince Peter that your majesty is not—er, just sane, and so, incompetent to rule Lutha. But we of Tann know differently, and with the help of the good God we will place your majesty upon the throne which Peter has kept from you all these years."

Barney sighed. They were determined that he should be king whether he would or no. He had often thought he would like to be a king; but now the realization of his boyish dreaming which seemed so imminent bade fair to be almost anything than pleasant.

Barney suddenly realized that the old fellow was talking. He was explaining how they might escape. It seemed that a secret passage led from this very chamber to the vaults beneath the castle and from there through a narrow tunnel below the moat to a cave in the hillside far beyond the structure.

"They will not return again tonight to see your majesty," said Joseph, "and so we had best make haste to leave at once. I have a rope and swords in readiness. We shall need the rope to make our way down the hillside, but let us hope that we shall not need the swords."

"I cannot leave Blentz," said Barney, "unless the Princess Emma goes with us."

"The Princess Emma!" cried the old man. "What Princess Emma?"

"Princess von der Tann," replied Barney. "Did you not know that she was captured with me!"

The old man was visibly affected by the knowledge that his young mistress was a prisoner within the walls of Blentz. He seemed torn by conflicting emotions—his duty toward his king and his love for the daughter of his old master. So it was that he seemed much relieved when he found that Barney insisted upon saving the girl before any thought of their own escape should be taken into consideration.

"My first duty, your majesty," said Joseph, "is to bring you safely out of the hands of your enemies, but if you command me to try to bring your betrothed with us I am sure that his highness, Prince Ludwig, would be the last to censure me for deviating thus from his instructions, for if he loves another more than he loves his king it is his daughter, the beautiful Princess Emma."

"What do you mean, Joseph," asked Barney, "by referring to the princess as my betrothed? I never saw her before today."

25

"It has slipped your majesty's mind," said the old man sadly; "but you and my young mistress were betrothed many years ago while you were yet but children. It was the old king's wish that you wed the daughter of his best friend and most loyal subject."

Here was a pretty pass, indeed, thought Barney. It was sufficiently embarrassing to be mistaken for the king, but to be thrown into this false position in company with a beautiful young woman to whom the king was engaged to be married, and who, with the others, thought him to be the king, was quite the last word in impossible positions.

Following this knowledge there came to Barney the first pangs of regret that he was not really the king, and then the realization, so sudden that it almost took his breath away, that the girl was very beautiful and very much to be desired. He had not thought about the matter until her utter impossibility was forced upon him.

It was decided that Joseph should leave the king's apartment at once and discover in what part of the castle Emma von der Tann was imprisoned. Their further plans were to depend upon the information gained by the old man during his tour of investigation of the castle.

In the interval of his absence Barney paced the length of his prison time and time again. He thought the fellow would never return. Perhaps he had been detected in the act of spying, and was himself a prisoner in some other part of the castle! The thought came to Barney like a blow in the face, for he realized that then he would be entirely at the mercy of his captors, and that there would be none to champion the cause of the Princess von der Tann.

When his nervous tension had about reached the breaking point there came a sound of stealthy movement just outside the door of his room. Barney halted close to the massive panels. He heard a key fitted quietly and then the lock grated as it turned.

Barney thought that they had surely detected Joseph's duplicity and had come to make short work of the king before other traitors arose in their midst entirely to frustrate their plans. The young American stepped to the wall behind the door that he might be out of sight of whoever entered. Should it prove other than Joseph, might the Lord help them! The clenched fists, square-set chin, and gleaming gray eyes of the prisoner presaged no good for any incoming enemy.

Slowly the door swung open and a man entered the room. Barney breathed a deep sigh of relief—it was Joseph.

"Well?" cried the young man from behind him, and Joseph started as though Peter of Blentz himself had laid an accusing finger upon his shoulder. "What news?"

"Your majesty," gasped Joseph, "how you did startle me! I found the apartments of the princess, sire. There is a bare chance that we may succeed in rescuing her, but a very bare one, indeed.

"We must traverse a main corridor of the castle to reach her suite, and then return by the same way. It will be a miracle if we are not discovered; but the worst of it is that next to her apartments, and between them and your majesty's, are the apartments of Captain Maenck.

"He is sure to be there and officers and servants may be coming and going throughout the entire night, for the man is a convivial fellow, sitting at cards and drink until sunrise nearly every day."

"And when we have brought the princess in safety to my quarters," asked Barney, "what then? How shall we conduct her from the castle? You have not told me that as yet."

The old man explained then the plan of escape. It seemed that one of the two huge tile panels that flanked the fireplace on either side was in reality a door hiding the entrance to a shaft that rose from the vaults beneath the castle to the roof. At each floor there was a similar secret door concealing the mouth of the passage. From the vaults a corridor led through another secret panel to the tunnel that wound downward to the cave in the hillside.

"Beyond that we shall find horses, your majesty," concluded the old man. "They have been hidden in the woods since I came to Blentz. Each day I go there to water and feed them."

During the servant's explanation Barney had been casting about in his mind for some means of rescuing the princess without so great risk of detection, and as the plan of the secret passageway became clear to him he thought that he saw a way to accomplish the thing with comparative safety in so far as detection was concerned.

"Who occupies the floor above us, Joseph?" he asked.

"It is vacant," replied the old man.

"Good! Come, show me the entrance to the shaft," directed Barney.

"You will go without attempting to succor the Princess Emma?" exclaimed the old fellow in ill-concealed chagrin.

"Far from it," replied Barney. "Bring your rope and the swords. I think we are going to find the rescuing of the Princess Emma the easiest part of our adventure."

The old man shook his head, but went to another room of the suite, from which he presently emerged with a stout rope about fifty feet in length and two swords. As he buckled one of the weapons to Barney his eyes fell upon the American's seal ring that encircled the third finger of his left hand.

"The Royal Ring of Lutha!" exclaimed Joseph. "Where is it, your majesty? What has become of the Royal Ring of the Kings of Lutha?"

"I'm sure I don't know, Joseph," replied the young man. "Should I be wearing a royal ring?"

"The profaning miscreants!" cried Joseph. "They have dared to filch from you the great ring that has been handed down from king to king for three hundred years. When did they take it from you?"

"I have never seen it, Joseph," replied the young man, "and possibly this fact may assure you where all else has failed that I am no true king of Lutha, after all."

"Ah, no, your majesty," replied the old servitor; "it but makes assurance doubly sure as to your true identity, for the fact that you have not the ring is positive proof that you are king

27

and that they have sought to hide the fact by removing the insignia of your divine right to rule in Lutha."

Barney could not but smile at the old fellow's remarkable logic. He saw that nothing short of a miracle would ever convince Joseph that he was not the real monarch, and so, as matters of greater importance were to the fore, he would have allowed the subject to drop had not the man attempted to recall to the impoverished memory of his king a recollection of the historic and venerated relic of the dead monarchs of Lutha.

"Do you not remember, sir," he asked, "the great ruby that glared, blood-red from its center, and the four sets of golden wings that formed the setting? From the blood of Charlemagne was the ruby made, so history tells us, and the setting represented the protecting wings of the power of the kings of Lutha spread to the four points of the compass. Now your majesty must recall the royal ring, I am sure."

Barney only shook his head, much to Joseph's evident sorrow.

"Never mind the ring, Joseph," said the young man. "Bring your rope and lead me to the floor above."

"The floor above? But, your majesty, we cannot reach the vaults and tunnel by going upward!"

"You forget, Joseph, that we are going to fetch the Princess Emma first."

"But she is not on the floor above us, sire; she is upon the same floor as we are," insisted the old man, hesitating.

"Joseph, who do you think I am?" asked Barney.

"You are the king, my lord," replied the old man.

"Then do as your king commands," said the American sharply.

Joseph turned with dubious mutterings and approached the tiled panel at the left of the fireplace. Here he fumbled about for a moment until his fingers found the hidden catch that held the cunningly devised door in place. An instant later the panel swung inward before his touch, and standing to one side, the old fellow bowed low as he ushered Barney into the Stygian darkness of the space beyond their vision.

Joseph halted the young man just within the doorway, cautioning him against the danger of falling into the shaft, then he closed the panel, and a moment later had found the lantern he had hidden there and lighted it. The rays disclosed to the American the rough masonry of the interior of a narrow, well-built shaft. A rude ladder standing upon a narrow ledge beside him extended upward to lose itself in the shadows above. At its foot the top of another ladder was visible protruding through the opening from the floor beneath.

No sooner had Joseph's lantern shown him the way than Barney was ascending the ladder toward the floor above. At the next landing he waited for the old man.

Joseph put out the light and placed the lantern where they could easily find it upon their return. Then he cautiously slipped the catch that held the panel in place and slowly opened the door until a narrow line of lesser darkness showed from without.

28

For a moment they stood in silence listening for any sound from the chamber beyond, but as nothing occurred to indicate that the apartment was occupied the old man opened the portal a trifle further, and finally far enough to permit his body to pass through. Barney followed him. They found themselves in a large, empty chamber, identical in size and shape with that which they had just quitted upon the floor below.

From this the two passed into the corridor beyond, and thence to the apartments at the far end of the wing, directly over those occupied by Emma von der Tann.

Barney hastened to a window overlooking the moat. By leaning far out he could see the light from the princess's chamber shining upon the sill. He wished that the light was not there, for the window was in plain view of the guard on the lookout upon the barbican.

Suddenly he caught the sound of voices from the chamber beneath. For an instant he listened, and then, catching a few words of the dialogue, he turned hurriedly toward his companion.

"The rope, Joseph! And for God's sake be quick about it."

V

THE ESCAPE

For half an hour the Princess von der Tann succeeded admirably in immersing herself in the periodical, to the exclusion of her unhappy thoughts and the depressing influence of the austere countenance of the Blentz Princess hanging upon the wall behind her.

But presently she became unaccountably nervous. At the slightest sound from the palace-life on the floor below she would start up with a tremor of excitement. Once she heard footsteps in the corridor before her door, but they passed on, and she thought she discerned the click of a latch a short distance further on along the passageway.

Again she attempted to gather up the thread of the article she had been reading, but she was unsuccessful. A stealthy scratching brought her round quickly, staring in the direction of the great portrait. The girl would have sworn that she had heard a noise within her chamber. She shuddered at the thought that it might have come from that painted thing upon the wall.

What was the matter with her? Was she losing all control of herself to be frightened like a little child by ghostly noises?

She tried to return to her reading, but for the life of her she could not keep her eyes off the silent, painted woman who stared and stared and stared in cold, threatening silence upon this ancient enemy of her house.

Presently the girl's eyes went wide in horror. She could feel the scalp upon her head contract with fright. Her terror-filled gaze was frozen upon that awful figure that loomed so large and sinister above her, for the thing had moved! She had seen it with her own eyes. There could be no mistake—no hallucination of overwrought nerves about it. The Blentz Princess was moving slowly toward her!

Like one in a trance the girl rose from her chair, her eyes glued upon the awful apparition that seemed creeping upon her. Slowly she withdrew toward the opposite side of the chamber. As the painting moved more quickly the truth flashed upon her—it was mounted on a door.

The crack of the door widened and beyond it the girl saw dimly, eyes fastened upon her. With difficulty she restrained a shriek. The portal swung wide and a man in uniform stepped into the room.

It was Maenck.

Emma von der Tann gazed in unveiled abhorrence upon the leering face of the governor of Blentz.

"What means this intrusion?" cried the girl.

"What would you have here?"

"You," replied Maenck.

The girl crimsoned.

Maenck regarded her sneeringly.

"You coward!" she cried. "Leave my apartments at once. Not even Peter of Blentz would countenance such abhorrent treatment of a prisoner."

"You do not know Peter, my dear," responded Maenck. "But you need not fear. You shall be my wife. Peter has promised me a baronetcy for the capture of Leopold, and before I am done I shall be made a prince, of that you may rest assured, so you see I am not so bad a match after all."

He crossed over toward her and would have laid a rough hand upon her arm.

The girl sprang away from him, running to the opposite side of the library table at which she had been reading. Maenck started to pursue her, when she seized a heavy, copper bowl that stood upon the table and hurled it full in his face. The missile struck him a glancing blow, but the edge laid open the flesh of one cheek almost to the jaw bone.

With a cry of pain and rage Captain Ernst Maenck leaped across the table full upon the young girl. With vicious, murderous fingers he seized upon her fair throat, shaking her as a terrier might shake a rat. Futilely the girl struck at the hate-contorted features so close to hers.

"Stop!" she cried. "You are killing me."

The fingers released their hold.

"No," muttered the man, and dragged the princess roughly across the room.

Half a dozen steps he had taken when there came a sudden crash of breaking glass from the window across the chamber. Both turned in astonishment to see the figure of a man leap into the room, carrying the shattered crystal and the casement with him. In one hand was a naked sword.

"The king!" cried Emma von der Tann.

"The devil!" muttered Maenck, as, dropping the girl, he scurried toward the great painting from behind which he had found ingress to the chambers of the princess.

Maenck was a coward, and he had seen murder in the eyes of the man rushing upon him. With a bound he reached the picture which still stood swung wide into the room.

Barney was close behind him, but fear lent wings to the governor of Blentz, so that he was able to dart into the passage behind the picture and slam the door behind him a moment before the infuriated man was upon him.

The American clawed at the edge of the massive frame, but all to no avail. Then he raised his sword and slashed the canvas, hoping to find a way into the place beyond, but mighty oaken panels barred his further progress. With a whispered oath he turned back toward the girl.

"Thank Heaven that I was in time, Emma," he cried.

"Oh, Leopold, my king, but at what a price," replied the girl. "He will return now with others and kill you. He is furious—so furious that he scarce knows what he does."

"He seemed to know what he was doing when he ran for that hole in the wall," replied Barney with a grin. "But come, it won't pay to let them find us should they return."

Together they hastened to the window beyond which the girl could see a rope dangling from above. The sight of it partially solved the riddle of the king's almost uncanny presence upon her window sill in the very nick of time.

Below, the lights in the watch tower at the outer gate were plainly visible, and the twinkling of them reminded Barney of the danger of detection from that quarter. Quickly he recrossed the apartment to the wall-switch that operated the recently installed electric lights, and an instant later the chamber was in total darkness.

Once more at the girl's side Barney drew in one end of the rope and made it fast about her body below her arms, leaving a sufficient length terminating in a small loop to permit her to support herself more comfortably with one foot within the noose. Then he stepped to the outer sill, and reaching down assisted her to his side.

Far below them the moonlight played upon the sluggish waters of the moat. In the distance twinkled the lights of the village of Blentz. From the courtyard and the palace came faintly the sound of voices, and the movement of men. A horse whinnied from the stables.

Barney turned his eyes upward. He could see the head and shoulders of Joseph leaning from the window of the chamber directly above them.

"Hoist away, Joseph!" whispered the American, and to the girl: "Be brave. Shut your eyes and trust to Joseph and—and—"

"And my king," finished the girl for him.

His arm was about her shoulders, supporting her upon the narrow sill. His cheek so close to hers that once he felt the soft velvet of it brush his own. Involuntarily his arm tightened about the supple body.

"My princess!" he murmured, and as he turned his face toward hers their lips almost touched.

Joseph was pulling upon the rope from above. They could feel it tighten beneath the girl's arms. Impulsively Barney Custer drew the sweet lips closer to his own. There was no resistance.

"I love you," he whispered. The words were smothered as their lips met.

Joseph, above, wondered at the great weight of the Princess Emma von der Tann.

"I love you, Leopold, forever," whispered the girl, and then as Joseph's Herculean tugging seemed likely to drag them both from the narrow sill, Barney lifted the girl upward with one hand while he clung to the window frame with the other. The distance to the sill above was short, and a moment later Joseph had grasped the princess's hand and was helping her over the ledge into the room beyond.

At the same instant there came a sudden commotion from the interior of the room in the window of which Barney still stood waiting for Joseph to remove the rope from about the princess and lower it for him. Barney heard the heavy feet of men, the clank of arms, and muttered oaths as the searchers stumbled against the furniture.

Presently one of them found the switch and instantly the room was flooded with light, which revealed to the American a dozen Luthanian troopers headed by the murderous Maenck.

Barney looked anxiously aloft. Would Joseph never lower that rope! Within the room the men were searching. He could hear Maenck directing them. Only a thin portiere screened him from their view. It was but a matter of seconds before they would investigate the window through which Maenck knew the king had found ingress.

Yes! It had come.

"Look to the window," commanded Maenck. "He may have gone as he came."

Two of the soldiers crossed the room toward the casement. From above Joseph was lowering the rope; but it was too late. The men would be at the window before he could clamber out of their reach.

"Hoist away!" he whispered to Joseph. "Quick now, my man, and make your escape with the Princess von der Tann. It is the king's command."

Already the soldiers were at the window. At the sound of his voice they tore aside the draperies; at the same instant the pseudo-king turned and leaped out into the blackness of the night.

There were exclamations of surprise and rage from the soldiers—a woman's scream. Then from far below came a dull splash as the body of Bernard Custer struck the surface of the moat.

Maenck, leaning from the window, heard the scream and the splash, and jumped to the conclusion that both the king and the princess had attempted to make their escape in this harebrained way. Immediately all the resources at his command were put to the task of searching the moat and the adjacent woods.

He was sure that one or both of the prisoners would be stunned by impact with the surface of the water, and then drowned before they regained consciousness, but he did not know Bernard Custer, nor the facility and almost uncanny ease with which that young man could negotiate a high dive into shallow water.

Nor did he know that upon the floor above him one Joseph was hastening along a dark corridor toward a secret panel in another apartment, and that with him was the Princess Emma bound for liberty and safety far from the frowning walls of Blentz.

As Barney's head emerged above the surface of the moat he shook it vigorously to free his eyes from water, and then struck out for the further bank.

Long before his pursuers had reached the courtyard and alarmed the watch at the barbican, the American had crawled out upon dry land and hastened across the broad clearing to the patch of stunted trees that grew lower down upon the steep hillside before the castle.

He shrank from the thought of leaving Blentz without knowing positively that Joseph had made good the escape of himself and the princess, but he finally argued that even if they had been retaken, he could serve her best by hastening to her father and fetching the only succor that might prevail against the strength of Blentz—armed men in sufficient force to storm the ancient fortress.

He had scarcely entered the wood when he heard the sound of the searchers at the moat, and saw the rays of their lanterns flitting hither and thither as they moved back and forth along the bank.

Then the young man turned his face from the castle and set forth across the unfamiliar country in the direction of the Old Forest and the castle Von der Tann.

The memory of the warm lips that had so recently been pressed to his urged him on in the service of the wondrous girl who had come so suddenly into his life, bringing to him the realization of a love that he knew must alter, for happiness or for sorrow, all the balance of his existence, even unto death.

He dreaded the day of reckoning when, at last, she must learn that he was no king. He did not have the temerity to hope that her courage would be equal to the great sacrifice which the acknowledgment of her love for one not of noble blood must entail; but he could not believe that she would cease to love him when she learned the truth.

So the future looked black and cheerless to Barney Custer as he trudged along the rocky, moonlit way. The only bright spot was the realization that for a while at least he might be serving the one woman in all the world.

All the balance of the long night the young man traversed valley and mountain, holding due south in the direction he supposed the Old Forest to lie. He passed many a little farm tucked away in the hollow of a hillside, and quaint hamlets, and now and then the ruins of an ancient feudal stronghold, but no great forest of black oaks loomed before him to apprise him of the nearness of his goal, nor did he dare to ask the correct route at any of the homes he passed.

His fatal likeness to the description of the mad king of Lutha warned him from intercourse with the men of Lutha until he might know which were friends and which enemies of the hapless monarch.

Dawn found him still upon his way, but with the determination fully crystallized to hail the first man he met and ask the way to Tann. He still avoided the main traveled roads, but from time to time he paralleled them close enough that he might have ample opportunity to hail the first passerby.

The road was becoming more and more mountainous and difficult. There were fewer homes and no hamlets, and now he began to despair entirely of meeting any who could give him direction unless he turned and retraced his steps to the nearest farm.

Directly before him the narrow trail he had been following for the past few miles wound sharply about the shoulder of a protruding cliff. He would see what lay beyond the turn— perhaps he would find the Old Forest there, after all.

But instead he found something very different, though in its way quite as interesting, for as he rounded the rugged bluff he came face to face with two evil-looking fellows astride stocky, rough-coated ponies.

At sight of him they drew in their mounts and eyed him suspiciously. Nor was there great cause for wonderment in that, for the American presented aught but a respectable appearance. His khaki motoring suit, soaked from immersion in the moat, had but partially dried upon him. Mud from the banks of the stagnant pool caked his legs to the knees, almost hiding his once tan puttees. More mud streaked his jacket front and stained its sleeves to the elbows. He was bare-headed, for his cap had remained in the moat at Blentz, and his disheveled hair was tousled upon his head, while his full beard had dried into a weird and tangled fringe about his face. At his side still hung the sword that Joseph had buckled there, and it was this that caused the two men the greatest suspicion of this strange looking character.

They continued to eye Barney in silence, every now and then casting apprehensive glances beyond him, as though expecting others of his kind to appear in the trail at his back. And that is precisely what they did fear, for the sword at Barney's side had convinced them that he must be an officer of the army, and they looked to see his command following in his wake.

The young man saluted them pleasantly, asking the direction to the Old Forest. They thought it strange that a soldier of Lutha should not know his own way about his native land, and so judged that his question was but a blind to deceive them.

"Why do you not ask your own men the way?" parried one of the fellows.

"I have no men, I am alone," replied Barney. "I am a stranger in Lutha and have lost my way."

He who had spoken before pointed to the sword at Barney's side.

34

"Strangers traveling in Lutha do not wear swords," he said. "You are an officer. Why should you desire to conceal the fact from two honest farmers? We have done nothing. Let us go our way."

Barney looked his astonishment at this reply.

"Most certainly, go your way, my friends," he said laughing. "I would not delay you if I could; but before you go please be good enough to tell me how to reach the Old Forest and the ancient castle of the Prince von der Tann."

For a moment the two men whispered together, then the spokesman turned to Barney.

"We will lead you upon the right road. Come," and the two turned their horses, one of them starting slowly back up the trail while the other remained waiting for Barney to pass him.

The American, suspecting nothing, voiced his thanks, and set out after him who had gone before. As he passed the fellow who waited the latter moved in behind him, so that Barney walked between the two. Occasionally the rider at his back turned in his saddle to scan the trail behind, as though still fearful that Barney had been lying to them and that he would discover a company of soldiers charging down upon them.

The trail became more and more difficult as they advanced, until Barney wondered how the little horses clung to the steep mountainside, where he himself had difficulty in walking without using his hand to keep from falling.

Twice the American attempted to break through the taciturnity of his guides, but his advances were met with nothing more than sultry grunts or silence, and presently a suspicion began to obtrude itself among his thoughts that possibly these "honest farmers" were something more sinister than they represented themselves to be.

A malign and threatening atmosphere seemed to surround them. Even the cat-like movement of their silent mounts breathed a sinister secrecy, and now, for the first time, Barney noticed the short, ugly looking carbines that were slung in boots at their saddle-horns. Then, prompted to further investigation, he dropped back beside the man who had been riding behind him, and as he did so he saw beneath the fellow's cloak the butts of two villainous-looking pistols.

As Barney dropped back beside him the man turned his mount across the narrow trail, and reining him in motioned Barney ahead.

"I have changed my mind," said the American, "about going to the Old Forest."

He had determined that he might as well have the thing out now as later, and discover at once how he stood with these two, and whether or not his suspicions of them were well grounded.

The man ahead had halted at the sound of Barney's voice, and swung about in the saddle.

"What's the trouble?" he asked.

"He don't want to go to the Old Forest," explained his companion, and for the first time Barney saw one of them grin. It was not at all a pleasant grin, nor reassuring.

"He don't, eh?" growled the other. "Well, he ain't goin', is he? Who ever said he was?"

And then he, too, laughed.

"I'm going back the way I came," said Barney, starting around the horse that blocked his way.

"No, you ain't," said the horseman. "You're goin' with us."

And Barney found himself gazing down the muzzle of one of the wicked looking pistols.

For a moment he stood in silence, debating mentally the wisdom of attempting to rush the fellow, and then, with a shake of his head, he turned back up the trail between his captors.

"Yes," he said, "on second thought I have decided to go with you. Your logic is most convincing."

VI

A KING'S RANSOM

For another mile the two brigands conducted their captor along the mountainside, then they turned into a narrow ravine near the summit of the hills—a deep, rocky, wooded ravine into whose black shadows it seemed the sun might never penetrate.

A winding path led crookedly among the pines that grew thickly in this sheltered hollow, until presently, after half an hour of rough going, they came upon a small natural clearing, rock-bound and impregnable.

As they filed from the wood Barney saw a score of villainous fellows clustered about a camp fire where they seemed engaged in cooking their noonday meal. Bits of meat were roasting upon iron skewers, and a great iron pot boiled vigorously at one side of the blaze.

At the sound of their approach the men sprang to their feet in alarm, and as many weapons as there were men leaped to view; but when they saw Barney's companions they returned their pistols to their holsters, and at sight of Barney they pressed forward to inspect the prisoner.

"Who have we here?" shouted a big blond giant, who affected extremely gaudy colors in his selection of wearing apparel, and whose pistols and knife had their grips heavily ornamented with pearl and silver.

"A stranger in Lutha he calls himself," replied one of Barney's captors. "But from the sword I take it he is one of old Peter's wolfhounds."

"Well, he's found the wolves at any rate," replied the giant, with a wide grin at his witticism. "And if Yellow Franz is the particular wolf you're after, my friend, why here I am," he concluded, addressing the American with a leer.

"I'm after no one," replied Barney. "I tell you I'm a stranger, and I lost my way in your infernal mountains. All I wish is to be set upon the right road to Tann, and if you will do that for me you shall be well paid for your trouble."

The giant, Yellow Franz, had come quite close to Barney and was inspecting him with an expression of considerable interest. Presently he drew a soiled and much-folded paper from his breast. Upon one side was a printed notice, and at the corners bits were torn away as though the paper had once been tacked upon wood, and then torn down without removing the tacks.

At sight of it Barney's heart sank. The look of the thing was all too familiar. Before the yellow one had commenced to read aloud from it Barney had repeated to himself the words he knew were coming.

"'Gray eyes,'" read the brigand, "'brown hair, and a full, reddish-brown beard.' Herman and Friedrich, my dear children, you have stumbled upon the richest haul in all Lutha. Down upon your marrow-bones, you swine, and rub your low-born noses in the dirt before your king."

The others looked their surprise.

"The king?" one cried.

"Behold!" cried Yellow Franz. "Leopold of Lutha!"

He waved a ham-like hand toward Barney.

Among the rough men was a young smooth-faced boy, and now with wide eyes he pressed forward to get a nearer view of the wonderful person of a king.

"Take a good look at him, Rudolph," cried Yellow Franz. "It is the first and will probably be the last time you will ever see a king. Kings seldom visit the court of their fellow monarch, Yellow Franz of the Black Mountains.

"Come, my children, remove his majesty's sword, lest he fall and stick himself upon it, and then prepare the royal chamber, seeing to it that it be made so comfortable that Leopold will remain with us a long time. Rudolph, fetch food and water for his majesty, and see to it that the silver plates and the golden goblets are well scoured and polished up."

They conducted Barney to a miserable lean-to shack at one side of the clearing, and for a while the motley crew loitered about bandying coarse jests at the expense of the "king." The boy, Rudolph, brought food and water, he alone of them all evincing the slightest respect or awe for the royalty of their unwilling guest.

After a time the men tired of the sport of king-baiting, for Barney showed neither rancor nor outraged majesty at their keenest thrusts, instead, often joining in the laugh with them at his own expense. They thought it odd that the king should hold his dignity in so low esteem, but that he was king they never doubted, attributing his denials to a disposition to deceive them, and rob them of the "king's ransom" they had already commenced to consider as their own.

Shortly after Barney arrived at the rendezvous he saw a messenger dispatched by Yellow Franz, and from the repeated gestures toward himself that had accompanied the giant's instructions to his emissary, Barney was positive that the man's errand had to do with him.

After the men had left his prison, leaving the boy standing awkwardly in wide-eyed contemplation of his august charge, the American ventured to open a conversation with his youthful keeper.

"Aren't you rather young to be starting in the bandit business, Rudolph?" asked Barney, who had taken a fancy to the youth.

"I do not want to be a bandit, your majesty," whispered the lad; "but my father owes Yellow Franz a great sum of money, and as he could not pay the debt Yellow Franz stole me from my home and says that he will keep me until my father pays him, and that if he does not pay he will make a bandit of me, and that then some day I shall be caught and hanged until I am dead."

"Can't you escape?" asked the young man. "It would seem to me that there would be many opportunities for you to get away undetected."

"There are, but I dare not. Yellow Franz says that if I run away he will be sure to come across me some day again and that then he will kill me."

Barney laughed.

"He is just talking, my boy," he said. "He thinks that by frightening you he will be able to keep you from running away."

"Your majesty does not know him," whispered the youth, shuddering. "He is the wickedest man in all the world. Nothing would please him more than killing me, and he would have done it long since but for two things. One is that I have made myself useful about his camp, doing chores and the like, and the other is that were he to kill me he knows that my father would never pay him."

"How much does your father owe him?"

"Five hundred marks, your majesty," replied Rudolph. "Two hundred of this amount is the original debt, and the balance Yellow Franz has added since he captured me, so that it is really ransom money. But my father is a poor man, so that it will take a long time before he can accumulate so large a sum.

"You would really like to go home again, Rudolph?"

"Oh, very much, your majesty, if I only dared." Barney was silent for some time, thinking. Possibly he could effect his own escape with the connivance of Rudolph, and at the same time free the boy. The paltry ransom he could pay out of his own pocket and send to Yellow Franz later, so that the youth need not fear the brigand's revenge. It was worth thinking about, at any rate.

"How long do you imagine they will keep me, Rudolph?" he asked after a time.

"Yellow Franz has already sent Herman to Lustadt with a message for Prince Peter, telling him that you are being held for ransom, and demanding the payment of a huge sum for your release. Day after tomorrow or the next day he should return with Prince Peter's reply.

"If it is favorable, arrangements will be made to turn you over to Prince Peter's agents, who will have to come to some distant meeting place with the money. A week, perhaps, it will take, maybe longer."

It was the second day before Herman returned from Lustadt. He rode in just at dark, his pony lathered from hard going.

Barney and the boy saw him coming, and the youth ran forward with the others to learn the news that he had brought; but Yellow Franz and his messenger withdrew to a hut which the brigand chief reserved for his own use, nor would he permit any beside the messenger to accompany him to hear the report.

For half an hour Barney sat alone waiting for word from Yellow Franz that arrangements had been consummated for his release, and then out of the darkness came Rudolph, wide-eyed and trembling.

"Oh, my king?" he whispered. "What shall we do? Peter has refused to ransom you alive, but he has offered a great sum for unquestioned proof of your death. Already he has caused a proclamation to be issued stating that you have been killed by bandits after escaping from Blentz, and ordering a period of national mourning. In three weeks he is to be crowned king of Lutha."

"When do they intend terminating my existence?" queried Barney.

There was a smile upon his lips, for even now he could scarce believe that in the twentieth century there could be any such medieval plotting against a king's life, and yet, on second thought, had he not ample proof of the lengths to which Peter of Blentz was willing to go to obtain the crown of Lutha!

"I do not know, your majesty," replied Rudolph, "when they will do it; but soon, doubtless, since the sooner it is done the sooner they can collect their pay."

Further conversation was interrupted by the sound of footsteps without, and an instant later Yellow Franz entered the squalid apartment and the dim circle of light which flickered feebly from the smoky lantern that hung suspended from the rafters.

He stopped just within the doorway and stood eyeing the American with an ugly grin upon his vicious face. Then his eyes fell upon the trembling Rudolph.

"Get out of here, you!" he growled. "I've got private business with this king. And see that you don't come nosing round either, or I'll slit that soft throat for you."

Rudolph slipped past the burly ruffian, barely dodging a brutal blow aimed at him by the giant, and escaped into the darkness without.

"And now for you, my fine fellow," said the brigand, turning toward Barney. "Peter says you ain't worth nothing to him—alive, but that your dead body will fetch us a hundred thousand marks."

"Rather cheap for a king, isn't it?" was Barney's only comment.

"That's what Herman tells him," replied Yellow Franz. "But he's a close one, Peter is, and so it was that or nothing."

"When are you going to pull off this little—er—ah—royal demise?" asked Barney.

"If you mean when am I going to kill you," replied the bandit, "why, there ain't no particular rush about it. I'm a tender-hearted chap, I am. I never should have been in this business at all, but here I be, and as there ain't nobody that can do a better job of the kind than me, or do it so painlessly, why I just got to do it myself, and that's all there is to it. But, as I says, there ain't no great rush. If you want to pray, why, go ahead and pray. I'll wait for you."

"I don't remember," said Barney, "when I have met so generous a party as you, my friend. Your self-sacrificing magnanimity quite overpowers me. It reminds me of another unloved Robin Hood whom I once met. It was in front of Burket's coal-yard on Ella Street, back in dear old Beatrice, at some unchristian hour of the night.

"After he had relieved me of a dollar and forty cents he remarked: 'I gotta good mind to kick yer slats in fer not havin' more of de cush on yeh; but I'm feelin' so good about de last guy I stuck up I'll let youse off dis time.'"

"I do not know what you are talking about," replied Yellow Franz; "but if you want to pray you'd better hurry up about it."

He drew his pistol from its holster on the belt at his hips.

Now Barney Custer had no mind to give up the ghost without a struggle; but just how he was to overcome the great beast who confronted him with menacing pistol was, to say the least, not precisely plain. He wished the man would come a little nearer where he might have some chance to close with him before the fellow could fire. To gain time the American assumed a prayerful attitude, but kept one eye on the bandit.

Presently Yellow Franz showed indications of impatience. He fingered the trigger of his weapon, and then slowly raised it on a line with Barney's chest.

"Hadn't you better come closer?" asked the young man. "You might miss at that distance, or just wound me."

Yellow Franz grinned.

"I don't miss," he said, and then: "You're certainly a game one. If it wasn't for the hundred thousand marks, I'd be hanged if I'd kill you."

"The chances are that you will be if you do," said Barney, "so wouldn't you rather take one hundred and fifty thousand marks and let me make my escape?"

Yellow Franz looked at the speaker a moment through narrowed lids.

"Where would you find any one willing to pay that amount for a crazy king?" he asked.

"I have told you that I am not the king," said Barney. "I am an American with a father who would gladly pay that amount on my safe delivery to any American consul."

Yellow Franz shook his head and tapped his brow significantly.

"Even if you was what you are dreaming, it wouldn't pay me," he said.

"I'll make it two hundred thousand," said Barney.

"No—it's a waste of time talking about it. It's worth more than money to me to know that I'll always have this thing on Peter, and that when he's king he won't dare bother me for fear I'll publish the details of this little deal. Come, you must be through praying by this time. I can't wait around here all night." Again Yellow Franz raised his pistol toward Barney's heart.

Before the brigand could pull the trigger, or Barney hurl himself upon his would-be assassin, there was a flash and a loud report from the open window of the shack.

With a groan Yellow Franz crumpled to the dirt floor, and simultaneously Barney was upon him and had wrested the pistol from his hand; but the precaution was unnecessary for Yellow Franz would never again press finger to trigger. He was dead even before Barney reached his side.

In possession of the weapon, the American turned toward the window from which had come the rescuing shot, and as he did so he saw the boy, Rudolph, clambering over the sill, white-faced and trembling. In his hand was a smoking carbine, and on his brow great beads of cold sweat.

"God forgive me!" murmured the youth. "I have killed a man."

"You have killed a dangerous wild beast, Rudolph," said Barney, "and both God and your fellow man will thank and reward you."

"I am glad that I killed him, though," went on the boy, "for he would have killed you, my king, had I not done so. Gladly would I go to the gallows to save my king."

"You are a brave lad, Rudolph," said Barney, "and if ever I get out of the pretty pickle I'm in you'll be well rewarded for your loyalty to Leopold of Lutha. After all," thought the young man, "being a kind has its redeeming features, for if the boy had not thought me his monarch he would never have risked the vengeance of the bloodthirsty brigands in this attempt to save me."

"Hasten, your majesty," whispered the boy, tugging at the sleeve of Barney's jacket. "There is no time to be lost. We must be far away from here when the others discover that Yellow Franz has been killed."

Barney stooped above the dead man, and removing his belt and cartridges transferred them to his own person. Then blowing out the lantern the two slipped out into the darkness of the night.

About the camp fire of the brigands the entire pack was congregated. They were talking together in low voices, ever and anon glancing expectantly toward the shack to which their chief had gone to dispatch the king. It is not every day that a king is murdered, and even these hardened cut-throats felt the spell of awe at the thought of what they believed the sharp report they had heard from the shack portended.

Keeping well to the far side of the clearing, Rudolph led Barney around the group of men and safely into the wood below them. From this point the boy followed the trail which Barney and his captors had traversed two days previously, until he came to a diverging ravine that led steeply up through the mountains upon their right hand.

In the distance behind them they suddenly heard, faintly, the shouting of men.

"They have discovered Yellow Franz," whispered the boy, shuddering.

"Then they'll be after us directly," said Barney.

"Yes, your majesty," replied Rudolph, "but in the darkness they will not see that we have turned up this ravine, and so they will ride on down the other. I have chosen this way because their horses cannot follow us here, and thus we shall be under no great disadvantage. It may be, however, that we shall have to hide in the mountains for a while, since there will be no place of safety for us between here and Lustadt until after the edge of their anger is dulled."

And such proved to be the case, for try as they would they found it impossible to reach Lustadt without detection by the brigands who patrolled every highway and byway from their rugged mountains to the capital of Lutha.

For nearly three weeks Barney and the boy hid in caves or dense underbrush by day, and by night sought some avenue which would lead them past the vigilant sentries that patrolled the ways to freedom.

Often they were wet by rains, nor were they ever in the warm sunlight for a sufficient length of time to become thoroughly dry and comfortable. Of food they had little, and of the poorest quality.

They dared not light a fire for warmth or cooking, and their light was so miserable that, but for the boy's pitiful terror at the thought of being recaptured by the bandits, Barney would long since have made a break for Lustadt, depending upon their arms and ammunition to carry them safely through were they discovered by their enemies.

Rudolph had contracted a severe cold the first night, and now, it having settled upon his lungs, he had developed a persistent and aggravating cough that caused Barney not a little apprehension. When, after nearly three weeks of suffering and privation, it became clear that the boy's lungs were affected, the American decided to take matters into his own hands and attempt to reach Lustadt and a good doctor; but before he had an opportunity to put his plan into execution the entire matter was removed from his jurisdiction.

It happened like this: After a particularly fatiguing and uncomfortable night spent in attempting to elude the sentinels who blocked their way from the mountains, daylight found them near a little spring, and here they decided to rest for an hour before resuming their way.

The little pool lay not far from a clump of heavy bushes which would offer them excellent shelter, as it was Barney's intention to go into hiding as soon as they had quenched their thirst at the spring.

42

Rudolph was coughing pitifully, his slender frame wracked by the convulsion of each new attack. Barney had placed an arm about the boy to support him, for the paroxysms always left him very weak.

The young man's heart went out to the poor boy, and pangs of regret filled his mind as he realized that the child's pathetic condition was the direct result of his self-sacrificing attempt to save his king. Barney felt much like a murderer and a thief, and dreaded the time when the boy should be brought to a realization of his mistake.

He had come to feel a warm affection for the loyal little lad, who had suffered so uncomplainingly and whose every thought had been for the safety and comfort of his king.

Today, thought Barney, I'll take this child through to Lustadt even if every ragged brigand in Lutha lies between us and the capital; but even as he spoke a sudden crashing of underbrush behind caused him to wheel about, and there, not twenty paces from them, stood two of Yellow Franz's cutthroats.

At sight of Barney and the lad they gave voice to a shout of triumph, and raising their carbines fired point-blank at the two fugitives.

But Barney had been equally as quick with his own weapon, and at the moment that they fired he grasped Rudolph and dragged him backward to a great boulder behind which their bodies might be protected from the fire of their enemies.

Both the bullets of the bandits' first volley had been directed at Barney, for it was upon his head that the great price rested. They had missed him by a narrow margin, due, perhaps, to the fact that the mounts of the brigands had been prancing in alarm at the unexpected sight of the two strangers at the very moment that their riders attempted to take aim and fire.

But now they had ridden back into the brush and dismounted, and after hiding their ponies they came creeping out upon their bellies upon opposite sides of Barney's shelter.

The American saw that it would be an easy thing for them to pick him off if he remained where he was, and so with a word to Rudolph he sprang up and the boy with him. Each delivered a quick shot at the bandit nearest him, and then together they broke for the bushes in which the brigand's mounts were hidden.

Two shots answered theirs. Rudolph, who was ahead of Barney, stumbled and threw up his hands. He would have fallen had not the American thrown a strong arm about him.

"I'm shot, your majesty," murmured the boy, his head dropping against Barney's breast.

With the lad grasped close to him, the young man turned at the edge of the brush to meet the charge of the two ruffians. The wounding of the youth had delayed them just enough to preclude their making this temporary refuge in safety.

As Barney turned both the men fired simultaneously, and both missed. The American raised his revolver, and with the flash of it the foremost brigand came to a sudden stop. An expression of bewilderment crossed his features. He extended his arms straight before him, the revolver slipped from his grasp, and then like a dying top he pivoted once drunkenly and collapsed upon the turf.

At the instant of his fall his companion and the American fired point-blank at one another.

Barney felt a burning sensation in his shoulder, but it was forgotten for the moment in the relief that came to him as he saw the second rascal sprawl headlong upon his face. Then he turned his attention to the limp little figure that hung across his left arm.

Gently Barney laid the boy upon the sward, and fetching water from the pool bathed his face and forced a few drops between the white lips. The cooling draft revived the wounded child, but brought on a paroxysm of coughing. When this had subsided Rudolph raised his eyes to those of the man bending above him.

"Thank God, your majesty is unharmed," he whispered. "Now I can die in peace."

The white lids drooped lower, and with a tired sigh the boy lay quiet. Tears came to the young man's eyes as he let the limp body gently to the ground.

"Brave little heart," he murmured, "you gave up your life in the service of your king as truly as though you had not been all mistaken in the object of your veneration, and if it lies within the power of Barney Custer you shall not have died in vain."

VII

THE REAL LEOPOLD

Two hours later a horseman pushed his way between tumbled and tangled briers along the bottom of a deep ravine.

He was hatless, and his stained and ragged khaki betokened much exposure to the elements and hard and continued usage. At his saddle-bow a carbine swung in its boot, and upon either hip was strapped a long revolver. Ammunition in plenty filled the cross belts that he had looped about his shoulders.

Grim and warlike as were his trappings, no less grim was the set of his strong jaw or the glint of his gray eyes, nor did the patch of brown stain that had soaked through the left shoulder of his jacket tend to lessen the martial atmosphere which surrounded him. Fortunate it was for the brigands of the late Yellow Franz that none of them chanced in the path of Barney Custer that day.

For nearly two hours the man had ridden downward out of the high hills in search of a dwelling at which he might ask the way to Tann; but as yet he had passed but a single house, and that a long untenanted ruin. He was wondering what had become of all the inhabitants of Lutha when his horse came to a sudden halt before an obstacle which entirely blocked the narrow trail at the bottom of the ravine.

As the horseman's eyes fell upon the thing they went wide in astonishment, for it was no less than the charred remnants of the once beautiful gray roadster that had brought him into this twentieth century land of medieval adventure and intrigue. Barney saw that the machine had been lifted from where it had fallen across the horse of the Princess von der Tann, for the animal's decaying carcass now lay entirely clear of it; but why this should have been done, or by whom, the young man could not imagine.

A glance aloft showed him the road far above him, from which he, the horse and the roadster had catapulted; and with the sight of it there flashed to his mind the fair face of the young girl in whose service the thing had happened. Barney wondered if Joseph had been successful in returning her to Tann, and he wondered, too, if she mourned for the man she had thought king—if she would be very angry should she ever learn the truth.

Then there came to the American's mind the figure of the shopkeeper of Tafelberg, and the fellow's evident loyalty to the mad king he had never seen. Here was one who might aid him, thought Barney. He would have the will, at least, and with the thought the young man turned his pony's head diagonally up the steep ravine side.

It was a tough and dangerous struggle to the road above, but at last by dint of strenuous efforts on the part of the sturdy little beast the two finally scrambled over the edge of the road and stood once more upon level footing.

After breathing his mount for a few minutes Barney swung himself into the saddle again and set off toward Tafelberg. He met no one upon the road, nor within the outskirts of the village, and so he came to the door of the shop he sought without attracting attention.

Swinging to the ground he tied the pony to one of the supporting columns of the porch-roof and a moment later had stepped within the shop.

From a back room the shopkeeper presently emerged, and when he saw who it was that stood before him his eyes went wide in consternation.

"In the name of all the saints, your majesty," cried the old fellow, "what has happened? How comes it that you are out of the hospital, and travel-stained as though from a long, hard ride? I cannot understand it, sire."

"Hospital?" queried the young man. "What do you mean, my good fellow? I have been in no hospital."

"You were there only last evening when I inquired after you of the doctor," insisted the shopkeeper, "nor did any there yet suspect your true identity."

"Last evening I was hiding far up in the mountains from Yellow Franz's band of cutthroats," replied Barney. "Tell me what manner of riddle you are propounding."

Then a sudden light of understanding flashed through Barney's mind.

"Man!" he exclaimed. "Tell me—you have found the true king? He is at a hospital in Tafelberg?"

"Yes, your majesty, I have found the true king, and it is so that he was at the Tafelberg sanatorium last evening. It was beside the remnants of your wrecked automobile that two of the men of Tafelberg found you.

"One leg was pinioned beneath the machine which was on fire when they discovered you. They brought you to my shop, which is the first on the road into town, and not guessing your

45

true identity they took my word for it that you were an old acquaintance of mine and without more ado turned you over to my care."

Barney scratched his head in puzzled bewilderment. He began to doubt if he were in truth himself, or, after all, Leopold of Lutha. As no one but himself could, by the wildest stretch of imagination, have been in such a position, he was almost forced to the conclusion that all that had passed since the instant that his car shot over the edge of the road into the ravine had been but the hallucinations of a fever-excited brain, and that for the past three weeks he had been lying in a hospital cot instead of experiencing the strange and inexplicable adventures that he had believed to have befallen him.

But yet the more he thought of it the more ridiculous such a conclusion appeared, for it did not in the least explain the pony tethered without, which he plainly could see from where he stood within the shop, nor did it satisfactorily account for the blotch of blood upon his shoulder from a wound so fresh that the stain still was damp; nor for the sword which Joseph had buckled about his waist within Blentz's forbidding walls; nor for the arms and ammunition he had taken from the dead brigands—all of which he had before him as tangible evidence of the rationality of the past few weeks.

"My friend," said Barney at last, "I cannot wonder that you have mistaken me for the king, since all those I have met within Lutha have leaped to the same error, though not one among them made the slightest pretense of ever having seen his majesty. A ridiculous beard started the trouble, and later a series of happenings, no one of which was particularly remarkable in itself, aggravated it, until but a moment since I myself was almost upon the point of believing that I am the king.

"But, my dear Herr Kramer, I am not the king; and when you have accompanied me to the hospital and seen that your patient still is there, you may be willing to admit that there is some justification for doubt as to my royalty."

The old man shook his head.

"I am not so sure of that," he said, "for he who lies at the hospital, providing you are not he, or he you, maintains as sturdily as do you that he is not Leopold. If one of you, whichever be king—providing that you are not one and the same, and that I be not the only maniac in the sad muddle—if one of you would but trust my loyalty and love for the true king and admit your identity, then I might be of some real service to that one of you who is really Leopold. Herr Gott! My words are as mixed as my poor brain."

"If you will listen to me, Herr Kramer," said Barney, "and believe what I tell you, I shall be able to unscramble your ideas in so far as they pertain to me and my identity. As to the man you say was found beneath my car, and who now lies in the sanatorium of Tafelberg, I cannot say until I have seen and talked with him. He may be the king and he may not; but if he insists that he is not, I shall be the last to wish a kingship upon him. I know from sad experience the hardships and burdens that the thing entails."

Then Barney narrated carefully and in detail the principal events of his life, from his birth in Beatrice to his coming to Lutha upon pleasure. He showed Herr Kramer his watch with his monogram upon it, his seal ring, and inside the pocket of his coat the label of his tailor, with his own name written beneath it and the date that the garment had been ordered.

When he had completed his narrative the old man shook his head.

"I cannot understand it," he said; "and yet I am almost forced to believe that you are not the king."

"Direct me to the sanatorium," suggested Barney, "and if it be within the range of possibility I shall learn whether the man who lies there is Leopold or another, and if he be the king I shall serve him as loyally as you would have served me. Together we may assist him to gain the safety of Tann and the protection of old Prince Ludwig."

"If you are not the king," said Kramer suspiciously, "why should you be so interested in aiding Leopold? You may even be an enemy. How can I know?"

"You cannot know, my good friend," replied Barney. "But had I been an enemy, how much more easily might I have encompassed my designs, whatever they might have been, had I encouraged you to believe that I was king. The fact that I did not, must assure you that I have no ulterior designs against Leopold."

This line of reasoning proved quite convincing to the old shopkeeper, and at last he consented to lead Barney to the sanatorium. Together they traversed the quiet village streets to the outskirts of the town, where in large, park-like grounds the well-known sanatorium of Tafelberg is situated in quiet surroundings. It is an institution for the treatment of nervous diseases to which patients are brought from all parts of Europe, and is doubtless Lutha's principal claim upon the attention of the outer world.

As the two crossed the gardens which lay between the gate and the main entrance and mounted the broad steps leading to the veranda an old servant opened the door, and recognizing Herr Kramer, nodded pleasantly to him.

"Your patient seems much brighter this morning, Herr Kramer," he said, "and has been asking to be allowed to sit up."

"He is still here, then?" questioned the shopkeeper with a sigh that might have indicated either relief or resignation.

"Why, certainly. You did not expect that he had entirely recovered overnight, did you?"

"No," replied Herr Kramer, "not exactly. In fact, I did not know what I should expect."

As the two passed him on their way to the room in which the patient lay, the servant eyed Herr Kramer in surprise, as though wondering what had occurred to his mentality since he had seen him the previous day. He paid no attention to Barney other than to bow to him as he passed, but there was another who did—an attendant standing in the hallway through which the two men walked toward the private room where one of them expected to find the real mad king of Lutha.

He was a dark-visaged fellow, sallow and small-eyed; and as his glance rested upon the features of the American a puzzled expression crossed his face. He let his gaze follow the two as they moved up the corridor until they turned in at the door of the room they sought, then he followed them, entering an apartment next to that in which Herr Kramer's patient lay.

As Barney and the shopkeeper entered the small, whitewashed room, the former saw upon the narrow iron cot the figure of a man of about his own height. The face that turned toward them as they entered was covered by a full, reddish-brown beard, and the eyes that looked up at them in troubled surprise were gray. Beyond these Barney could see no likenesses to himself; yet they were sufficient, he realized, to have deceived any who might have compared one solely to the printed description of the other.

At the doorway Kramer halted, motioning Barney within.

"It will be better if you talk with him alone," he said. "I am sure that before both of us he will admit nothing."

Barney nodded, and the shopkeeper of Tafelberg withdrew and closed the door behind him. The American approached the bedside with a cheery "Good morning."

The man returned the salutation with a slight inclination of his head. There was a questioning look in his eyes; but dominating that was a pitiful, hunted expression that touched the American's heart.

The man's left hand lay upon the coverlet. Barney glanced at the third finger. About it was a plain gold band. There was no royal ring of the kings of Lutha in evidence, yet that was no indication that the man was not Leopold; for were he the king and desirous of concealing his identity, his first act would be to remove every symbol of his kingship.

Barney took the hand in his.

"They tell me that you are well on the road to recovery," he said. "I am very glad that it is so."

"Who are you?" asked the man.

"I am Bernard Custer, an American. You were found beneath my car at the bottom of a ravine. I feel that I owe you full reparation for the injuries you received, though it is beyond me how you happened to be found under the machine. Unless I am truly mad, I was the only occupant of the roadster when it plunged over the embankment."

"It is very simple," replied the man upon the cot. "I chanced to be at the bottom of the ravine at the time and the car fell upon me."

"What were you doing at the bottom of the ravine?" asked Barney quite suddenly, after the manner of one who administers a third degree.

The man started and flushed with suspicion.

"That is my own affair," he said.

He tried to disengage his hand from Barney's, and as he did so the American felt something within the fingers of the other. For an instant his own fingers tightened upon those that lay within them, so that as the others were withdrawn his index finger pressed close upon the thing that had aroused his curiosity.

It was a large setting turned inward upon the third finger of the left hand. The gold band that Barney had seen was but the opposite side of the same ring.

48

A quick look of comprehension came to Barney's eyes. The man upon the cot evidently noted it and rightly interpreted its cause, for, having freed his hand, he now slipped it quickly beneath the coverlet.

"I have passed through a series of rather remarkable adventures since I came to Lutha," said Barney apparently quite irrelevantly, after the two had remained silent for a moment. "Shortly after my car fell upon you I was mistaken for the fugitive King Leopold by the young lady whose horse fell into the ravine with my car. She is a most loyal supporter of the king, being none other than the Princess Emma von der Tann. From her I learned to espouse the cause of Leopold."

Step by step Barney took the man through the adventures that had befallen him during the past three weeks, closing with the story of the death of the boy, Rudolph.

"Above his dead body I swore to serve Leopold of Lutha as loyally as the poor, mistaken child had served me, your majesty," and Barney looked straight into the eyes of him who lay upon the little iron cot.

For a moment the man held his eyes upon those of the American, but finally, under the latter's steady gaze, they dropped and wandered.

"Why do you address me as 'your majesty'?" he asked irritably.

"With my forefinger I felt the ruby and the four wings of the setting of the royal ring of the kings of Lutha upon the third finger of your left hand," replied Barney.

The king started up upon his elbow, his eyes wild with apprehension.

"It is not so," he cried. "It is a lie! I am not the king."

"Hush!" admonished Barney. "You have nothing to fear from me. There are good friends and loyal subjects in plenty to serve and protect your majesty, and place you upon the throne that has been stolen from you. I have sworn to serve you. The old shopkeeper, Herr Kramer, who brought me here, is an honest, loyal old soul. He would die for you, your majesty. Trust us. Let us help you. Tomorrow, Kramer tells me, Peter of Blentz is to have himself crowned as king in the cathedral at Lustadt.

"Will you sit supinely by and see another rob you of your kingdom, and then continue to rob and throttle your subjects as he has been doing for the past ten years? No, you will not. Even if you do not want the crown, you were born to the duties and obligations it entails, and for the sake of your people you must assume them now."

"How am I to know that you are not another of the creatures of that fiend of Blentz?" cried the king. "How am I to know that you will not drag me back to the terrors of that awful castle, and to the poisonous potions of the new physician Peter has employed to assassinate me? I can trust none.

"Go away and leave me. I do not want to be king. I wish only to go away as far from Lutha as I can get and pass the balance of my life in peace and security. Peter may have the crown. He is welcome to it, for all of me. All I ask is my life and my liberty."

49

Barney saw that while the king was evidently of sound mind, his was not one of those iron characters and courageous hearts that would willingly fight to the death for his own rights and the rights and happiness of his people. Perhaps the long years of bitter disappointment and misery, the tedious hours of imprisonment, and the constant haunting fears for his life had reduced him to this pitiable condition.

Whatever the cause, Barney Custer was determined to overcome the man's aversion to assuming the duties which were rightly his, for in his memory were the words of Emma von der Tann, in which she had made plain to him the fate that would doubtless befall her father and his house were Peter of Blentz to become king of Lutha. Then, too, there was the life of the little peasant boy. Was that to be given up uselessly for a king with so mean a spirit that he would not take a scepter when it was forced upon him?

And the people of Lutha? Were they to be further and continually robbed and downtrodden beneath the heel of Peter's scoundrelly officials because their true king chose to evade the responsibilities that were his by birth?

For half an hour Barney pleaded and argued with the king, until he infused in the weak character of the young man a part of his own tireless enthusiasm and courage. Leopold commenced to take heart and see things in a brighter and more engaging light. Finally he became quite excited about the prospects, and at last Barney obtained a willing promise from him that he would consent to being placed upon his throne and would go to Lustadt at any time that Barney should come for him with a force from the retainers of Prince Ludwig von der Tann.

"Let us hope," cried the king, "that the luck of the reigning house of Lutha has been at last restored. Not since my aunt, the Princess Victoria, ran away with a foreigner has good fortune shone upon my house. It was when my father was still a young man—before he had yet come to the throne—and though his reign was marked with great peace and prosperity for the people of Lutha, his own private fortunes were most unhappy.

"My mother died at my birth, and the last days of my father's life were filled with suffering from the cancer that was slowly killing him. Let us pray, Herr Custer, that you have brought new life to the fortunes of my house."

"Amen, your majesty," said Barney. "And now I'll be off for Tann—there must not be a moment lost if we are to bring you to Lustadt in time for the coronation. Herr Kramer will watch over you, but as none here guesses your true identity you are safer here than anywhere else in Lutha. Good-bye, your majesty. Be of good heart. We'll have you on the road to Lustadt and the throne tomorrow morning."

After Barney Custer had closed the door of the king's chamber behind him and hurried down the corridor, the door of the room next the king's opened quietly and a dark-visaged fellow, sallow and small-eyed, emerged. Upon his lips was a smile of cunning satisfaction, as he hastened to the office of the medical director and obtained a leave of absence for twenty-four hours.

VIII

Toward dusk of the day upon which the mad king of Lutha had been found, a dust-covered horseman reined in before the great gate of the castle of Prince Ludwig von der Tann. The unsettled political conditions which overhung the little kingdom of Lutha were evident in the return to medievalism which the raised portcullis and the armed guard upon the barbican of the ancient feudal fortress revealed. Not for a hundred years before had these things been done other than as a part of the ceremonials of a fete day, or in honor of visiting royalty.

At the challenge from the gate Barney replied that he bore a message for the prince. Slowly the portcullis sank into position across the moat and an officer advanced to meet the rider.

"The prince has ridden to Lustadt with a large retinue," he said, "to attend the coronation of Peter of Blentz tomorrow."

"Prince Ludwig von der Tann has gone to attend the coronation of Peter!" cried Barney in amazement. "Has the Princess Emma returned from her captivity in the castle of Blentz?"

"She is with her father now, having returned nearly three weeks ago," replied the officer, "and Peter has disclaimed responsibility for the outrage, promising that those responsible shall be punished. He has convinced Prince Ludwig that Leopold is dead, and for the sake of Lutha— to save her from civil strife—my prince has patched a truce with Peter; though unless I mistake the character of the latter and the temper of the former it will be short-lived.

"To demonstrate to the people," continued the officer, "that Prince Ludwig and Peter are good friends, the great Von der Tann will attend the coronation, but that he takes little stock in the sincerity of the Prince of Blentz would be apparent could the latter have a peep beneath the cloaks and look into the loyal hearts of the men of Tann who rode down to Lustadt today."

Barney did not wait to hear more. He was glad that in the gathering dusk the officer had not seen his face plainly enough to mistake him for the king. With a parting, "Then I must ride to Lustadt with my message for the prince," he wheeled his tired mount and trotted down the steep trail from Tann toward the highway which leads to the capital.

All night Barney rode. Three times he wandered from the way and was forced to stop at farmhouses to inquire the proper direction; but darkness hid his features from the sleepy eyes of those who answered his summons, and daylight found him still forging ahead in the direction of the capital of Lutha.

The American was sunk in unhappy meditation as his weary little mount plodded slowly along the dusty road. For hours the man had not been able to urge the beast out of a walk. The loss of time consequent upon his having followed wrong roads during the night and the exhaustion of the pony which retarded his speed to what seemed little better than a snail's pace seemed to assure the failure of his mission, for at best he could not reach Lustadt before noon.

There was no possibility of bringing Leopold to his capital in time for the coronation, and but a bare possibility that Prince Ludwig would accept the word of an entire stranger that Leopold lived, for the acknowledgment of such a condition by the old prince could result in nothing less than an immediate resort to arms by the two factions. It was certain that Peter would be infinitely more anxious to proceed with his coronation should it be rumored that Leopold lived, and equally certain that Prince Ludwig would interpose every obstacle, even to armed resistance, to prevent the consummation of the ceremony.

Yet there seemed to Barney no other alternative than to place before the king's one powerful friend the information that he had. It would then rest with Ludwig to do what he thought advisable.

An hour from Lustadt the road wound through a dense forest, whose pleasant shade was a grateful relief to both horse and rider from the hot sun beneath which they had been journeying the greater part of the morning. Barney was still lost in thought, his eyes bent forward, when at a sudden turning of the road he came face to face with a troop of horse that were entering the main highway at this point from an unfrequented byroad.

At sight of them the American instinctively wheeled his mount in an effort to escape, but at a command from an officer a half dozen troopers spurred after him, their fresh horses soon overtaking his jaded pony.

For a moment Barney contemplated resistance, for these were troopers of the Royal Horse, the body which was now Peter's most effective personal tool; but even as his hand slipped to the butt of one of the revolvers at his hip, the young man saw the foolish futility of such a course, and with a shrug and a smile he drew rein and turned to face the advancing soldiers.

As he did so the officer rode up, and at sight of Barney's face gave an exclamation of astonishment. The officer was Butzow.

"Well met, your majesty," he cried saluting. "We are riding to the coronation. We shall be just in time."

"To see Peter of Blentz rob Leopold of a crown," said the American in a disgusted tone.

"To see Leopold of Lutha come into his own, your majesty. Long live the king!" cried the officer.

Barney thought the man either poking fun at him because he was not the king, or, thinking he was Leopold, taking a mean advantage of his helplessness to bait him. Yet this last suspicion seemed unfair to Butzow, who at Blentz had given ample evidence that he was a gentleman, and of far different caliber from Maenck and the others who served Peter.

If he could but convince the man that he was no king and thus gain his liberty long enough to reach Prince Ludwig's ear, his mission would have been served in so far as it lay in his power to serve it. For some minutes Barney expended his best eloquence and logic upon the cavalry officer in an effort to convince him that he was not Leopold.

The king had given the American his great ring to safeguard for him until it should be less dangerous for Leopold to wear it, and for fear that at the last moment someone within the sanatorium might recognize it and bear word to Peter of the king's whereabouts. Barney had worn it turned in upon the third finger of his left hand, and now he slipped it surreptitiously into his breeches pocket lest Butzow should see and by it be convinced that Barney was indeed Leopold.

"Never mind who you are," cried Butzow, thinking to humor the king's strange obsession. "You look enough like Leopold to be his twin, and you must help us save Lutha from Peter of Blentz."

The American showed in his expression the surprise he felt at these words from an officer of the prince regent.

"You wonder at my change of heart?" asked Butzow.

"How can I do otherwise?"

"I cannot blame you," said the officer. "Yet I think that when you know the truth you will see that I have done only that which I believed to be the duty of a patriotic officer and a true gentleman."

They had rejoined the troop by this time, and the entire company was once more headed toward Lustadt. Butzow had commanded one of the troopers to exchange horses with Barney, bringing the jaded animal into the city slowly, and now freshly mounted the American was making better time toward his destination. His spirits rose, and as they galloped along the highway, he listened with renewed interest to the story which Lieutenant Butzow narrated in detail.

It seemed that Butzow had been absent from Lutha for a number of years as military attache to the Luthanian legation at a foreign court. He had known nothing of the true condition at home until his return, when he saw such scoundrels as Coblich, Maenck, and Stein high in the favor of the prince regent. For some time before the events that had transpired after he had brought Barney and the Princess Emma to Blentz he had commenced to have his doubts as to the true patriotism of Peter of Blentz; and when he had learned through the unguarded words of Schonau that there was a real foundation for the rumor that the regent had plotted the assassination of the king his suspicions had crystallized into knowledge, and he had sworn to serve his king before all others—were he sane or mad. From this loyalty he could not be shaken.

"And what do you intend doing now?" asked Barney.

"I intend placing you upon the throne of your ancestors, sire," replied Butzow; "nor will Peter of Blentz dare the wrath of the people by attempting to interpose any obstacle. When he sees Leopold of Lutha ride into the capital of his kingdom at the head of even so small a force as ours he will know that the end of his own power is at hand, for he is not such a fool that he does not perfectly realize that he is the most cordially hated man in all Lutha, and that only those attend upon him who hope to profit through his success or who fear his evil nature."

"If Peter is crowned today," asked Barney, "will it prevent Leopold regaining his throne?"

"It is difficult to say," replied Butzow; "but the chances are that the throne would be lost to him forever. To regain it he would have to plunge Lutha into a bitter civil war, for once Peter is proclaimed king he will have the law upon his side, and with the resources of the State behind him—the treasury and the army—he will feel in no mood to relinquish the scepter without a struggle. I doubt much that you will ever sit upon your throne, sire, unless you do so within the very next hour."

For some time Barney rode in silence. He saw that only by a master stroke could the crown be saved for the true king. Was it worth it? The man was happier without a crown. Barney had come to believe that no man lived who could be happy in possession of one. Then there came before his mind's eye the delicate, patrician face of Emma von der Tann.

Would Peter of Blentz be true to his new promises to the house of Von der Tann? Barney doubted it. He recalled all that it might mean of danger and suffering to the girl whose kisses he still felt upon his lips as though it had been but now that hers had placed them there. He recalled the limp little body of the boy, Rudolph, and the Spartan loyalty with which the little fellow had given his life in the service of the man he had thought king. The pitiful figure of the fear-haunted man upon the iron cot at Tafelberg rose before him and cried for vengeance.

To this man was the woman he loved betrothed! He knew that he might never wed the Princess Emma. Even were she not promised to another, the iron shackles of convention and age-old customs must forever separate her from an untitled American. But if he couldn't have her he still could serve her!

"For her sake," he muttered.

"Did your majesty speak?" asked Butzow.

"Yes, lieutenant. We urge greater haste, for if we are to be crowned today we have no time to lose."

Butzow smiled a relieved smile. The king had at last regained his senses!

Within the ancient cathedral at Lustadt a great and gorgeously attired assemblage had congregated. All the nobles of Lutha were gathered there with their wives, their children, and their retainers. There were the newer nobility of the lowlands—many whose patents dated but since the regency of Peter—and there were the proud nobility of the highlands—the old nobility of which Prince Ludwig von der Tann was the chief.

It was noticeable that though a truce had been made between Ludwig and Peter, yet the former chancellor of the kingdom did not stand upon the chancel with the other dignitaries of the State and court.

Few there were who knew that he had been invited to occupy a place of honor there, and had replied that he would take no active part in the making of any king in Lutha whose veins did not pulse to the flow of the blood of the house in whose service he had grown gray.

Close packed were the retainers of the old prince so that their great number was scarcely noticeable, though quite so was the fact that they kept their cloaks on, presenting a somber appearance in the midst of all the glitter of gold and gleam of jewels that surrounded them— a grim, business-like appearance that cast a chill upon Peter of Blentz as his eyes scanned the multitude of faces below him.

He would have shown his indignation at this seeming affront had he dared; but until the crown was safely upon his head and the royal scepter in his hand Peter had no mind to do aught that might jeopardize the attainment of the power he had sought for the past ten years.

The solemn ceremony was all but completed; the Bishop of Lustadt had received the great golden crown from the purple cushion upon which it had been borne at the head of the procession which accompanied Peter up the broad center aisle of the cathedral. He had raised it above the head of the prince regent, and was repeating the solemn words which precede the placing of the golden circlet upon the man's brow. In another moment Peter of Blentz would be proclaimed the king of Lutha.

By her father's side stood Emma von der Tann. Upon her haughty, high-bred face there was no sign of the emotions which ran riot within her fair bosom. In the act that she was witnessing she saw the eventual ruin of her father's house. That Peter would long want for an excuse to break and humble his ancient enemy she did not believe; but this was not the only cause for the sorrow that overwhelmed her.

Her most poignant grief, like that of her father, was for the dead king, Leopold; but to the sorrow of the loyal subject was added the grief of the loving woman, bereft. Close to her heart she hugged the memory of the brief hours spent with the man whom she had been taught since childhood to look upon as her future husband, but for whom the all-consuming fires of love had only been fanned to life within her since that moment, now three weeks gone, that he had crushed her to his breast to cover her lips with kisses for the short moment ere he sacrificed his life to save her from a fate worse than death.

Before her stood the Nemesis of her dead king. The last act of the hideous crime against the man she had loved was nearing its close. As the crown, poised over the head of Peter of Blentz, sank slowly downward the girl felt that she could scarce restrain her desire to shriek aloud a protest against the wicked act—the crowning of a murderer king of her beloved Lutha.

A glance at the old man at her side showed her the stern, commanding features of her sire molded in an expression of haughty dignity; only the slight movement of the muscles of the strong jaw revealed the tensity of the hidden emotions of the stern old warrior. He was meeting disappointment and defeat as a Von der Tann should—brave to the end.

The crown had all but touched the head of Peter of Blentz when a sudden commotion at the back of the cathedral caused the bishop to look up in ill-concealed annoyance. At the sight that met his eyes his hands halted in mid-air.

The great audience turned as one toward the doors at the end of the long central aisle. There, through the wide-swung portals, they saw mounted men forcing their way into the cathedral. The great horses shouldered aside the foot-soldiers that attempted to bar their way, and twenty troopers of the Royal Horse thundered to the very foot of the chancel steps.

At their head rode Lieutenant Butzow and a tall young man in soiled and tattered khaki, whose gray eyes and full reddish-brown beard brought an exclamation from Captain Maenck who commanded the guard about Peter of Blentz.

"Mein Gott—the king!" cried Maenck, and at the words Peter went white.

In open-mouthed astonishment the spectators saw the hurrying troopers and heard Butzow's "The king! The king! Make way for Leopold, King of Lutha!"

And a girl saw, and as she saw her heart leaped to her mouth. Her small hand gripped the sleeve of her father's coat. "The king, father," she cried. "It is the king."

Old Von der Tann, the light of a new hope firing his eyes, threw aside his cloak and leaped to the chancel steps beside Butzow and the others who were mounting them. Behind him a hundred cloaks dropped from the shoulders of his fighting men, exposing not silks and satins and fine velvet, but the coarse tan of khaki, and grim cartridge belts well filled, and stern revolvers slung to well-worn service belts.

As Butzow and Barney stepped upon the chancel Peter of Blentz leaped forward. "What mad treason is this?" he fairly screamed.

"The days of treason are now past, prince," replied Butzow meaningly. "Here is not treason, but Leopold of Lutha come to claim his crown which he inherited from his father."

"It is a plot," cried Peter, "to place an impostor upon the throne! This man is not the king."

For a moment there was silence. The people had not taken sides as yet. They awaited a leader. Old Von der Tann scrutinized the American closely.

"How may we know that you are Leopold?" he asked. "For ten years we have not seen our king."

"The governor of Blentz has already acknowledged his identity," cried Butzow. "Maenck was the first to proclaim the presence of the putative king."

At that someone near the chancel cried: "Long live Leopold, king of Lutha!" and at the words the whole assemblage raised their voices in a tumultuous: "Long live the king!"

Peter of Blentz turned toward Maenck. "The guard!" he cried. "Arrest those traitors, and restore order in the cathedral. Let the coronation proceed."

Maenck took a step toward Barney and Butzow, when old Prince von der Tann interposed his giant frame with grim resolve.

"Hold!" He spoke in a low, stern voice that brought the cowardly Maenck to a sudden halt.

The men of Tann had pressed eagerly forward until they stood, with bared swords, a solid rank of fighting men in grim semicircle behind their chief. There were cries from different parts of the cathedral of: "Crown Leopold, our true king! Down with Peter! Down with the assassin!"

"Enough of this," cried Peter. "Clear the cathedral!"

He drew his own sword, and with half a hundred loyal retainers at his back pressed forward to clear the chancel. There was a brief fight, from which Barney, much to his disgust, was barred by the mighty figure of the old prince and the stalwart sword-arm of Butzow. He did get one crack at Maenck, and had the satisfaction of seeing blood spurt from a flesh wound across the fellow's cheek.

"That for the Princess Emma," he called to the governor of Blentz, and then men crowded between them and he did not see the captain again during the battle.

When Peter saw that more than half of the palace guard were shouting for Leopold, and fighting side by side with the men of Tann, he realized the futility of further armed resistance

56

at this time. Slowly he withdrew, and at last the fighting ceased and some semblance of order was restored within the cathedral.

Fearfully, the bishop emerged from hiding, his robes disheveled and his miter askew. Butzow grasped him none too reverently by the arm and dragged him before Barney. The crown of Lutha dangled in the priest's palsied hands.

"Crown the king!" cried the lieutenant. "Crown Leopold, king of Lutha!"

A mad roar of acclaim greeted this demand, and again from all parts of the cathedral rose the same wild cry. But in the lull that followed there were some who demanded proof of the tattered young man who stood before them and claimed that he was king.

"Let Prince Ludwig speak!" cried a dozen voices.

"Yes, Prince Ludwig! Prince Ludwig!" took up the throng.

Prince Ludwig von der Tann turned toward the bearded young man. Silence fell upon the crowded cathedral. Peter of Blentz stood awaiting the outcome, ready to demand the crown upon the first indication of wavering belief in the man he knew was not Leopold.

"How may we know that you are really Leopold?" again asked Ludwig of Barney.

The American raised his left hand, upon the third finger of which gleamed the great ruby of the royal ring of the kings of Lutha. Even Peter of Blentz started back in surprise as his eyes fell upon the ring.

Where had the man come upon it?

Prince von der Tann dropped to one knee before Mr. Bernard Custer of Beatrice, Nebraska, U.S.A., and lifted that gentleman's hand to his lips, and as the people of Lutha saw the act they went mad with joy.

Slowly Prince Ludwig rose and addressed the bishop. "Leopold, the rightful heir to the throne of Lutha, is here. Let the coronation proceed."

The quiet of the sepulcher fell upon the assemblage as the holy man raised the crown above the head of the king. Barney saw from the corner of his eye the sea of faces upturned toward him. He saw the relief and happiness upon the stern countenance of the old prince.

He hated to dash all their new found joy by the announcement that he was not the king. He could not do that, for the moment he did Peter would step forward and demand that his own coronation continue. How was he to save the throne for Leopold?

Among the faces beneath him he suddenly descried that of a beautiful young girl whose eyes, filled with the tears of a great happiness and a greater love, were upturned to his. To reveal his true identity would lose him this girl forever. None save Peter knew that he was not the king. All save Peter would hail him gladly as Leopold of Lutha. How easily he might win a throne and the woman he loved by a moment of seeming passive compliance.

The temptation was great, and then he recalled the boy, lying dead for his king in the desolate mountains, and the pathetic light in the eyes of the sorrowful man at Tafelberg, and the great trust and confidence in the heart of the woman who had shown that she loved him.

Slowly Barney Custer raised his palm toward the bishop in a gesture of restraint.

"There are those who doubt that I am king," he said. "In these circumstances there should be no coronation in Lutha until all doubts are allayed and all may unite in accepting without question the royal right of the true Leopold to the crown of his father. Let the coronation wait, then, until another day, and all will be well."

"It must take place before noon of the fifth day of November, or not until a year later," said Prince Ludwig. "In the meantime the Prince Regent must continue to rule. For the sake of Lutha the coronation must take place today, your majesty."

"What is the date?" asked Barney.

"The third, sire."

"Let the coronation wait until the fifth."

"But your majesty," interposed Von der Tann, "all may be lost in two days."

"It is the king's command," said Barney quietly.

"But Peter of Blentz will rule for these two days, and in that time with the army at his command there is no telling what he may accomplish," insisted the old man.

"Peter of Blentz shall not rule Lutha for two days, or two minutes," replied Barney. "We shall rule. Lieutenant Butzow, you may place Prince Peter, Coblich, Maenck, and Stein under arrest. We charge them with treason against their king, and conspiring to assassinate their rightful monarch."

Butzow smiled as he turned with his troopers at his back to execute this most welcome of commissions; but in a moment he was again at Barney's side.

"They have fled, your majesty," he said. "Shall I ride to Blentz after them?"

"Let them go," replied the American, and then, with his retinue about him the new king of Lutha passed down the broad aisle of the cathedral of Lustadt and took his way to the royal palace between ranks of saluting soldiery backed by cheering thousands.

IX

THE KING'S GUESTS

Once within the palace Barney sought the seclusion of a small room off the audience chamber. Here he summoned Butzow.

"Lieutenant," said the American, "for the sake of a woman, a dead child and an unhappy king I have become dictator of Lutha for forty-eight hours; but at noon upon the fifth this farce must cease. Then we must place the true Leopold upon the throne, or a new dictator must replace me.

"In vain I have tried to convince you that I am not the king, and today in the cathedral so great was the temptation to take advantage of the odd train of circumstances that had placed a crown within my reach that I all but surrendered to it—not for the crown of gold, Butzow, but for an infinitely more sacred diadem which belongs to him to whom by right of birth and lineage, belongs the crown of Lutha. I do not ask you to understand—it is not necessary—but this you must know and believe: that I am not Leopold, and that the true Leopold lies in hiding in the sanatorium at Tafelberg, from which you and I, Butzow, must fetch him to Lustadt before noon on the fifth."

"But, sire—" commenced Butzow, when Barney raised his hand.

"Enough of that, Butzow!" he cried almost irritably. "I am sick of being 'sired' and 'majestied'—my name is Custer. Call me that when others are not present. Believe what you will, but ride with me in secrecy to Tafelberg tonight, and together we shall bring back Leopold of Lutha. Then we may call Prince Ludwig into our confidence, and none need ever know of the substitution.

"I doubt if many had a sufficiently close view of me today to realize the trick that I have played upon them, and if they note a difference they will attribute it to the change in apparel, for we shall see to it that the king is fittingly garbed before we exhibit him to his subjects, while hereafter I shall continue in khaki, which becomes me better than ermine."

Butzow shook his head.

"King or dictator," he said, "it is all the same, and I must obey whatever commands you see fit to give, and so I will ride to Tafelberg tonight, though what we shall find there I cannot imagine, unless there are two Leopolds of Lutha. But shall we also find another royal ring upon the finger of this other king?"

Barney smiled. "You're a typical hard-headed Dutchman, Butzow," he said.

The lieutenant drew himself up haughtily. "I am not a Dutchman, your majesty. I am a Luthanian."

Barney laughed. "Whatever else you may be, Butzow, you're a brick," he said, laying his hand upon the other's arm.

Butzow looked at him narrowly.

"From your speech," he said, "and the occasional Americanisms into which you fall I might believe that you were other than the king but for the ring."

"It is my commission from the king," replied Barney. "Leopold placed it upon my finger in token of his royal authority to act in his behalf. Tonight, then Butzow, you and I shall ride to Tafelberg. Have three good horses. We must lead one for the king."

Butzow saluted and left the apartment. For an hour or two the American was busy with tailors whom he had ordered sent to the palace to measure him for the numerous garments of a royal wardrobe, for he knew the king to be near enough his own size that he might easily wear clothes that had been fitted to Barney; and it was part of his plan to have everything in readiness for the substitution which was to take place the morning of the coronation.

Then there were foreign dignitaries, and the heads of numerous domestic and civic delegations to be given audience. Old Von der Tann stood close behind Barney prompting him upon the royal duties that had fallen so suddenly upon his shoulders, and none thought it strange that he was unfamiliar with the craft of kingship, for was it not common knowledge that he had been kept a close prisoner in Blentz since boyhood, nor been given any coaching for the duties Peter of Blentz never intended he should perform?

After it was all over Prince Ludwig's grim and leathery face relaxed into a smile of satisfaction.

"None who witnessed the conduct of your first audience, sire," he said, "could for a moment doubt your royal lineage—if ever a man was born to kingship, your majesty, it be you."

Barney smiled, a bit ruefully, however, for in his mind's eye he saw a future moment when the proud old Prince von der Tann would know the truth of the imposture that had been played upon him, and the young man foresaw that he would have a rather unpleasant half-hour.

At a little distance from them Barney saw Emma von der Tann surrounded by a group of officials and palace officers. Since he had come to Lustadt that day he had had no word with her, and now he crossed toward her, amused as the throng parted to form an aisle for him, the men saluting and the women curtsying low.

He took both of the girl's hands in his, and, drawing one through his arm, took advantage of the prerogatives of kingship to lead her away from the throng of courtiers.

"I thought that I should never be done with all the tiresome business which seems to devolve upon kings," he said, laughing. "All the while that I should have been bending my royal intellect to matters of state, I was wondering just how a king might find a way to see the woman he loves without interruptions from the horde that dogs his footsteps."

"You seem to have found a way, Leopold," she whispered, pressing his arm close to her. "Kings usually do."

"It is not because I am a king that I found a way, Emma," he replied. "It is because I am an American."

She looked up at him with an expression of pleading in her eyes.

"Why do you persist?" she cried. "You have come into your own, and there is no longer aught to fear from Peter or any other. To me at least, it is most unkind still to deny your identity."

"I wonder," said Barney, "if your love could withstand the knowledge that I am not the king."

"It is the MAN I love, Leopold," the girl replied.

"You think so now," he said, "but wait until the test comes, and when it does, remember that I have always done my best to undeceive you. I know that you are not for such as I, my princess, and when I have returned your true king to you all that I shall ask is that you be happy with him."

"I shall always be happy with my king," she whispered, and the look that she gave him made Barney Custer curse the fate that had failed to make him a king by birth.

An hour later darkness had fallen upon the little city of Lustadt, and from a small gateway in the rear of the palace grounds two horsemen rode out into the ill-paved street and turned their mounts' heads toward the north. At the side of one trotted a led horse.

As they passed beneath the glare of an arc-light before a cafe at the side of the public square, a diner sitting at a table upon the walk spied the tall figure and the bearded face of him who rode a few feet in advance of his companion. Leaping to his feet the man waved his napkin above his head.

"Long live the king!" he cried. "God save Leopold of Lutha!"

And amid the din of cheering that followed, Barney Custer of Beatrice and Lieutenant Butzow of the Royal Horse rode out into the night upon the road to Tafelberg.

When Peter of Blentz had escaped from the cathedral he had hastily mounted with a handful of his followers and hurried out of Lustadt along the road toward his formidable fortress at Blentz. Half way upon the journey he had met a dusty and travel-stained horseman hastening toward the capital city that Peter and his lieutenants had just left.

At sight of the prince regent the fellow reined in and saluted.

"May I have a word in private with your highness?" he asked. "I have news of the greatest importance for your ears alone."

Peter drew to one side with the man.

"Well," he asked, "and what news have you for Peter of Blentz?"

The man leaned from his horse close to Peter's ear.

"The king is in Tafelberg, your highness," he said.

"The king is dead," snapped Peter. "There is an impostor in the palace at Lustadt. But the real Leopold of Lutha was slain by Yellow Franz's band of brigands weeks ago."

"I heard the man at Tafelberg tell another that he was the king," insisted the fellow. "Through the keyhole of his room I saw him take a great ring from his finger—a ring with a mighty ruby set in its center—and give it to the other. Both were bearded men with gray eyes—either might have passed for the king by the description upon the placards that have covered Lutha for the past month. At first he denied his identity, but when the other had convinced him that he sought only the king's welfare he at last admitted that he was Leopold."

"Where is he now?" cried Peter.

"He is still in the sanatorium at Tafelberg. In room twenty-seven. The other promised to return for him and take him to Lustadt, but when I left Tafelberg he had not yet done so, and if you hasten you may reach there before they take him away, and if there be any reward for my loyalty to you, prince, my name is Ferrath."

"Ride with us and if you have told the truth, fellow, there shall be a reward and if not—then there shall be deserts," and Peter of Blentz wheeled his horse and with his company galloped on toward Tafelberg.

As he rode he talked with his lieutenants Coblich, Maenck, and Stein, and among them it was decided that it would be best that Peter stop at Blentz for the night while the others rode on to Tafelberg.

"Do not bring Leopold to Blentz," directed Peter, "for if it be he who lies at Tafelberg and they find him gone it will be toward Blentz that they will first look. Take him—"

The Regent leaned from his saddle so that his mouth was close to the ear of Coblich, that none of the troopers might hear.

Coblich nodded his head.

"And, Coblich, the fewer that ride to Tafelberg tonight the surer the success of the mission. Take Maenck, Stein and one other with you. I shall keep this man with me, for it may prove but a plot to lure me to Tafelberg."

Peter scowled at the now frightened hospital attendant.

"Tomorrow I shall be riding through the lowlands, Coblich, and so you may not find means to communicate with me, but before noon of the fifth have word at your town house in Lustadt for me of the success of your venture."

They had reached the point now where the road to Tafelberg branches from that to Blentz, and the four who were to fetch the king wheeled their horses into the left-hand fork and cantered off upon their mission.

The direct road between Lustadt and Tafelberg is but little more than half the distance of that which Coblich and his companions had to traverse because of the wide detour they had made by riding almost to Blentz first, and so it was that when they cantered into the little mountain town near midnight Barney Custer and Lieutenant Butzow were but a mile or two behind them.

Had the latter had even the faintest of suspicions that the identity of the hiding place of the king might come to the knowledge of Peter of Blentz they could have reached Tafelberg ahead of Coblich and his party, but all unsuspecting they rode slowly to conserve the energy of their mounts for the return trip.

In silence the two men approached the grounds surrounding the sanatorium. In the soft dirt of the road the hoofs of their mounts made no sound, and the shadows of the trees that border the front of the enclosure hid them from the view of the trooper who held four riderless horses in a little patch of moonlight that broke through the opening in the trees at the main gate of the institution.

Barney was the first to see the animals and the man.

"S-s-st," he hissed, reining in his horse.

Butzow drew alongside the American.

"What can it mean?" asked Barney. "That fellow is a trooper, but I cannot make out his uniform."

"Wait here," said Butzow, and slipping from his horse he crept closer to the man, hugging the dense shadows close to the trees.

Barney reined in nearer the low wall. From his saddle he could see the grounds beyond through the branches of a tree. As he looked his attention was suddenly riveted upon a sight that sent his heart into his throat.

Three men were dragging a struggling, half-naked figure down the gravel walk from the sanatorium toward the gate. One kept a hand clapped across the mouth of the prisoner, who struck and fought his assailants with all the frenzy of despair.

Barney leaped from his saddle and ran headlong after Butzow. The lieutenant had reached the gate but an instant ahead of him when the trooper, turning suddenly at some slight sound of the officer's foot upon the ground, detected the man creeping upon him. In an instant the fellow had whipped out a revolver, and raising it fired point-blank at Butzow's chest; but in the same instant a figure shot out of the shadows beside him, and with the report of the revolver a heavy fist caught the trooper on the side of the chin, crumpling him to the ground as if he were dead.

The blow had been in time to deflect the muzzle of the firearm, and the bullet whistled harmlessly past the lieutenant.

"Your majesty!" exclaimed Butzow excitedly. "Go back. He might have killed you."

Barney leaped to the other's side and grasping him by the shoulders wheeled him about so that he faced the gate.

"There, Butzow," he cried, "there is your king, and from the looks of it he never needed a loyal subject more than he does this moment. Come!" Without waiting to see if the other followed him, Barney Custer leaped through the gate full in the faces of the astonished trio that was dragging Leopold of Lutha from his sanctuary.

At sight of the American the king gave a muffled cry of relief, and then Barney was upon those who held him. A stinging uppercut lifted Coblich clear of the ground to drop him, dazed and bewildered, at the foot of the monarch he had outraged. Maenck drew a revolver only to have it struck from his hand by the sword of Butzow, who had followed closely upon the American's heels.

Barney, seizing the king by the arm, started on a run for the gateway. In his wake came Butzow with a drawn sword beating back Stein, who was armed with a cavalry saber, and Maenck who had now drawn his own sword.

The American saw that the two were pressing Butzow much too closely for safety and that Coblich had now recovered from the effects of the blow and was in pursuit, drawing his saber as he ran. Barney thrust the king behind him and turned to face the enemy, at Butzow's side.

The three men rushed upon the two who stood between them and their prey. The moonlight was now full in the faces of Butzow and the American. For the first time Maenck and the others saw who it was that had interrupted them.

"The impostor!" cried the governor of Blentz. "The false king!"

Imbued with temporary courage by the knowledge that his side had the advantage of superior numbers he launched himself full upon the American. To his surprise he met a sword-arm that none might have expected in an American, for Barney Custer had been a pupil of the redoubtable Colonel Monstery, who was, as Barney was wont to say, "one of the thanwhomest of fencing masters."

Quickly Maenck fell back to give place to Stein, but not before the American's point had found him twice to leave him streaming blood from two deep flesh wounds.

Neither of those who fought in the service of the king saw the trembling, weak-kneed figure, which had stood behind them, turn and scurry through the gateway, leaving the men who battled for him to their fate.

The trooper whom Barney had felled had regained consciousness and as he came to his feet rubbing his swollen jaw he saw a disheveled, half-dressed figure running toward him from the sanatorium grounds. The fellow was no fool, and knowing the purpose of the expedition as he did he was quick to jump to the conclusion that this fleeing personification of abject terror was Leopold of Lutha; and so it was that as the king emerged from the gateway in search of freedom he ran straight into the widespread arms of the trooper.

Maenck and Coblich had seen the king's break for liberty, and the latter maneuvered to get himself between Butzow and the open gate that he might follow after the fleeing monarch.

At the same instant Maenck, seeing that Stein was being worsted by the American, rushed in upon the latter, and thus relieved, the rat-faced doctor was enabled to swing a heavy cut at Barney which struck him a glancing blow upon the head, sending him stunned and bleeding to the sward.

Coblich and the governor of Blentz hastened toward the gate, pausing for an instant to overwhelm Butzow. In the fierce scrimmage that followed the lieutenant was overthrown, though not before his sword had passed through the heart of the rat-faced one. Deserting their fallen comrade the two dashed through the gate, where to their immense relief they found Leopold safe in the hands of the trooper.

An instant later the precious trio, with Leopold upon the horse of the late Dr. Stein, were galloping swiftly into the darkness of the wood that lies at the outskirts of Tafelberg.

When Barney regained consciousness he found himself upon a cot within the sanatorium. Close beside him lay Butzow, and above them stood an interne and several nurses. No sooner had the American regained his scattered wits than he leaped to the floor. The interne and the nurses tried to force him back upon the cot, thinking that he was in the throes of a delirium, and it required his best efforts to convince them that he was quite rational.

During the melee Butzow regained consciousness; his wound being as superficial as that of the American, the two men were soon donning their clothing, and, half-dressed, rushing toward the outer gate.

The interne had told them that when he had reached the scene of the conflict in company with the gardener he had found them and another lying upon the sward.

Their companion, he said, was quite dead.

"That must have been Stein," said Butzow. "And the others had escaped with the king!"

"The king?" cried the interne.

"Yes, the king, man—Leopold of Lutha. Did you not know that he who has lain here for three weeks was the king?" replied Butzow.

The interne accompanied them to the gate and beyond, but everywhere was silence. The king was gone.

X

ON THE BATTLEFIELD

All that night and the following day Barney Custer and his aide rode in search of the missing king.

They came to Blentz, and there Butzow rode boldly into the great court, admitted by virtue of the fact that the guard upon the gate knew him only as an officer of the royal guard whom they believed still loyal to Peter of Blentz.

The lieutenant learned that the king was not there, nor had he been since his escape. He also learned that Peter was abroad in the lowland recruiting followers to aid him forcibly to regain the crown of Lutha.

The lieutenant did not wait to hear more, but, hurrying from the castle, rode to Barney where the latter had remained in hiding in the wood below the moat—the same wood through which he had stumbled a few weeks previously after his escape from the stagnant waters of the moat.

"The king is not here," said Butzow to him, as soon as the former reached his side. "Peter is recruiting an army to aid him in seizing the palace at Lustadt, and king or no king, we must ride for the capital in time to check that move. Thank God," he added, "that we shall have a king to place upon the throne of Lutha at noon tomorrow in spite of all that Peter can do."

"What do you mean?" asked Barney. "Have you any clue to the whereabouts of Leopold?"

"I saw the man at Tafelberg whom you say is king," replied Butzow. "I saw him tremble and whimper in the face of danger. I saw him run when he might have seized something, even a stone, and fought at the sides of the men who were come to rescue him. And I saw you there also.

"The truth and the falsity of this whole strange business is beyond me, but this I know: if you are not the king today I pray God that the other may not find his way to Lustadt before noon tomorrow, for by then a brave man will sit upon the throne of Lutha, your majesty."

Barney laid his hand upon the shoulder of the other.

"It cannot be, my friend," he said. "There is more than a throne at stake for me, but to win them both I could not do the thing you suggest. If Leopold of Lutha lives he must be crowned tomorrow."

"And if he does not live?" asked Butzow.

Barney Custer shrugged his shoulders.

It was dusk when the two entered the palace grounds in Lustadt. The sight of Barney threw the servants and functionaries of the royal household into wild excitement and confusion. Men ran hither and thither bearing the glad tidings that the king had returned.

Old von der Tann was announced within ten minutes after Barney reached his apartments. He urged upon the American the necessity for greater caution in the future.

"Your majesty's life is never safe while Peter of Blentz is abroad in Lutha," cried he.

"It was to save your king from Peter that we rode from Lustadt last night," replied Barney, but the old prince did not catch the double meaning of the words.

While they talked a young officer of cavalry begged an audience. He had important news for the king, he said. From him Barney learned that Peter of Blentz had succeeded in recruiting a fair-sized army in the lowlands. Two regiments of government infantry and a squadron of cavalry had united forces with him, for there were those who still accepted him as regent, believing his contention that the true king was dead, and that he whose coronation was to be attempted was but the puppet of old Von der Tann.

The morning of November 5 broke clear and cold. The old town of Lustadt was awakened with a start at daybreak by the booming of cannon. Mounted messengers galloped hither and thither through the steep, winding streets. Troops, foot and horse, moved at the double from the barracks along the King's Road to the fortifications which guard the entrance to the city at the foot of Margaretha Street.

Upon the heights above the town Barney Custer and the old Prince von der Tann stood surrounded by officers and aides watching the advance of a skirmish line up the slopes toward Lustadt. Behind, the thin line columns of troops were marching under cover of two batteries of field artillery that Peter of Blentz had placed upon a wooden knoll to the southeast of the city.

The guns upon the single fort that, overlooking the broad valley, guarded the entire southern exposure of the city were answering the fire of Prince Peter's artillery, while several machine guns had been placed to sweep the slope up which the skirmish line was advancing.

The trees that masked the enemy's pieces extended upward along the ridge and the eastern edge of the city. Barney saw that a force of men might easily reach a commanding position from that direction and enter Lustadt almost in rear of the fortifications. Below him a squadron of the Royal Horse were just emerging from their stables, taking their way toward the plain to join in a concerted movement against the troops that were advancing toward the fort.

He turned to an aide de camp standing just behind him.

"Intercept that squadron and direct the major to move due east along the King's Road to the grove," he commanded. "We will join him there."

And as the officer spurred down the steep and narrow street the American, followed by Von der Tann and his staff, wheeled and galloped eastward.

Ten minutes later the party entered the wood at the edge of town, where the squadron soon joined them. Von der Tann was mystified at the purpose of this change in the position of the general staff, since from the wood they could see nothing of the battle waging upon the slope. During his brief intercourse with the man he thought king he had quite forgotten that there had been any question as to the young man's sanity, for he had given no indication of possessing aught but a well-balanced mind. Now, however, he commenced to have misgivings, if not of his sanity, then as to his judgment at least.

"I fear, your majesty," he ventured, "that we are putting ourselves too much out of touch with the main body of the army. We can neither see nor accomplish anything from this position."

"We were too far away to accomplish much upon the top of that mountain," replied Barney, "but we're going to commence doing things now. You will please to ride back along the King's Road and take direct command of the troops mobilized near the fort.

"Direct the artillery to redouble their fire upon the enemy's battery for five minutes, and then to cease firing into the wood entirely. At the same instant you may order a cautious advance against the troops advancing up the slope.

"When you see us emerge upon the west side of the grove where the enemy's guns are now, you may order a charge, and we will take them simultaneously upon their right flank with a cavalry charge."

"But, your majesty," exclaimed Von der Tann dubiously, "where will you be in the mean time?"

"We shall be with the major's squadron, and when you see us emerging from the grove, you will know that we have taken Peter's guns and that everything is over except the shouting."

"You are not going to accompany the charge!" cried the old prince.

"We are going to lead it," and the pseudo-king of Lutha wheeled his mount as though to indicate that the time for talking was past.

With a signal to the major commanding the squadron of Royal Horse, he moved eastward into the wood. Prince Ludwig hesitated a moment as though to question further the wisdom of the move, but finally with a shake of his head he trotted off in the direction of the fort.

Five minutes later the enemy were delighted to note that the fire upon their concealed battery had suddenly ceased.

Then Peter saw a force of foot-soldiers deploy from the city and advance slowly in line of skirmishers down the slope to meet his own firing line.

Immediately he did what Barney had expected that he would—turned the fire of his artillery toward the southwest, directly away from the point from which the American and the crack squadron were advancing.

So it came that the cavalrymen crept through the woods upon the rear of the guns, unseen; the noise of their advance was drowned by the detonation of the cannon.

The first that the artillerymen knew of the enemy in their rear was a shout of warning from one of the powder-men at a caisson, who had caught a glimpse of the grim line advancing through the trees at his rear.

Instantly an effort was made to wheel several of the pieces about and train them upon the advancing horsemen; but even had there been time, a shout that rose from several of Peter's artillerymen as the Royal Horse broke into full view would doubtless have prevented the maneuver, for at sight of the tall, bearded, young man who galloped in front of the now charging cavalrymen there rose a shout of "The king! The king!"

With the force of an avalanche the Royal Horse rode through those two batteries of field artillery; and in the thick of the fight that followed rode the American, a smile upon his face, for in his ears rang the wild shouts of his troopers: "For the king! For the king!"

In the moment that the enemy made their first determined stand a bullet brought down the great bay upon which Barney rode. A dozen of Peter's men rushed forward to seize the man stumbling to his feet. As many more of the Royal Horse closed around him, and there, for five minutes, was waged as fierce a battle for possession of a king as was ever fought.

But already many of the artillerymen had deserted the guns that had not yet been attacked, for the magic name of king had turned their blood to water. Fifty or more raised a white flag and surrendered without striking a blow, and when, at last, Barney and his little bodyguard fought their way through those who surrounded them they found the balance of the field already won.

Upon the slope below the city the loyal troops were advancing upon the enemy. Old Prince Ludwig paced back and forth behind them, apparently oblivious to the rain of bullets about him. Every moment he turned his eyes toward the wooded ridge from which there now belched an almost continuous fusillade of shells upon the advancing royalists.

Quite suddenly the cannonading ceased and the old man halted in his tracks, his gaze riveted upon the wood. For several minutes he saw no sign of what was transpiring behind that screen of sere and yellow autumn leaves, and then a man came running out, and after him another and another.

The prince raised his field glasses to his eyes. He almost cried aloud in his relief—the uniforms of the fugitives were those of artillerymen, and only cavalry had accompanied the king. A moment later there appeared in the center of his lenses a tall figure with a full beard. He rode, swinging his saber above his head, and behind him at full gallop came a squadron of the Royal Horse.

Old von der Tann could restrain himself no longer.

"The king! The king!" he cried to those about him, pointing in the direction of the wood.

The officers gathered there and the soldiery before him heard and took up the cry, and then from the old man's lips came the command, "Charge!" and a thousand men tore down the slopes of Lustadt upon the forces of Peter of Blentz, while from the east the king charged their right flank at the head of the Royal Horse.

Peter of Blentz saw that the day was lost, for the troops upon the right were crumpling before the false king while he and his cavalrymen were yet a half mile distant. Before the retreat could become a rout the prince regent ordered his forces to fall back slowly upon a suburb that lies in the valley below the city.

Once safely there he raised a white flag, asking a conference with Prince Ludwig.

"Your majesty," said the old man, "what answer shall we send the traitor who even now ignores the presence of his king?"

"Treat with him," replied the American. "He may be honest enough in his belief that I am an impostor."

Von der Tann shrugged his shoulders, but did as Barney bid, and for half an hour the young man waited with Butzow while Von der Tann and Peter met halfway between the forces for their conference.

A dozen members of the most powerful of the older nobility accompanied Ludwig. When they returned their faces were a picture of puzzled bewilderment. With them were several officers, soldiers and civilians from Peter's contingency.

"What said he?" asked Barney.

"He said, your majesty," replied Von der Tann, "that he is confident you are not the king, and that these men he has sent with me knew the king well at Blentz. As proof that you are not the king he has offered the evidence of your own denials—made not only to his officers and soldiers, but to the man who is now your loyal lieutenant, Butzow, and to the Princess Emma von der Tann, my daughter.

"He insists that he is fighting for the welfare of Lutha, while we are traitors, attempting to seat an impostor upon the throne of the dead Leopold. I will admit that we are at a loss, your majesty, to know where lies the truth and where the falsity in this matter.

"We seek only to serve our country and our king but there are those among us who, to be entirely frank, are not yet convinced that you are Leopold. The result of the conference may not, then, meet with the hearty approval of your majesty."

"What was the result?" asked Barney.

"It was decided that all hostilities cease, and that Prince Peter be given an opportunity to establish the validity of his claim that your majesty is an impostor. If he is able to do so to the entire satisfaction of a majority of the old nobility, we have agreed to support him in a return to his regency."

For a moment there was deep silence. Many of the nobles stood with averted faces and eyes upon the ground.

The American, a half-smile upon his face, turned toward the men of Peter who had come to denounce him. He knew what their verdict would be. He knew that if he were to save the throne for Leopold he must hold it at any cost until Leopold should be found.

Troopers were scouring the country about Lustadt as far as Blentz in search of Maenck and Coblich. Could they locate these two and arrest them "with all found in their company," as his order read, he felt sure that he would be able to deliver the missing king to his subjects in time for the coronation at noon.

Barney looked straight into the eyes of old Von der Tann.

"You have given us the opinion of others, Prince Ludwig," he said. "Now you may tell us your own views of the matter."

"I shall have to abide by the decision of the majority," replied the old man. "But I have seen your majesty under fire, and if you are not the king, for Lutha's sake you ought to be."

"He is not Leopold," said one of the officers who had accompanied the prince from Peter's camp. "I was governor of Blentz for three years and as familiar with the king's face as with that of my own brother."

"No," cried several of the others, "this man is not the king."

Several of the nobles drew away from Barney. Others looked at him questioningly.

Butzow stepped close to his side, and it was noticeable that the troopers, and even the officers, of the Royal Horse which Barney had led in the charge upon the two batteries in the wood, pressed a little closer to the American. This fact did not escape Butzow's notice.

"If you are content to take the word of the servants of a traitor and a would-be regicide," he cried, "I am not. There has been no proof advanced that this man is not the king. In so far as I am concerned he is the king, nor ever do I expect to serve another more worthy of the title.

"If Peter of Blentz has real proof—not the testimony of his own faction—that Leopold of Lutha is dead, let him bring it forward before noon today, for at noon we shall crown a king in the cathedral at Lustadt, and I for one pray to God that it may be he who has led us in battle today."

70

A shout of applause rose from the Royal Horse, and from the foot-soldiers who had seen the king charge across the plain, scattering the enemy before him.

Barney, appreciating the advantage in the sudden turn affairs had taken following Butzow's words, swung to his saddle.

"Until Peter of Blentz brings to Lustadt one with a better claim to the throne," he said, "we shall continue to rule Lutha, nor shall other than Leopold be crowned her king. We approve of the amnesty you have granted, Prince Ludwig, and Peter of Blentz is free to enter Lustadt, as he will, so long as he does not plot against the true king.

"Major," he added, turning to the commander of the squadron at his back, "we are returning to the palace. Your squadron will escort us, remaining on guard there about the grounds. Prince Ludwig, you will see that machine guns are placed about the palace and commanding the approaches to the cathedral."

With a nod to the cavalry major he wheeled his horse and trotted up the slope toward Lustadt.

With a grim smile Prince Ludwig von der Tann mounted his horse and rode toward the fort. At his side were several of the nobles of Lutha. They looked at him in astonishment.

"You are doing his bidding, although you do not know that he is the true king?" asked one of them.

"Were he an impostor," replied the old man, "he would have insisted by word of mouth that he is king. But not once has he said that he is Leopold. Instead, he has proved his kingship by his acts."

XI

A TIMELY INTERVENTION

Nine o'clock found Barney Custer pacing up and down his apartments in the palace. No clue as to the whereabouts of Coblich, Maenck or the king had been discovered. One by one his troopers had returned to Butzow empty-handed, and as much at a loss as to the hiding-place of their quarry as when they had set out upon their search.

Peter of Blentz and his retainers had entered the city and already had commenced to gather at the cathedral.

Peter, at the residence of Coblich, had succeeded in gathering about him many of the older nobility whom he pledged to support him in case he could prove to them that the man who occupied the royal palace was not Leopold of Lutha.

They agreed to support him in his regency if he produced proof that the true Leopold was dead, and Peter of Blentz waited with growing anxiety the coming of Coblich with word that he had the king in custody. Peter was staking all on a single daring move which he had decided to make in his game of intrigue.

As Barney paced within the palace, waiting for word that Leopold had been found, Peter of Blentz was filled with equal apprehension as he, too, waited for the same tidings. At last he heard the pound of hoofs upon the pavement without and a moment later Coblich, his clothing streaked with dirt, blood caked upon his face from a wound across the forehead, rushed into the presence of the prince regent.

Peter drew him hurriedly into a small study on the first floor.

"Well?" he whispered, as the two faced each other.

"We have him," replied Coblich. "But we had the devil's own time getting him. Stein was killed and Maenck and I both wounded, and all morning we have spent the time hiding from troopers who seemed to be searching for us. Only fifteen minutes since did we reach the hiding-place that you instructed us to use. But we have him, your highness, and he is in such a state of cowardly terror that he is ready to agree to anything, if you will but spare his life and set him free across the border."

"It is too late for that now, Coblich," replied Peter. "There is but one way that Leopold of Lutha can serve me now, and that is—dead. Were his corpse to be carried into the cathedral of Lustadt before noon today, and were those who fetched it to swear that the king was killed by the impostor after being dragged from the hospital at Tafelberg where you and Maenck had located him, and from which you were attempting to rescue him, I believe that the people would tear our enemies to pieces. What say you, Coblich?"

The other stared at Peter of Blentz for several seconds while the atrocity of his chief's plan filtered through his brain.

"My God!" he exclaimed at last. "You mean that you wish me to murder Leopold with my own hands?"

"You put it too crudely, my dear Coblich," replied the other.

"I cannot do it," muttered Coblich. "I have never killed a man in my life. I am getting old. No, I could never do it. I should not sleep nights."

"If it is not done, Coblich, and Leopold comes into his own," said Peter slowly, "you will be caught and hanged higher than Haman. And if you do not do it, and the impostor is crowned today, then you will be either hanged officially or knifed unofficially, and without any choice in the matter whatsoever. Nothing, Coblich, but the dead body of the true Leopold can save your neck. You have your choice, therefore, of letting him live to prove your treason, or letting him die and becoming chancellor of Lutha."

Slowly Coblich turned toward the door. "You are right," he said, "but may God have mercy on my soul. I never thought that I should have to do it with my own hands."

So saying he left the room and a moment later Peter of Blentz smiled as he heard the pounding of a horse's hoofs upon the pavement without.

Then the Regent entered the room he had recently quitted and spoke to the nobles of Lutha who were gathered there.

"Coblich has found the body of the murdered king," he said. "I have directed him to bring it to the cathedral. He came upon the impostor and his confederate, Lieutenant Butzow, as they were bearing the corpse from the hospital at Tafelberg where the king has lain unknown since the rumor was spread by Von der Tann that he had been killed by bandits.

"He was not killed until last evening, my lords, and you shall see today the fresh wounds upon him. When the time comes that we can present this grisly evidence of the guilt of the impostor and those who uphold him, I shall expect you all to stand at my side, as you have promised."

With one accord the noblemen pledged anew their allegiance to Peter of Blentz if he could produce one-quarter of the evidence he claimed to possess.

"All that we wish to know positively is," said one, "that the man who bears the title of king today is really Leopold of Lutha, or that he is not. If not then he stands convicted of treason, and we shall know how to conduct ourselves."

Together the party rode to the cathedral, the majority of the older nobility now openly espousing the cause of the Regent.

At the palace Barney was about distracted. Butzow was urging him to take the crown whether he was Leopold or not, for the young lieutenant saw no hope for Lutha, if either the scoundrelly Regent or the cowardly man whom Barney had assured him was the true king should come into power.

It was eleven o'clock. In another hour Barney knew that he must have found some new solution of his dilemma, for there seemed little probability that the king would be located in the brief interval that remained before the coronation. He wondered what they did to people who stole thrones. For a time he figured his chances of reaching the border ahead of the enraged populace. All had depended upon the finding of the king, and he had been so sure that it could be accomplished in time, for Coblich and Maenck had had but a few hours in which to conceal the monarch before the search was well under way.

Armed with the king's warrants, his troopers had ridden through the country, searching houses, and questioning all whom they met. Patrols had guarded every road that the fugitives might take either to Lustadt, Blentz, or the border; but no king had been found and no trace of his abductors.

Prince von der Tann, Barney was convinced, was on the point of deserting him, and going over to the other side. It was true that the old man had carried out his instructions relative to the placing of the machine guns; but they might be used as well against him, where they stood, as for him.

From his window he could see the broad avenue which passes before the royal palace of Lutha. It was crowded with throngs moving toward the cathedral. Presently there came a knock upon the closed door of his chamber.

At his "Enter" a functionary announced: "His Royal Highness Ludwig, Prince von der Tann!"

The old man was much perturbed at the rumors he had heard relative to the assassination of the true Leopold. Soldier-like, he blurted out his suspicions and his ultimatum.

"None but the royal blood of Rubinroth may reign in Lutha while there be a Rubinroth left to reign and old Von der Tann lives," he cried in conclusion.

At the name "Rubinroth" Barney started. It was his mother's name. Suddenly the truth flashed upon him. He understood now the reticence of both his father and mother relative to her early life.

"Prince Ludwig," said the young man earnestly, "I have only the good of Lutha in my heart. For three weeks I have labored and risked death a hundred times to place the legitimate heir to the crown of Lutha upon his throne. I—"

He hesitated, not knowing just how to commence the confession he was determined to make, though he was positive that it would place Peter of Blentz upon the throne, since the old prince had promised to support the Regent could it be proved that Barney was an impostor.

"I," he started again, and then there came an interruption at the door.

"A messenger, your majesty," announced the doorman, "who says that he must have audience at once upon a matter of life and death to the king."

"We will see him in the ante-chamber," replied Barney, moving toward the door. "Await us here, Prince Ludwig."

A moment later he re-entered the apartment. There was an expression of renewed hope upon his face.

"As we were about to remark, my dear prince," he said, "I swear that the royal blood of the Rubinroths flows in my veins, and as God is my judge, none other than the true Leopold of Lutha shall be crowned today. And now we must prepare for the coronation. If there be trouble in the cathedral, Prince Ludwig, we look to your sword in protection of the king."

"When I am with you, sire," said Von der Tann, "I know that you are king. When I saw how you led the troops in battle, I prayed that there could be no mistake. God give that I am right. But God help you if you are playing with old Ludwig von der Tann."

When the old man had left the apartment Barney summoned an aide and sent for Butzow. Then he hurried to the bath that adjoined the apartment, and when the lieutenant of horse was announced Barney called through a soapy lather for his confederate to enter.

"What are you doing, sire?" cried Butzow in amazement.

"Cut out the 'sire,' old man," shouted Barney Custer of Beatrice. "this is the fifth of November and I am shaving off this alfalfa. The king is found!"

"What?" cried Butzow, and upon his face there was little to indicate the rejoicing that a loyal subject of Leopold of Lutha should have felt at that announcement.

"There is a man in the next room," went on Barney, "who can lead us to the spot where Coblich and Maenck guard the king. Get him in here."

74

Butzow hastened to comply with the American's instructions, and a moment later returned to the apartment with the old shopkeeper of Tafelberg.

As Barney shaved he issued directions to the two. Within the room to the east, he said, there were the king's coronation robes, and in a smaller dressingroom beyond they would find a long gray cloak.

They were to wrap all these in a bundle which the old shopkeeper was to carry.

"And, Butzow," added Barney, "look to my revolvers and your own, and lay my sword out as well. The chances are that we shall have to use them before we are ten minutes older."

In an incredibly short space of time the young man emerged from the bath, his luxuriant beard gone forever, he hoped. Butzow looked at him with a smile.

"I must say that the beard did not add greatly to your majesty's good looks," he said.

"Never mind the bouquets, old man," cried Barney, cramming his arms into the sleeves of his khaki jacket and buckling sword and revolver about him, as he hurried toward a small door that opened upon the opposite side of the apartment to that through which his visitors had been conducted.

Together the three hastened through a narrow, little-used corridor and down a flight of well-worn stone steps to a door that let upon the rear court of the palace.

There were grooms and servants there, and soldiers too, who saluted Butzow, according the old shopkeeper and the smooth-faced young stranger only cursory glances. It was evident that without his beard it was not likely that Barney would be again mistaken for the king.

At the stables Butzow requisitioned three horses, and soon the trio was galloping through a little-frequented street toward the northern, hilly environs of Lustadt. They rode in silence until they came to an old stone building, whose boarded windows and general appearance of dilapidation proclaimed its long tenantless condition. Rank weeds, now rustling dry and yellow in the November wind, choked what once might have been a luxuriant garden. A stone wall, which had at one time entirely surrounded the grounds, had been almost completely removed from the front to serve as foundation stone for a smaller edifice farther down the mountainside.

The horsemen avoided this break in the wall, coming up instead upon the rear side where their approach was wholly screened from the building by the wall upon that exposure.

Close in they dismounted, and leaving the animals in charge of the shopkeeper of Tafelberg, Barney and Butzow hastened toward a small postern-gate which swung, groaning, upon a single rusted hinge. Each felt that there was no time for caution or stratagem. Instead all depended upon the very boldness and rashness of their attack, and so as they came through into the courtyard the two dashed headlong for the building.

Chance accomplished for them what no amount of careful execution might have done, and they came within the ruin unnoticed by the four who occupied the old, darkened library.

Possibly the fact that one of the men had himself just entered and was excitedly talking to the others may have drowned the noisy approach of the two. However that may be, it is a fact that Barney and the cavalry officer came to the very door of the library unheard.

There they halted, listening. Coblich was speaking.

"The Regent commands it, Maenck," he was saying. "It is the only thing that can save our necks. He said that you had better be the one to do it, since it was your carelessness that permitted the fellow to escape from Blentz."

Huddled in a far corner of the room was an abject figure trembling in terror. At the words of Coblich it staggered to its feet. It was the king.

"Have pity—have pity!" he cried. "Do not kill me, and I will go away where none will ever know that I live. You can tell Peter that I am dead. Tell him anything, only spare my life. Oh, why did I ever listen to the cursed fool who tempted me to think of regaining the crown that has brought me only misery and suffering—the crown that has now placed the sentence of death upon me."

"Why not let him go?" suggested the trooper, who up to this time had not spoken. "If we don't kill him, we can't be hanged for his murder."

"Don't be too sure of that," exclaimed Maenck. "If he goes away and never returns, what proof can we offer that we did not kill him, should we be charged with the crime? And if we let him go, and later he returns and gains his throne, he will see that we are hanged anyway for treason.

"The safest thing to do is to put him where he at least cannot come back to threaten us, and having done so upon the orders of Peter, let the king's blood be upon Peter's head. I, at least, shall obey my master, and let you two bear witness that I did the thing with my own hand." So saying he drew his sword and crossed toward the king.

But Captain Ernst Maenck never reached his sovereign.

As the terrified shriek of the sorry monarch rang through the interior of the desolate ruin another sound mingled with it, half-drowning the piercing wail of terror.

It was the sharp crack of a revolver, and even as it spoke Maenck lunged awkwardly forward, stumbled, and collapsed at Leopold's feet. With a moan the king shrank back from the grisly thing that touched his boot, and then two men were in the center of the room, and things were happening with a rapidity that was bewildering.

About all that he could afterward recall with any distinctness was the terrified face of Coblich, as he rushed past him toward a door in the opposite side of the room, and the horrid leer upon the face of the dead trooper, who foolishly, had made a move to draw his revolver.

Within the cathedral at Lustadt excitement was at fever heat. It lacked but two minutes of noon, and as yet no king had come to claim the crown. Rumors were running riot through the close-packed audience.

One man had heard the king's chamberlain report to Prince von der Tann that the master of ceremonies had found the king's apartments vacant when he had gone to urge the monarch to hasten his preparations for the coronation.

Another had seen Butzow and two strangers galloping north through the city. A third told of a little old man who had come to the king with an urgent message.

Peter of Blentz and Prince Ludwig were talking in whispers at the foot of the chancel steps. Peter ascended the steps and facing the assemblage raised a silencing hand.

"He who claimed to be Leopold of Lutha," he said, "was but a mad adventurer. He would have seized the throne of the Rubinroths had his nerve not failed him at the last moment. He has fled. The true king is dead. Now I, Prince Regent of Lutha, declare the throne vacant, and announce myself king!"

There were a few scattered cheers and some hissing. A score of the nobles rose as though to protest, but before any could take a step the attention of all was directed toward the sorry figure of a white-faced man who scurried up the broad center aisle.

It was Coblich.

He ran to Peter's side, and though he attempted to speak in a whisper, so out of breath, and so filled with hysterical terror was he that his words came out in gasps that were audible to many of those who stood near by.

"Maenck is dead," he cried. "The impostor has stolen the king."

Peter of Blentz went white as his lieutenant. Von der Tann heard and demanded an explanation.

"You said that Leopold was dead," he said accusingly.

Peter regained his self-control quickly.

"Coblich is excited," he explained. "He means that the impostor has stolen the body of the king that Coblich and Maenck had discovered and were bringing to Lustadt."

Von der Tann looked troubled.

He knew not what to make of the series of wild tales that had come to his ears within the past hour. He had hoped that the young man whom he had last seen in the king's apartments was the true Leopold. He would have been glad to have served such a one, but there had been many inexplicable occurrences which tended to cast a doubt upon the man's claims— and yet, had he ever claimed to be the king? It suddenly occurred to the old prince that he had not. On the contrary he had repeatedly stated to Prince Ludwig's daughter and to Lieutenant Butzow that he was not Leopold.

It seemed that they had all been so anxious to believe him king that they had forced the false position upon him, and now if he had indeed committed the atrocity that Coblich charged against him, who could wonder? With less provocation men had before attempted to seize thrones by more dastardly means.

Peter of Blentz was speaking.

"Let the coronation proceed," he cried, "that Lutha may have a true king to frustrate the plans of the impostor and the traitors who had supported him."

He cast a meaning glance at Prince von der Tann.

There were many cries for Peter of Blentz. "Let's have done with treason, and place upon the throne of Lutha one whom we know to be both a Luthanian and sane. Down with the mad king! Down with the impostor!"

Peter turned to ascend the chancel steps.

Von der Tann still hesitated. Below him upon one side of the aisle were massed his own retainers. Opposite them were the men of the Regent, and dividing the two the parallel ranks of Horse Guards stretched from the chancel down the broad aisle to the great doors. These were strongly for the impostor, if impostor he was, who had led them to victory over the men of the Blentz faction.

Von der Tann knew that they would fight to the last ditch for their hero should he come to claim the crown. Yet how would they fight—to which side would they cleave, were he to attempt to frustrate the design of the Regent to seize the throne of Lutha?

Already Peter of Blentz had approached the bishop, who, eager to propitiate whoever seemed most likely to become king, gave the signal for the procession that was to mark the solemn bearing of the crown of Lutha up the aisle to the chancel.

Outside the cathedral there was the sudden blare of trumpets. The great doors swung violently open, and the entire throng were upon their feet in an instant as a trooper of the Royal Horse shouted: "The king! The king! Make way for Leopold of Lutha!"

XII

THE GRATITUDE OF A KING

At the cry silence fell upon the throng. Every head was turned toward the great doors through which the head of a procession was just visible. It was a grim looking procession—the head of it, at least.

There were four khaki-clad trumpeters from the Royal Horse Guards, the gay and resplendent uniforms which they should have donned today conspicuous for their absence. From their brazen bugles sounded another loud fanfare, and then they separated, two upon each side of the aisle, and between them marched three men.

One was tall, with gray eyes and had a reddish-brown beard. He was fully clothed in the coronation robes of Leopold. Upon his either hand walked the others—Lieutenant Butzow and a gray-eyed, smooth-faced, square-jawed stranger.

Behind them marched the balance of the Royal Horse Guards that were not already on duty within the cathedral. As the eyes of the multitude fell upon the man in the coronation robes there were cries of: "The king! Impostor!" and "Von der Tann's puppet!"

"Denounce him!" whispered one of Peter's henchmen in his master's ear.

The Regent moved closer to the aisle, that he might meet the impostor at the foot of the chancel steps. The procession was moving steadily up the aisle.

Among the clan of Von der Tann a young girl with wide eyes was bending forward that she might have a better look at the face of the king. As he came opposite her her eyes filled with horror, and then she saw the eyes of the smooth-faced stranger at the king's side. They were brave, laughing eyes, and as they looked straight into her own the truth flashed upon her, and the girl gave a gasp of dismay as she realized that the king of Lutha and the king of her heart were not one and the same.

At last the head of the procession was almost at the foot of the chancel steps. There were murmurs of: "It is not the king," and "Who is this new impostor?"

Leopold's eyes were searching the faces of the close-packed nobility about the chancel. At last they fell upon the face of Peter. The young man halted not two paces from the Regent. The man went white as the king's eyes bored straight into his miserable soul.

"Peter of Blentz," cried the young man, "as God is your judge, tell the truth today. Who am I?"

The legs of the Prince Regent trembled. He sank upon his knees, raising his hands in supplication toward the other. "Have pity on me, your majesty, have pity!" he cried.

"Who am I, man?" insisted the king.

"You are Leopold Rubinroth, sire, by the grace of God, king of Lutha," cried the frightened man. "Have mercy on an old man, your majesty."

"Wait! Am I mad? Was I ever mad?"

"As God is my judge, sire, no!" replied Peter of Blentz.

Leopold turned to Butzow.

"Remove the traitor from our presence," he commanded, and at a word from the lieutenant a dozen guardsmen seized the trembling man and hustled him from the cathedral amid hisses and execrations.

Following the coronation the king was closeted in his private audience chamber in the palace with Prince Ludwig.

"I cannot understand what has happened, even now, your majesty," the old man was saying. "That you are the true Leopold is all that I am positive of, for the discomfiture of Prince Peter evidenced that fact all too plainly. But who the impostor was who ruled Lutha in your name for two days, disappearing as miraculously as he came, I cannot guess.

79

"But for another miracle which preserved you for us in the nick of time he might now be wearing the crown of Lutha in your stead. Having Peter of Blentz safely in custody our next immediate task should be to hunt down the impostor and bring him to justice also; though"— and the old prince sighed—"he was indeed a brave man, and a noble figure of a king as he led your troops to battle."

The king had been smiling as Von der Tann first spoke of the "impostor," but at the old man's praise of the other's bravery a slight flush tinged his cheek, and the shadow of a scowl crossed his brow.

"Wait," he said, "we shall not have to look far for your 'impostor,'" and summoning an aide he dispatched him for "Lieutenant Butzow and Mr. Custer."

A moment later the two entered the audience chamber. Barney found that Leopold the king, surrounded by comforts and safety, was a very different person from Leopold the fugitive. The weak face now wore an expression of arrogance, though the king spoke most graciously to the American.

"Here, Von der Tann," said Leopold, "is your 'impostor.' But for him I should doubtless be dead by now, or once again a prisoner at Blentz."

Barney and Butzow found it necessary to repeat their stories several times before the old man could fully grasp all that had transpired beneath his very nose without his being aware of scarce a single detail of it.

When he was finally convinced that they were telling the truth, he extended his hand to the American.

"I knelt to you once, young man," he said, "and kissed your hand. I should be filled with bitterness and rage toward you. On the contrary, I find that I am proud to have served in the retinue of such an impostor as you, for you upheld the prestige of the house of Rubinroth upon the battlefield, and though you might have had a crown, you refused it and brought the true king into his own."

Leopold sat tapping his foot upon the carpet. It was all very well if he, the king, chose to praise the American, but there was no need for old von der Tann to slop over so. The king did not like it. As a matter of fact, he found himself becoming very jealous of the man who had placed him upon his throne.

"There is only one thing that I can harbor against you," continued Prince Ludwig, "and that is that in a single instance you deceived me, for an hour before the coronation you told me that you were a Rubinroth."

"I told you, prince," corrected Barney, "that the royal blood of Rubinroth flowed in my veins, and so it does. I am the son of the runaway Princess Victoria of Lutha."

Both Leopold and Ludwig looked their surprise, and to the king's eyes came a sudden look of fear. With the royal blood in his veins, what was there to prevent this popular hero from some day striving for the throne he had once refused? Leopold knew that the minds of men were wont to change most unaccountably.

"Butzow," he said suddenly to the lieutenant of horse, "how many do you imagine know positively that he who has ruled Lutha for the past two days and he who was crowned in the cathedral this noon are not one and the same?"

"Only a few besides those who are in this room, your majesty," replied Butzow. "Peter and Coblich have known it from the first, and then there is Kramer, the loyal old shopkeeper of Tafelberg, who followed Coblich and Maenck all night and half a day as they dragged the king to the hiding-place where we found him. Other than these there may be those who guess the truth, but there are none who know."

For a moment the king sat in thought. Then he rose and commenced pacing back and forth the length of the apartment.

"Why should they ever know?" he said at last, halting before the three men who had been standing watching him. "For the sake of Lutha they should never know that another than the true king sat upon the throne even for an hour."

He was thinking of the comparison that might be drawn between the heroic figure of the American and his own colorless part in the events which had led up to his coronation. In his heart of hearts he felt that old Von der Tann rather regretted that the American had not been the king, and he hated the old man accordingly, and was commencing to hate the American as well.

Prince Ludwig stood looking at the carpet after the king had spoken. His judgment told him that the king's suggestion was a wise one; but he was sorry and ashamed that it had come from Leopold. Butzow's lips almost showed the contempt that he felt for the ingratitude of his king.

Barney Custer was the first to speak.

"I think his majesty is quite right," he said, "and tonight I can leave the palace after dark and cross the border some time tomorrow evening. The people need never know the truth."

Leopold looked relieved.

"We must reward you, Mr. Custer," he said. "Name that which it lies within our power to grant you and it shall be yours."

Barney thought of the girl he loved; but he did not mention her name, for he knew that she was not for him now.

"There is nothing, your majesty," he said.

"A money reward," Leopold started to suggest, and then Barney Custer lost his temper.

A flush mounted to his face, his chin went up, and there came to his lips bitter words of sarcasm. With an effort, however, he held his tongue, and, turning his back upon the king, his broad shoulders proclaiming the contempt he felt, he walked slowly out of the room.

Von der Tann and Butzow and Leopold of Lutha stood in silence as the American passed out of sight beyond the portal.

81

The manner of his going had been an affront to the king, and the young ruler had gone red with anger.

"Butzow," he cried, "bring the fellow back; he shall be taught a lesson in the deference that is due kings."

Butzow hesitated. "He has risked his life a dozen times for your majesty," said the lieutenant.

Leopold flushed.

"Do not humiliate him, sire," advised Von der Tann. "He has earned a greater reward at your hands than that."

The king resumed his pacing for a moment, coming to a halt once more before the two.

"We shall take no notice of his insolence," he said, "and that shall be our royal reward for his services. More than he deserves, we dare say, at that."

As Barney hastened through the palace on his way to his new quarters to obtain his arms and order his horse saddled, he came suddenly upon a girlish figure gazing sadly from a window upon the drear November world—her heart as sad as the day.

At the sound of his footstep she turned, and as her eyes met the gray ones of the man she stood poised as though of half a mind to fly. For a moment neither spoke.

"Can your highness forgive?" he asked.

For answer the girl buried her face in her hands and dropped upon the cushioned window seat before her. The American came close and knelt at her side.

"Don't," he begged as he saw her shoulders rise to the sudden sobbing that racked her slender frame. "Don't!"

He thought that she wept from mortification that she had given her kisses to another than the king.

"None knows," he continued, "what has passed between us. None but you and I need ever know. I tried to make you understand that I was not Leopold; but you would not believe. It is not my fault that I loved you. It is not my fault that I shall always love you. Tell me that you forgive me my part in the chain of strange circumstances that deceived you into an acknowledgment of a love that you intended for another. Forgive me, Emma!"

Down the corridor behind them a tall figure approached on silent, noiseless feet. At sight of the two at the window seat it halted. It was the king.

The girl looked up suddenly into the eyes of the American bending so close above her.

"I can never forgive you," she cried, "for not being the king, for I am betrothed to him—and I love you!"

Before she could prevent him, Barney Custer had taken her in his arms, and though at first she made a pretense of attempting to escape, at last she lay quite still. Her arms found their way about the man's neck, and her lips returned the kisses that his were showering upon her upturned mouth.

Presently her glance wandered above the shoulder of the American, and of a sudden her eyes filled with terror, and, with a little gasp of consternation, she struggled to free herself.

"Let me go!" she whispered. "Let me go—the king!"

Barney sprang to his feet and, turning, faced Leopold. The king had gone quite white.

"Failing to rob me of my crown," he cried in a trembling voice, "you now seek to rob me of my betrothed! Go to your father at once, and as for you—you shall learn what it means for you thus to meddle in the affairs of kings."

Barney saw the terrible position in which his love had placed the Princess Emma. His only thought now was for her. Bowing low before her he spoke so that the king might hear, yet as though his words were for her ears alone.

"Your highness knows the truth, now," he said, "and that after all I am not the king. I can only ask that you will forgive me the deception. Now go to your father as the king commands."

Slowly the girl turned away. Her heart was torn between love for this man, and her duty toward the other to whom she had been betrothed in childhood. The hereditary instinct of obedience to her sovereign was strong within her, and the bonds of custom and society held her in their relentless shackles. With a sob she passed up the corridor, curtsying to the king as she passed him.

When she had gone Leopold turned to the American. There was an evil look in the little gray eyes of the monarch.

"You may go your way," he said coldly. "We shall give you forty-eight hours to leave Lutha. Should you ever return your life shall be the forfeit."

The American kept back the hot words that were ready upon the end of his tongue. For her sake he must bow to fate. With a slight inclination of his head toward Leopold he wheeled and resumed his way toward his quarters.

Half an hour later as he was about to descend to the courtyard where a trooper of the Royal Horse held his waiting mount, Butzow burst suddenly into his room.

"For God's sake," cried the lieutenant, "get out of this. The king has changed his mind, and there is an officer of the guard on his way here now with a file of soldiers to place you under arrest. Leopold swears that he will hang you for treason. Princess Emma has spurned him, and he is wild with rage."

The dismal November twilight had given place to bleak night as two men cantered from the palace courtyard and turned their horses' heads northward toward Lutha's nearest boundary. All night they rode, stopping at daylight before a distant farm to feed and water their mounts and snatch a mouthful for themselves. Then onward once again they pressed in their mad flight.

Now that day had come they caught occasional glimpses of a body of horsemen far behind them, but the border was near, and their start such that there was no danger of their being overtaken.

"For the thousandth time, Butzow," said one of the men, "will you turn back before it is too late?"

But the other only shook his head obstinately, and so they came to the great granite monument which marks the boundary between Lutha and her powerful neighbor upon the north.

Barney held out his hand. "Good-bye, old man," he said. "If I've learned the ingratitude of kings here in Lutha, I have found something that more than compensates me—the friendship of a brave man. Now hurry back and tell them that I escaped across the border just as I was about to fall into your hands and they will think that you have been pursuing me instead of aiding in my escape across the border."

But again Butzow shook his head.

"I have fought shoulder to shoulder with you, my friend," he said. "I have called you king, and after that I could never serve the coward who sits now upon the throne of Lutha. I have made up my mind during this long ride from Lustadt, and I have come to the decision that I should prefer to raise corn in Nebraska with you rather than serve in the court of an ingrate."

"Well, you are an obstinate Dutchman, after all," replied the American with a smile, placing his hand affectionately upon the shoulder of his comrade.

There was a clatter of horses' hoofs upon the gravel of the road behind them.

The two men put spurs to their mounts, and Barney Custer galloped across the northern boundary of Lutha just ahead of a troop of Luthanian cavalry, as had his father thirty years before; but a royal princess had accompanied the father—only a soldier accompanied the son.

PART II

I

BARNEY RETURNS TO LUTHA

"What's the matter, Vic?" asked Barney Custer of his sister. "You look peeved."

"I am peeved," replied the girl, smiling. "I am terribly peeved. I don't want to play bridge this afternoon. I want to go motoring with Lieutenant Butzow. This is his last day with us."

"Yes. I know it is, and I hate to think of it," replied Barney; "but why in the world do you have to play bridge if you don't want to?"

"I promised Margaret that I'd go. They're short one, and she's coming after me in her car."

"Where are you going to play—at the champion lady bridge player's on Fourth Street?" asked Barney, grinning.

His sister answered with a nod and a smile. "Where you brought down the wrath of the lady champion upon your head the other night when you were letting your mind wander across to Lutha and the Old Forest, instead of paying attention to the game," she added.

"Well, cheer up, Vic," cried her brother. "Bert'll probably set fire to the car, the way he did to their first one, and then you won't have to go."

"Oh, yes, I would; Margaret would send him after me in that awful-looking, unwashed Ford runabout of his," answered the girl.

"And then you WOULD go," said Barney.

"You bet I would," laughed Victoria. "I'd go in a wheelbarrow with Bert."

But she didn't have to; and after she had driven off with her chum, Barney and Butzow strolled down through the little city of Beatrice to the corn mill in which the former was interested.

"I'm mighty sorry that you have to leave us, Butzow," said Barney's partner. "It's bad enough to lose you, but I'm afraid it will mean the loss of Barney, too. He's been hunting for some excuse to get back to Lutha, and with you there and a war in sight I'm afraid nothing can hold him."

"I don't know but that it may be just as well for my friends here that I leave," said Butzow seriously. "I did not tell you, Barney, all there is in this letter"—he tapped his breastpocket, where the foreign-looking envelope reposed with its contents.

Custer looked at him inquiringly.

"Besides saying that war between Austria and Serbia seems unavoidable and that Lutha doubtless will be drawn into it, my informant warns me that Leopold had sent emissaries to America to search for you, Barney, and myself. What his purpose may be my friend does not know, but he warns us to be upon our guard. Von der Tann wants me to return to Lutha. He has promised to protect me, and with the country in danger there is nothing else for me to do. I must go."

"I wish I could go with you," said Barney. "If it wasn't for this dinged old mill I would; but Bert wants to go away this summer, and as I have been away most of the time for the past two years, it's up to me to stay."

As the three men talked the afternoon wore on. Heavy clouds gathered in the sky; a storm was brewing. Outside, a man, skulking behind a box car on the siding, watched the entrance through which the three had gone. He watched the workmen, and as quitting time came and he saw them leaving for their homes he moved more restlessly, transferring the package which he held from one hand to another many times, yet always gingerly.

At last all had left. The man started from behind the box car, only to jump back as the watchman appeared around the end of one of the buildings. He watched the guardian of the property make his rounds; he saw him enter his office, and then he crept forward toward the building, holding his queer package in his right hand.

In the office the watchman came upon the three friends. At sight of him they looked at one another in surprise.

"Why, what time is it?" exclaimed Custer, and as he looked at his watch he rose with a laugh. "Late to dinner again," he cried. "Come on, we'll go out this other way." And with a cheery good night to the watchman Barney and his friends hastened from the building.

Upon the opposite side the stranger approached the doorway to the mill. The rain was falling in blinding sheets. Ominously the thunder roared. Vivid flashes of lightning shot the heavens. The watchman, coming suddenly from the doorway, his hat brim pulled low over his eyes, passed within a couple of paces of the stranger without seeing him.

Five minutes later there was a blinding glare accompanied by a deafening roar. It was as though nature had marshaled all her forces in one mighty, devastating effort. At the same instant the walls of the great mill burst asunder, a nebulous mass of burning gas shot heavenward, and then the flames settled down to complete the destruction of the ruin.

It was the following morning that Victoria and Barney Custer, with Lieutenant Butzow and Custer's partner, stood contemplating the smoldering wreckage.

"And to think," said Barney, "that yesterday this muss was the largest corn mill west of anywhere. I guess we can both take vacations now, Bert."

"Who would have thought that a single bolt of lightning could have resulted in such havoc?" mused Victoria.

"Who would?" agreed Lieutenant Butzow, and then, with a sudden narrowing of his eyes and a quick glance at Barney, "if it WAS lightning."

The American looked at the Luthanian. "You think—" he started.

"I don't dare think," replied Butzow, "because of the fear of what this may mean to you and Miss Victoria if it was not lightning that destroyed the mill. I shouldn't have spoken of it but that it may urge you to greater caution, which I cannot but think is most necessary since the warning I received from Lutha."

"Why should Leopold seek to harm me now?" asked Barney. "It has been almost two years since you and I placed him upon his throne, only to be rewarded with threats and hatred. In that time neither of us has returned to Lutha nor in any way conspired against the king. I cannot fathom his motives."

"There is the Princess Emma von der Tann," Butzow reminded him. "She still repulses him. He may think that, with you removed definitely and permanently, all will then be plain sailing for him in that direction. Evidently he does not know the princess."

An hour later they were all bidding Butzow good-bye at the station. Victoria Custer was genuinely grieved to see him go, for she liked this soldierly young officer of the Royal Horse Guards immensely.

"You must come back to America soon," she urged.

He looked down at her from the steps of the moving train. There was something in his expression that she had never seen there before.

"I want to come back soon," he answered, "to—to Beatrice," and he flushed and smiled at his own stumbling tongue.

For about a week Barney Custer moped disconsolately, principally about the ruins of the corn mill. He was in everyone's way and accomplished nothing.

"I was never intended for a captain of industry," he confided to his partner for the hundredth time. "I wish some excuse would pop up to which I might hang a reason for beating it to Europe. There's something doing there. Nearly everybody has declared war upon everybody else, and here I am stagnating in peace. I'd even welcome a tornado."

His excuse was to come sooner than he imagined. That night, after the other members of his family had retired, Barney sat smoking within a screened porch off the living-room. His thoughts were upon a trim little figure in riding togs, as he had first seen it nearly two years before, clinging desperately to a runaway horse upon the narrow mountain road above Tafelberg.

He lived that thrilling experience through again as he had many times before. He even smiled as he recalled the series of events that had resulted from his resemblance to the mad king of Lutha.

They had come to a culmination at the time when the king, whom Barney had placed upon a throne at the risk of his own life, discovered that his savior loved the girl to whom the king had been betrothed since childhood and that the girl returned the American's love even after she knew that he had but played the part of a king.

Barney's cigar, forgotten, had long since died out. Not even its former fitful glow proclaimed his presence upon the porch, whose black shadows completely enveloped him. Before him stretched a wide acreage of lawn, tree dotted at the side of the house. Bushes hid the stone wall that marked the boundary of the Custer grounds and extended here and there out upon the sward among the trees. The night was moonless but clear. A faint light pervaded the scene.

Barney sat staring straight ahead, but his gaze did not stop upon the familiar objects of the foreground. Instead it spanned two continents and an ocean to rest upon the little spot of woodland and rugged mountain and lowland that is Lutha. It was with an effort that the man suddenly focused his attention upon that which lay directly before him. A shadow among the trees had moved!

Barney Custer sat perfectly still, but now he was suddenly alert and watchful. Again the shadow moved where no shadow should be moving. It crossed from the shade of one tree to another. Barney came cautiously to his feet. Silently he entered the house, running quickly to a side door that opened upon the grounds. As he drew it back its hinges gave forth no sound. Barney looked toward the spot where he had seen the shadow. Again he saw it scuttle hurriedly beneath another tree nearer the house. This time there was no doubt. It was a man!

Directly before the door where Barney stood was a pergola, ivy-covered. Behind this he slid, and, running its length, came out among the trees behind the night prowler. Now he saw him distinctly. The fellow was bearded, and in his right hand he carried a package. Instantly Barney recalled Butzow's comment upon the destruction of the mill—"if it WAS lightning!"

Cold sweat broke from every pore of his body. His mother and father were there in the house, and Vic—all sleeping peacefully. He ran quickly toward the menacing figure, and as he did so he saw the other halt behind a great tree and strike a match. In the glow of the flame he saw it touch close to the package that the fellow held, and then he was upon him.

There was a brief and terrific struggle. The stranger hurled the package toward the house. Barney caught him by the throat, beating him heavily in the face; and then, realizing what the package was, he hurled the fellow from him, and sprang toward the hissing and sputtering missile where it lay close to the foundation wall of the house, though in the instant of his close contact with the man he had recognized through the disguising beard the features of Captain Ernst Maenck, the principal tool of Peter of Blentz.

Quick though Barney was to reach the bomb and extinguish the fuse, Maenck had disappeared before he returned to search for him; and, though he roused the gardener and chauffeur and took turns with them in standing guard the balance of the night, the would-be assassin did not return.

There was no question in Barney Custer's mind as to whom the bomb was intended for. That Maenck had hurled it toward the house after Barney had seized him was merely the result of accident and the man's desire to get the death-dealing missile as far from himself as possible before it exploded. That it would have wrecked the house in the hope of reaching him, had he not fortunately interfered, was too evident to the American to be questioned.

And so he decided before the night was spent to put himself as far from his family as possible, lest some future attempt upon his life might endanger theirs. Then, too, righteous anger and a desire for revenge prompted his decision. He would run Maenck to earth and have an accounting with him. It was evident that his life would not be worth a farthing so long as the fellow was at liberty.

Before dawn he swore the gardener and chauffeur to silence, and at breakfast announced his intention of leaving that day for New York to seek a commission as correspondent with an old classmate, who owned the New York Evening National. At the hotel Barney inquired of the proprietor relative to a bearded stranger, but the man had had no one of that description registered. Chance, however, gave him a clue. His roadster was in a repair shop, and as he stopped in to get it he overheard a conversation that told him all he wanted to know. As he stood talking with the foreman a dust-covered automobile pulled into the garage.

"Hello, Bill," called the foreman to the driver. "Where you been so early?"

"Took a guy to Lincoln," replied the other. "He was in an awful hurry. I bet we broke all the records for that stretch of road this morning—I never knew the old boat had it in her."

"Who was it?" asked Barney.

88

"I dunno," replied the driver. "Talked like a furriner, and looked the part. Bushy black beard. Said he was a German army officer, an' had to beat it back on account of the war. Seemed to me like he was mighty anxious to get back there an' be killed."

Barney waited to hear no more. He did not even go home to say good-bye to his family. Instead he leaped into his gray roadster—a later model of the one he had lost in Lutha—and the last that Beatrice, Nebraska, saw of him was a whirling cloud of dust as he raced north out of town toward Lincoln.

He was five minutes too late into the capital city to catch the eastbound limited that Maenck must have taken; but he caught the next through train for Chicago, and the second day thereafter found him in New York. There he had little difficulty in obtaining the desired credentials from his newspaper friend, especially since Barney offered to pay all his own expenses and donate to the paper anything he found time to write.

Passenger steamers were still sailing, though irregularly, and after scanning the passenger-lists of three he found the name he sought. "Captain Ernst Maenck, Lutha." So he had not been mistaken, after all. It was Maenck he had apprehended on his father's grounds. Evidently the man had little fear of being followed, for he had made no effort to hide his identity in booking passage for Europe.

The steamer he had caught had sailed that very morning. Barney was not so sorry, after all, for he had had time during his trip from Beatrice to do considerable thinking, and had found it rather difficult to determine just what to do should he have overtaken Maenck in the United States. He couldn't kill the man in cold blood, justly as he may have deserved the fate, and the thought of causing his arrest and dragging his own name into the publicity of court proceedings was little less distasteful to him.

Furthermore, the pursuit of Maenck now gave Barney a legitimate excuse for returning to Lutha, or at least to the close neighborhood of the little kingdom, where he might await the outcome of events and be ready to give his services in the cause of the house of Von der Tann should they be required.

By going directly to Italy and entering Austria from that country Barney managed to arrive within the boundaries of the dual monarchy with comparatively few delays. Nor did he encounter any considerable bodies of troops until he reached the little town of Burgova, which lies not far from the Serbian frontier. Beyond this point his credentials would not carry him. The emperor's officers were polite, but firm. No newspaper correspondents could be permitted nearer the front than Burgova.

There was nothing to be done, therefore, but wait until some propitious event gave him the opportunity to approach more closely the Serbian boundary and Lutha. In the meantime he would communicate with Butzow, who might be able to obtain passes for him to some village nearer the Luthanian frontier, when it should be an easy matter to cross through to Serbia. He was sure the Serbian authorities would object less strenuously to his presence.

The inn at which he applied for accommodations was already overrun by officers, but the proprietor, with scant apologies for a civilian, offered him a little box of a room in the attic. The place was scarce more than a closet, and for that Barney was in a way thankful since the limited space could accommodate but a single cot, thus insuring him the privacy that a larger chamber would have precluded.

He was very tired after his long and comfortless land journey, so after an early dinner he went immediately to his room and to bed. How long he slept he did not know, but some time during the night he was awakened by the sound of voices apparently close to his ear.

For a moment he thought the speakers must be in his own room, so distinctly did he overhear each word of their conversation; but presently he discovered that they were upon the opposite side of a thin partition in an adjoining room. But half awake, and with the sole idea of getting back to sleep again as quickly as possible, Barney paid only the slightest attention to the meaning of the words that fell upon his ears, until, like a bomb, a sentence broke through his sleepy faculties, banishing Morpheus upon the instant.

"It will take but little now to turn Leopold against Von der Tann." The speaker evidently was an Austrian. "Already I have half convinced him that the old man aspires to the throne. Leopold fears the loyalty of his army, which is for Von der Tann body and soul. He knows that Von der Tann is strongly anti-Austrian, and I have made it plain to him that if he allows his kingdom to take sides with Serbia he will have no kingdom when the war is over—it will be a part of Austria.

"It was with greater difficulty, however, my dear Peter, that I convinced him that you, Von Coblich, and Captain Maenck were his most loyal friends. He fears you yet, but, nevertheless, he has pardoned you all. Do not forget when you return to your dear Lutha that you owe your repatriation to Count Zellerndorf of Austria."

"You may be assured that we shall never forget," replied another voice that Barney recognized at once as belonging to Prince Peter of Blentz, the one time regent of Lutha.

"It is not for myself," continued Count Zellerndorf, "that I crave your gratitude, but for my emperor. You may do much to win his undying gratitude, while for yourselves you may win to almost any height with the friendship of Austria behind you. I am sure that should any accident, which God forfend, deprive Lutha of her king, none would make a more welcome successor in the eyes of Austria than our good friend Peter."

Barney could almost see the smile of satisfaction upon the thin lips of Peter of Blentz as this broad hint fell from the lips of the Austrian diplomat—a hint that seemed to the American little short of the death sentence of Leopold, King of Lutha.

"We owed you much before, count," said Peter. "But for you we should have been hanged a year ago—without your aid we should never have been able to escape from the fortress of Lustadt or cross the border into Austria-Hungary. I am sorry that Maenck failed in his mission, for had he not we would have had concrete evidence to present to the king that we are indeed his loyal supporters. It would have dispelled at once such fears and doubts as he may still entertain of our fealty."

"Yes, I, too, am sorry," agreed Zellerndorf. "I can assure you that the news we hoped Captain Maenck would bring from America would have gone a long way toward restoring you to the confidence and good graces of the king."

"I did my best," came another voice that caused Barney's eyes to go wide in astonishment, for it was none other than the voice of Maenck himself. "Twice I risked hanging to get him and only came away after I had been recognized."

90

"It is too bad," sighed Zellerndorf; "though it may not be without its advantages after all, for now we still have this second bugbear to frighten Leopold with. So long, of course, as the American lives there is always the chance that he may return and seek to gain the throne. The fact that his mother was a Rubinroth princess might make it easy for Von der Tann to place him upon the throne without much opposition, and if he married the old man's daughter it is easy to conceive that the prince might favor such a move. At any rate, it should not be difficult to persuade Leopold of the possibility of such a thing.

"Under the circumstances Leopold is almost convinced that his only hope of salvation lies in cementing friendly relations with the most powerful of Von der Tann's enemies, of which you three gentlemen stand preeminently in the foreground, and of assuring to himself the support of Austria. And now, gentlemen," he went on after a pause, "good night. I have handed Prince Peter the necessary military passes to carry you safely through our lines, and tomorrow you may be in Blentz if you wish."

II

CONDEMNED TO DEATH

For some time Barney Custer lay there in the dark revolving in his mind all that he had overheard through the partition—the thin partition which alone lay between himself and three men who would be only too glad to embrace the first opportunity to destroy him. But his fears were not for himself so much as for the daughter of old Von der Tann, and for all that might befall that princely house were these three unhung rascals to gain Lutha and have their way with the weak and cowardly king who reigned there.

If he could but reach Von der Tann's ear and through him the king before the conspirators came to Lutha! But how might he accomplish it? Count Zellerndorf's parting words to the three had shown that military passes were necessary to enable one to reach Lutha.

His papers were practically worthless even inside the lines. That they would carry him through the lines he had not the slightest hope. There were two things to be accomplished if possible. One was to cross the frontier into Lutha; and the other, which of course was quite out of the question, was to prevent Peter of Blentz, Von Coblich, and Maenck from doing so. But was that altogether impossible?

The idea that followed that question came so suddenly that it brought Barney Custer out onto the floor in a bound, to don his clothes and sneak into the hall outside his room with the stealth of a professional second-story man.

To the right of his own door was the door to the apartment in which the three conspirators slept. At least, Barney hoped they slept. He bent close to the keyhole and listened. From within came no sound other than the regular breathing of the inmates. It had been at least half an hour since the American had heard the conversation cease. A glance through the keyhole showed no light within the room. Stealthily Barney turned the knob. Had they bolted the door? He felt the tumbler move to the pressure—soundlessly. Then he pushed gently inward. The door swung.

A moment later he stood in the room. Dimly he could see two beds—a large one and a smaller. Peter of Blentz would be alone upon the smaller bed, his henchmen sleeping together in the larger. Barney crept toward the lone sleeper. At the bedside he fumbled in the dark groping for the man's clothing—for the coat, in the breastpocket of which he hoped to find the military pass that might carry him safely out of Austria-Hungary and into Lutha. On the foot of the bed he found some garments. Gingerly he felt them over, seeking the coat.

At last he found it. His fingers, steady even under the nervous tension of this unaccustomed labor, discovered the inner pocket and the folded paper. There were several of them; Barney took them all.

So far he made no noise. None of the sleepers had stirred. Now he took a step toward the doorway and—kicked a shoe that lay in his path. The slight noise in that quiet room sounded to Barney's ears like the fall of a brick wall. Peter of Blentz stirred, turning in his sleep. Behind him Barney heard one of the men in the other bed move. He turned his head in that direction. Either Maenck or Coblich was sitting up peering through the darkness.

"Is that you, Prince Peter?" The voice was Maenck's.

"What's the matter?" persisted Maenck.

"I'm going for a drink of water," replied the American, and stepped toward the door.

Behind him Peter of Blentz sat up in bed.

"That you, Maenck?" he called.

Instantly Maenck was out of bed, for the first voice had come from the vicinity of the doorway; both could not be Peter's.

"Quick!" he cried; "there's someone in our room."

Barney leaped for the doorway, and upon his heels came the three conspirators. Maenck was closest to him—so close that Barney was forced to turn at the top of the stairs. In the darkness he was just conscious of the form of the man who was almost upon him. Then he swung a vicious blow for the other's face—a blow that landed, for there was a cry of pain and anger as Maenck stumbled back into the arms of the two behind him. From below came the sound of footsteps hurrying up the stairs to the accompaniment of a clanking saber. Barney's retreat was cut off.

Turning, he dodged into his own room before the enemy could locate him or even extricate themselves from the confusion of Maenck's sudden collision with the other two. But what could Barney gain by the slight delay that would be immediately followed by his apprehension?

He didn't know. All that he was sure of was that there had been no other place to go than this little room. As he entered the first thing that his eyes fell upon was the small square window. Here at least was some slight encouragement.

He ran toward it. The lower sash was raised. As the door behind him opened to admit Peter of Blentz and his companions, Barney slipped through into the night, hanging by his hands from the sill without. What lay beneath or how far the drop he could not guess, but that

92

certain death menaced him from above he knew from the conversation he had overheard earlier in the evening.

For an instant he hung suspended. He heard the men groping about the room. Evidently they were in some fear of the unknown assailant they sought, for they did not move about with undue rashness. Presently one of them struck a light—Barney could see its flare lighten the window casing for an instant.

"The room is empty," came a voice from above him.

"Look to the window!" cried Peter of Blentz, and then Barney Custer let go his hold upon the sill and dropped into the blackness below.

His fall was a short one, for the window had been directly over a low shed at the side of the inn. Upon the roof of this the American landed, and from there he dropped to the courtyard without mishap. Glancing up, he saw the heads of three men peering from the window of the room he had just quitted.

"There he is!" cried one, and instantly the three turned back into the room. As Barney fled from the courtyard he heard the rattle of hasty footsteps upon the rickety stairway of the inn.

Choosing an alley rather than a street in which he might run upon soldiers at any moment, he moved quickly yet cautiously away from the inn. Behind him he could hear the voices of many men. They were raised to a high pitch by excitement. It was clear to Barney that there were many more than the original three—Prince Peter had, in all probability, enlisted the aid of the military.

Could he but reach the frontier with his stolen passes he would be comparatively safe, for the rugged mountains of Lutha offered many places of concealment, and, too, there were few Luthanians who did not hate Peter of Blentz most cordially—among the men of the mountains at least. Once there he could defy a dozen Blentz princes for the little time that would be required to carry him into Serbia and comparative safety.

As he approached a cross street a couple of squares from the inn he found it necessary to pass beneath a street lamp. For a moment he paused in the shadows of the alley listening. Hearing nothing moving in the street, Barney was about to make a swift spring for the shadows upon the opposite side when it occurred to him that it might be safer to make assurance doubly sure by having a look up and down the street before emerging into the light.

It was just as well that he did, for as he thrust his head around the corner of the building the first thing that his eyes fell upon was the figure of an Austrian sentry, scarcely three paces from him. The soldier was standing in a listening attitude, his head half turned away from the American. The sounds coming from the direction of the inn were apparently what had attracted his attention.

Behind him, Barney was sure he heard evidences of pursuit. Before him was certain detection should he attempt to cross the street. On either hand rose the walls of buildings. That he was trapped there seemed little doubt.

He continued to stand motionless, watching the Austrian soldier. Should the fellow turn toward him, he had but to withdraw his head within the shadow of the building that hid his body. Possibly the man might turn and take his beat in the opposite direction. In which case Barney was sure he could dodge across the street, undetected.

Already the vague threat of pursuit from the direction of the inn had developed into a certainty—he could hear men moving toward him through the alley from the rear. Would the sentry never move! Evidently not, until he heard the others coming through the alley. Then he would turn, and the devil would be to pay for the American.

Barney was about hopeless. He had been in the war zone long enough to know that it might prove a very disagreeable matter to be caught sneaking through back alleys at night. There was a single chance—a sort of forlorn hope—and that was to risk fate and make a dash beneath the sentry's nose for the opposite alley mouth.

"Well, here goes," thought Barney. He had heard that many of the Austrians were excellent shots. Visions of Beatrice, Nebraska, swarmed his memory. They were pleasant visions, made doubly alluring by the thought that the realities of them might never again be for him.

He turned once more toward the sounds of pursuit—the men upon his track could not be over a square away—there was not an instant to be lost. And then from above him, upon the opposite side of the alley, came a low: "S-s-t!"

Barney looked up. Very dimly he could see the dark outline of a window some dozen feet from the pavement, and framed within it the lighter blotch that might have been a human face. Again came the challenging: "S-s-t!" Yes, there was someone above, signaling to him.

"S-s-t!" replied Barney. He knew that he had been discovered, and could think of no better plan for throwing the discoverer off his guard than to reply.

Then a soft voice floated down to him—a woman's voice!

"Is that you?" The tongue was Serbian. Barney could understand it, though he spoke it but indifferently.

"Yes," he replied truthfully.

"Thank Heaven!" came the voice from above. "I have been watching you, and thought you one of the Austrian pigs. Quick! They are coming—I can hear them;" and at the same instant Barney saw something drop from the window to the ground. He crossed the alley quickly, and could have shouted in relief for what he found there—the end of a knotted rope dangling from above.

His pursuers were almost upon him when he seized the rude ladder to clamber upward. At the window's ledge a firm, young hand reached out and, seizing his own, almost dragged him through the window. He turned to look back into the alley. He had been just in time; the Austrian sentry, alarmed by the sound of approaching footsteps down the alley, had stepped into view. He stood there now with leveled rifle, a challenge upon his lips. From the advancing party came a satisfactory reply.

At the same instant the girl beside him in the Stygian blackness of the room threw her arms about Barney's neck and drew his face down to hers.

"Oh, Stefan," she whispered, "what a narrow escape! It makes me tremble to think of it. They would have shot you, my Stefan!"

The American put an arm about the girl's shoulders, and raised one hand to her cheek—it might have been in caress, but it wasn't. It was to smother the cry of alarm he anticipated would follow the discovery that he was not "Stefan." He bent his lips close to her ear.

"Do not make an outcry," he whispered in very poor Serbian. "I am not Stefan; but I am a friend."

The exclamation of surprise or fright that he had expected was not forthcoming. The girl lowered her arms from about his neck.

"Who are you?" she asked in a low whisper.

"I am an American war correspondent," replied Barney, "but if the Austrians get hold of me now it will be mighty difficult to convince them that I am not a spy." And then a sudden determination came to him to trust his fate to this unknown girl, whose face, even, he had never seen. "I am entirely at your mercy," he said. "There are Austrian soldiers in the street below. You have but to call to them to send me before the firing squad—or, you can let me remain here until I can find an opportunity to get away in safety. I am trying to reach Serbia."

"Why do you wish to reach Serbia?" asked the girl suspiciously.

"I have discovered too many enemies in Austria tonight to make it safe for me to remain," he replied, "and, further, my original intention was to report the war from the Serbian side."

The girl hesitated for a while, evidently in thought.

"They are moving on," suggested Barney. "If you are going to give me up you'd better do it at once."

"I'm not going to give you up," replied the girl. "I'm going to keep you prisoner until Stefan returns—he will know best what to do with you. Now you must come with me and be locked up. Do not try to escape—I have a revolver in my hand," and to give her prisoner physical proof of the weapon he could not see she thrust the muzzle against his side.

"I'll take your word for the gun," said Barney, "if you'll just turn it in the other direction. Go ahead—I'll follow you."

"No, you won't," replied the girl. "You'll go first; but before that you'll raise your hands above your head. I want to search you."

Barney did as he was bid and a moment later felt deft fingers running over his clothing in search of concealed weapons. Satisfied at last that he was unarmed, the girl directed him to precede her, guiding his steps from behind with a hand upon his arm. Occasionally he felt the muzzle of her revolver touch his body. It was a most unpleasant sensation.

They crossed the room to a door which his captor directed him to open, and after they had passed through and she had closed it behind them the girl struck a match and lit a candle which stood upon a little bracket on the partition wall. The dim light of the tallow dip showed Barney that he was in a narrow hall from which several doors opened into different rooms.

At one end of the hall a stairway led to the floor below, while at the opposite end another flight disappeared into the darkness above.

"This way," said the girl, motioning toward the stairs that led upward.

Barney had turned toward her as she struck the match, obtaining an excellent view of her features. They were clear-cut and regular. Her eyes were large and very dark. Dark also was her hair, which was piled in great heaps upon her finely shaped head. Altogether the face was one not easily to be forgotten. Barney could scarce have told whether the girl was beautiful or not, but that she was striking there could be no doubt.

He preceded her up the stairway to a door at the top. At her direction he turned the knob and entered a small room in which was a cot, an ancient dresser and a single chair.

"You will remain here," she said, "until Stefan returns. Stefan will know what to do with you." Then she left him, taking the light with her, and Barney heard a key turn in the lock of the door after she had closed it. Presently her footfalls died out as she descended to the lower floors.

"Anyhow," thought the American, "this is better than the Austrians. I don't know what Stefan will do with me, but I have a rather vivid idea of what the Austrians would have done to me if they'd caught me sneaking through the alleys of Burgova at midnight."

Throwing himself on the cot Barney was soon asleep, for though his predicament was one that, under ordinary circumstances might have made sleep impossible, yet he had so long been without the boon of slumber that tired nature would no longer be denied.

When he awoke it was broad daylight. The sun was pouring in through a skylight in the ceiling of his tiny chamber. Aside from this there were no windows in the room. The sound of voices came to him with an uncanny distinctness that made it seem that the speakers must be in this very chamber, but a glance about the blank walls convinced him that he was alone.

Presently he espied a small opening in the wall at the head of his cot. He rose and examined it. The voices appeared to be coming from it. In fact, they were. The opening was at the top of a narrow shaft that seemed to lead to the basement of the structure—apparently once the shaft of a dumb-waiter or a chute for refuse or soiled clothes.

Barney put his ear close to it. The voices that came from below were those of a man and a woman. He heard every word distinctly.

"We must search the house, fraulein," came in the deep voice of a man.

"Whom do you seek?" inquired a woman's voice. Barney recognized it as the voice of his captor.

"A Serbian spy, Stefan Drontoff," replied the man. "Do you know him?"

There was a considerable pause on the girl's part before she answered, and then her reply was in such a low voice that Barney could barely hear it.

"I do not know him," she said. "There are several men who lodge here. What may this Stefan Drontoff look like?"

"I have never seen him," replied the officer; "but by arresting all the men in the house we must get this Stefan also, if he is here."

"Oh!" cried the girl, a new note in her voice, "I guess I know now whom you mean. There is one man here I have heard them call Stefan, though for the moment I had forgotten it. He is in the small attic-room at the head of the stairs. Here is a key that will fit the lock. Yes, I am sure that he is Stefan. You will find him there, and it should be easy to take him, for I know that he is unarmed. He told me so last night when he came in."

"The devil!" muttered Barney Custer; but whether he referred to his predicament or to the girl it would be impossible to tell. Already the sound of heavy boots on the stairs announced the coming of men—several of them. Barney heard the rattle of accouterments—the clank of a scabbard—the scraping of gun butts against the walls. The Austrians were coming!

He looked about. There was no way of escape except the door and the skylight, and the door was impossible.

Quickly he tilted the cot against the door, wedging its legs against a crack in the floor—that would stop them for a minute or two. Then he wheeled the dresser beneath the skylight and, placing the chair on top of it, scrambled to the seat of the latter. His head was at the height of the skylight. To force the skylight from its frame required but a moment. A key entered the lock of the door from the opposite side and turned. He knew that someone without was pushing. Then he heard an oath and heavy battering upon the panels. A moment later he had drawn himself through the skylight and stood upon the roof of the building. Before him stretched a series of uneven roofs to the end of the street. Barney did not hesitate. He started on a rapid trot toward the adjoining roof. From that he clambered to a higher one beyond.

On he went, now leaping narrow courts, now dropping to low sheds and again clambering to the heights of the higher buildings, until he had come almost to the end of the row. Suddenly, behind him he heard a hoarse shout, followed by the report of a rifle. With a whir, a bullet flew a few inches above his head. He had gained the last roof—a large, level roof—and at the shot he turned to see how near to him were his pursuers.

Fatal turn!

Scarce had he taken his eyes from the path ahead than his foot fell upon a glass skylight, and with a loud crash he plunged through amid a shower of broken glass.

His fall was a short one. Directly beneath the skylight was a bed, and on the bed a fat Austrian infantry captain. Barney lit upon the pit of the captain's stomach. With a howl of pain the officer catapulted Barney to the floor. There were three other beds in the room, and in each bed one or two other officers. Before the American could regain his feet they were all sitting on him—all except the infantry captain. He lay shrieking and cursing in a painful attempt to regain his breath, every atom of which Barney had knocked out of him.

The officers sitting on Barney alternately beat him and questioned him, interspersing their interrogations with lurid profanity.

"If you will get off of me," at last shouted the American, "I shall be glad to explain—and apologize."

They let him up, scowling ferociously. He had promised to explain, but now that he was confronted by the immediate necessity of an explanation that would prove at all satisfactory as to how he happened to be wandering around the rooftops of Burgova, he discovered that his powers of invention were entirely inadequate. The need for explaining, however, was suddenly removed. A shadow fell upon them from above, and as they glanced up Barney saw the figure of an officer surrounded by several soldiers looking down upon him.

"Ah, you have him!" cried the newcomer in evident satisfaction. "It is well. Hold him until we descend."

A moment later he and his escort had dropped through the broken skylight to the floor beside them.

"Who is the mad man?" cried the captain who had broken Barney's fall. "The assassin! He tried to murder me."

"I cannot doubt it," replied the officer who had just descended, "for the fellow is no other than Stefan Drontoff, the famous Serbian spy!"

"Himmel!" ejaculated the officers in chorus. "You have done a good day's work, lieutenant."

"The firing squad will do a better work in a few minutes," replied the lieutenant, with a grim pointedness that took Barney's breath away.

III

BEFORE THE FIRING SQUAD

They marched Barney before the staff where he urged his American nationality, pointing to his credentials and passes in support of his contention.

The general before whom he had been brought shrugged his shoulders. "They are all Americans as soon as they are caught," he said; "but why did you not claim to be Prince Peter of Blentz? You have his passes as well. How can you expect us to believe your story when you have in your possession passes for different men?

"We have every respect for our friends the Americans. I would even stretch a point rather than chance harming an American; but you will admit that the evidence is all against you. You were found in the very building where Drontoff was known to stay while in Burgova. The young woman whose mother keeps the place directed our officer to your room, and you tried to escape, which I do not think that an innocent American would have done.

"However, as I have said, I will go to almost any length rather than chance a mistake in the case of one who from his appearance might pass more readily for an American than a Serbian. I have sent for Prince Peter of Blentz. If you can satisfactorily explain to him how you chance to be in possession of military passes bearing his name I shall be very glad to give you the benefit of every other doubt."

Peter of Blentz. Send for Peter of Blentz! Barney wondered just what kind of a sensation it was to stand facing a firing squad. He hoped that his knees wouldn't tremble—they felt a trifle weak even now. There was a chance that the man might not recall his face, but a very slight chance. It had been his remarkable likeness to Leopold of Lutha that had resulted in the snatching of a crown from Prince Peter's head.

Likely indeed that he would ever forget his, Barney's, face, though he had seen it but once without the red beard that had so added to Barney's likeness to the king. But Maenck would be along, of course, and Maenck would have no doubts—he had seen Barney too recently in Beatrice to fail to recognize him now.

Several men were entering the room where Barney stood before the general and his staff. A glance revealed to the prisoner that Peter of Blentz had come, and with him Von Coblich and Maenck. At the same instant Peter's eyes met Barney's, and the former, white and wide-eyed came almost to a dead halt, grasping hurriedly at the arm of Maenck who walked beside him.

"My God!" was all that Barney heard him say, but he spoke a name that the American did not hear. Maenck also looked his surprise, but his expression was suddenly changed to one of malevolent cunning and gratification. He turned toward Prince Peter with a few low-whispered words. A look of relief crossed the face of the Blentz prince.

"You appear to know the gentleman," said the general who had been conducting Barney's examination. "He has been arrested as a Serbian spy, and military passes in your name were found upon his person together with the papers of an American newspaper correspondent, which he claims to be. He is charged with being Stefan Drontoff, whom we long have been anxious to apprehend. Do you chance to know anything about him, Prince Peter?"

"Yes," replied Peter of Blentz, "I know him well by sight. He entered my room last night and stole the military passes from my coat—we all saw him and pursued him, but he got away in the dark. There can be no doubt but that he is the Serbian spy."

"He insists that he is Bernard Custer, an American," urged the general, who, it seemed to Barney, was anxious to make no mistake, and to give the prisoner every reasonable chance—a state of mind that rather surprised him in a European military chieftain, all of whom appeared to share the popular obsession regarding the prevalence of spies.

"Pardon me, general," interrupted Maenck. "I am well acquainted with Mr. Custer, who spent some time in Lutha a couple of years ago. This man is not he."

"That is sufficient, gentlemen, I thank you," said the general. He did not again look at the prisoner, but turned to a lieutenant who stood near-by. "You may remove the prisoner," he directed. "He will be destroyed with the others—here is the order," and he handed the subaltern a printed form upon which many names were filled in and at the bottom of which the general had just signed his own. It had evidently been waiting the outcome of the examination of Stefan Drontoff.

Surrounded by soldiers, Barney Custer walked from the presence of the military court. It was to him as though he moved in a strange world of dreams. He saw the look of satisfaction upon the face of Peter of Blentz as he passed him, and the open sneer of Maenck. As yet he did not fully realize what it all meant—that he was marching to his death! For the last time he was looking upon the faces of his fellow men; for the last time he had seen the sun rise, never again to see it set.

He was to be "destroyed." He had heard that expression used many times in connection with useless horses, or vicious dogs. Mechanically he drew a cigarette from his pocket and lighted it. There was no bravado in the act. On the contrary it was done almost unconsciously. The soldiers marched him through the streets of Burgova. The men were entirely impassive— even so early in the war they had become accustomed to this grim duty. The young officer who commanded them was more nervous than the prisoner—it was his first detail with a firing squad. He looked wonderingly at Barney, expecting momentarily to see the man collapse, or at least show some sign of terror at his close impending fate; but the American walked silently toward his death, puffing leisurely at his cigarette.

At last, after what seemed a long time, his guard turned in at a large gateway in a brick wall surrounding a factory. As they entered Barney saw twenty or thirty men in civilian dress, guarded by a dozen infantrymen. They were standing before the wall of a low brick building. Barney noticed that there were no windows in the wall. It suddenly occurred to him that there was something peculiarly grim and sinister in the appearance of the dead, blank surface of weather-stained brick. For the first time since he had faced the military court he awakened to a full realization of what it all meant to him—he was going to be lined up against that ominous brick wall with these other men—they were going to shoot them.

A momentary madness seized him. He looked about upon the other prisoners and guards. A sudden break for liberty might give him temporary respite. He could seize a rifle from the nearest soldier, and at least have the satisfaction of selling his life dearly. As he looked he saw more soldiers entering the factory yard.

A sudden apathy overwhelmed him. What was the use? He could not escape. Why should he wish to kill these soldiers? It was not they who were responsible for his plight—they were but obeying orders. The close presence of death made life seem very desirable. These men, too, desired life. Why should he take it from them uselessly? At best he might kill one or two, but in the end he would be killed as surely as though he took his place before the brick wall with the others.

He noticed now that these others evinced no inclination to contest their fates. Why should he, then? Doubtless many of them were as innocent as he, and all loved life as well. He saw that several were weeping silently. Others stood with bowed heads gazing at the hard-packed earth of the factory yard. Ah, what visions were their eyes beholding for the last time! What memories of happy firesides! What dear, loved faces were limned upon that sordid clay!

His reveries were interrupted by the hoarse voice of a sergeant, breaking rudely in upon the silence and the dumb terror. The fellow was herding the prisoners into position. When he was done Barney found himself in the front rank of the little, hopeless band. Opposite them, at a few paces, stood the firing squad, their gun butts resting upon the ground.

The young lieutenant stood at one side. He issued some instructions in a low tone, then he raised his voice.

"Ready!" he commanded. Fascinated by the horror of it, Barney watched the rifles raised smartly to the soldiers' hips—the movement was as precise as though the men were upon parade. Every bolt clicked in unison with its fellows.

"Aim!" the pieces leaped to the hollows of the men's shoulders. The leveled barrels were upon a line with the breasts of the condemned. A man at Barney's right moaned. Another sobbed.

"Fire!" There was the hideous roar of the volley. Barney Custer crumpled forward to the ground, and three bodies fell upon his. A moment later there was a second volley—all had not fallen at the first. Then the soldiers came among the bodies, searching for signs of life; but evidently the two volleys had done their work. The sergeant formed his men in line. The lieutenant marched them away. Only silence remained on guard above the pitiful dead in the factory yard.

The day wore on and still the stiffening corpses lay where they had fallen. Twilight came and then darkness. A head appeared above the top of the wall that had enclosed the grounds. Eyes peered through the night and keen ears listened for any sign of life within. At last, evidently satisfied that the place was deserted, a man crawled over the summit of the wall and dropped to the ground within. Here again he paused, peering and listening.

What strange business had he here among the dead that demanded such caution in its pursuit? Presently he advanced toward the pile of corpses. Quickly he tore open coats and searched pockets. He ran his fingers along the fingers of the dead. Two rings had rewarded his search and he was busy with a third that encircled the finger of a body that lay beneath three others. It would not come off. He pulled and tugged, and then he drew a knife from his pocket.

But he did not sever the digit. Instead he shrank back with a muffled scream of terror. The corpse that he would have mutilated had staggered suddenly to its feet, flinging the dead bodies to one side as it rose.

"You fiend!" broke from the lips of the dead man, and the ghoul turned and fled, gibbering in his fright.

The tramp of soldiers in the street beyond ceased suddenly at the sound from within the factory yard. It was a detail of the guard marching to the relief of sentries. A moment later the gates swung open and a score of soldiers entered. They saw a figure dodging toward the wall a dozen paces from them, but they did not see the other that ran swiftly around the corner of the factory.

This other was Barney Custer of Beatrice. When the command to fire had been given to the squad of riflemen, a single bullet had creased the top of his head, stunning him. All day he had lain there unconscious. It had been the tugging of the ghoul at his ring that had roused him to life at last.

Behind him, as he scurried around the end of the factory building, he heard the scattering fire of half a dozen rifles, followed by a scream—the fleeing hyena had been hit. Barney crouched in the shadow of a pile of junk. He heard the voices of soldiers as they gathered about the wounded man, questioning him, and a moment later the imperious tones of an officer issuing instructions to his men to search the yard. That he must be discovered seemed a certainty to the American. He crouched further back in the shadows close to the wall, stepping with the utmost caution.

Presently to his chagrin his foot touched the metal cover of a manhole; there was a resultant rattling that smote upon Barney's ears and nerves with all the hideous clatter of a boiler shop. He halted, petrified, for an instant. He was no coward, but after being so near death, life had

101

never looked more inviting, and he knew that to be discovered meant certain extinction this time.

The soldiers were circling the building. Already he could hear them nearing his position. In another moment they would round the corner of the building and be upon him. For an instant he contemplated a bold rush for the fence. In fact, he had gathered himself for the leaping start and the quick sprint across the open under the noses of the soldiers who still remained beside the dying ghoul, when his mind suddenly reverted to the manhole beneath his feet. Here lay a hiding place, at least until the soldiers had departed.

Barney stooped and raised the heavy lid, sliding it to one side. How deep was the black chasm beneath he could not even guess. Doubtless it led into a coal bunker, or it might open over a pit of great depth. There was no way to discover other than to plumb the abyss with his body. Above was death—below, a chance of safety.

The soldiers were quite close when Barney lowered himself through the manhole. Clinging with his fingers to the upper edge his feet still swung in space. How far beneath was the bottom? He heard the scraping of the heavy shoes of the searchers close above him, and then he closed his eyes, released the grasp of his fingers, and dropped.

IV

A RACE TO LUTHA

Barney's fall was not more than four or five feet. He found himself upon a slippery floor of masonry over which two or three inches of water ran sluggishly. Above him he heard the soldiers pass the open manhole. It was evident that in the darkness they had missed it.

For a few minutes the fugitive remained motionless, then, hearing no sounds from above he started to grope about his retreat. Upon two sides were blank, circular walls, upon the other two circular openings about four feet in diameter. It was through these openings that the tiny stream of water trickled.

Barney came to the conclusion that he had dropped into a sewer. To get out the way he had entered appeared impossible. He could not leap upward from the slimy, concave bottom the distance he had dropped. To follow the sewer upward would lead him nowhere nearer escape. There remained no hope but to follow the trickling stream downward toward the river, into which his judgment told him the entire sewer system of the city must lead.

Stooping, he entered the ill-smelling circular conduit, groping his way slowly along. As he went the water deepened. It was half way to his knees when he plunged unexpectedly into another tube running at right angles to the first. The bottom of this tube was lower than that of the one which emptied into it, so that Barney now found himself in a swiftly running stream of filth that reached above his knees. Downward he followed this flood—faster now for the fear of the deadly gases which might overpower him before he could reach the river.

The water deepened gradually as he went on. At last he reached a point where, with his head scraping against the roof of the sewer, his chin was just above the surface of the stream. A few more steps would be all that he could take in this direction without drowning. Could he retrace his way against the swift current? He did not know. He was weakened from the effects of his wound, from lack of food and from the exertions of the past hour. Well, he would go on as far as he could. The river lay ahead of him somewhere. Behind was only the hostile city.

He took another step. His foot found no support. He surged backward in an attempt to regain his footing, but the power of the flood was too much for him. He was swept forward to plunge into water that surged above his head as he sank. An instant later he had regained the surface and as his head emerged he opened his eyes.

He looked up into a starlit heaven! He had reached the mouth of the sewer and was in the river. For a moment he lay still, floating upon his back to rest. Above him he heard the tread of a sentry along the river front, and the sound of men's voices.

The sweet, fresh air, the star-shot void above, acted as a powerful tonic to his shattered hopes and overwrought nerves. He lay inhaling great lungsful of pure, invigorating air. He listened to the voices of the Austrian soldiery above him. All the buoyancy of his inherent Americanism returned to him.

"This is no place for a minister's son," he murmured, and turning over struck out for the opposite shore. The river was not wide, and Barney was soon nearing the bank along which he could see occasional camp fires. Here, too, were Austrians. He dropped down-stream below these, and at last approached the shore where a wood grew close to the water's edge. The bank here was steep, and the American had some difficulty in finding a place where he could clamber up the precipitous wall of rock. But finally he was successful, finding himself in a little clump of bushes on the river's brim. Here he lay resting and listening—always listening. It seemed to Barney that his ears ached with the constant strain of unflagging duty that his very existence demanded of them.

Hearing nothing, he crawled at last from his hiding place with the purpose of making his way toward the south and to the frontier as rapidly as possible. He could hope only to travel by night, and he guessed that this night must be nearly spent. Stooping, he moved cautiously away from the river. Through the shadows of the wood he made his way for perhaps a hundred yards when he was suddenly confronted by a figure that stepped from behind the bole of a tree.

"Halt! Who goes there?" came the challenge.

Barney's heart stood still. With all his care he had run straight into the arms of an Austrian sentry. To run would be to be shot. To advance would mean capture, and that too would mean death.

For the barest fraction of an instant he hesitated, and then his quick American wits came to his aid. Feigning intoxication he answered the challenge in dubious Austrian that he hoped his maudlin tongue would excuse.

"Friend," he answered thickly. "Friend with a drink—have one?" And he staggered drunkenly forward, banking all upon the credulity and thirst of the soldier who confronted him with fixed bayonet.

That the sentry was both credulous and thirsty was evidenced by the fact that he let Barney come within reach of his gun. Instantly the drunken Austrian was transformed into a very

103

sober and active engine of destruction. Seizing the barrel of the piece Barney jerked it to one side and toward him, and at the same instant he leaped for the throat of the sentry.

So quickly was this accomplished that the Austrian had time only for a single cry, and that was choked in his windpipe by the steel fingers of the American. Together both men fell heavily to the ground, Barney retaining his hold upon the other's throat.

Striking and clutching at one another they fought in silence for a couple of minutes, then the soldier's struggles began to weaken. He squirmed and gasped for breath. His mouth opened and his tongue protruded. His eyes started from their sockets. Barney closed his fingers more tightly upon the bearded throat. He rained heavy blows upon the upturned face. The beating fists of his adversary waved wildly now—the blows that reached Barney were pitifully weak. Presently they ceased. The man struggled violently for an instant, twitched spasmodically and lay still.

Barney clung to him for several minutes longer, until there was not the slightest indication of remaining life. The perpetration of the deed sickened him; but he knew that his act was warranted, for it had been either his life or the other's. He dragged the body back to the bushes in which he had been hiding. There he stripped off the Austrian uniform, put his own clothes upon the corpse and rolled it into the river.

Dressed as an Austrian private, Barney Custer shouldered the dead soldier's gun and walked boldly through the wood to the south. Momentarily he expected to run upon other soldiers, but though he kept straight on his way for hours he encountered none. The thin line of sentries along the river had been posted only to double the preventive measures that had been taken to keep Serbian spies either from entering or leaving the city.

Toward dawn, at the darkest period of the night, Barney saw lights ahead of him. Apparently he was approaching a village. He went more cautiously now, but all his care did not prevent him from running for the second time that night almost into the arms of a sentry. This time, however, Barney saw the soldier before he himself was discovered. It was upon the edge of the town, in an orchard, that the sentinel was posted. Barney, approaching through the trees, darting from one to another, was within a few paces of the man before he saw him.

The American remained quietly in the shadow of a tree waiting for an opportunity to escape, but before it came he heard the approach of a small body of troops. They were coming from the village directly toward the orchard. They passed the sentry and marched within a dozen feet of the tree behind which Barney was hiding.

As they came opposite him he slipped around the tree to the opposite side. The sentry had resumed his pacing, and was now out of sight momentarily among the trees further on. He could not see the American, but there were others who could. They came in the shape of a non-commissioned officer and a detachment of the guard to relieve the sentry. Barney almost bumped into them as he rounded the tree. There was no escape—the non-commissioned officer was within two feet of him when Barney discovered him. "What are you doing here?" shouted the sergeant with an oath. "Your post is there," and he pointed toward the position where Barney had seen the sentry.

At first Barney could scarce believe his ears. In the darkness the sergeant had mistaken him for the sentinel! Could he carry it out? And if so might it not lead him into worse predicament? No, Barney decided, nothing could be worse. To be caught masquerading in the uniform of an Austrian soldier within the Austrian lines was to plumb the uttermost depth of guilt—nothing that he might do now could make his position worse.

He faced the sergeant, snapping his piece to present, hoping that this was the proper thing to do. Then he stumbled through a brief excuse. The officer in command of the troops that had just passed had demanded the way of him, and he had but stepped a few paces from his post to point out the road to his superior.

The sergeant grunted and ordered him to fall in. Another man took his place on duty. They were far from the enemy and discipline was lax, so the thing was accomplished which under other circumstances would have been well nigh impossible. A moment later Barney found himself marching back toward the village, to all intents and purposes an Austrian private.

Before a low, windowless shed that had been converted into barracks for the guard, the detail was dismissed. The men broke ranks and sought their blankets within the shed, tired from their lonely vigil upon sentry duty.

Barney loitered until the last. All the others had entered. He dared not, for he knew that any moment the sentry upon the post from which he had been taken would appear upon the scene, after discovering another of his comrades. He was certain to inquire of the sergeant. They would be puzzled, of course, and, being soldiers, they would be suspicious. There would be an investigation, which would start in the barracks of the guard. That neighborhood would at once become a most unhealthy spot for Barney Custer, of Beatrice, Nebraska.

When the last of the soldiers had entered the shed Barney glanced quickly about. No one appeared to notice him. He walked directly past the doorway to the end of the building. Around this he found a yard, deeply shadowed. He entered it, crossed it, and passed out into an alley beyond. At the first cross-street his way was blocked by the sight of another sentry—the world seemed composed entirely of Austrian sentries. Barney wondered if the entire Austrian army was kept perpetually upon sentry duty; he had scarce been able to turn without bumping into one.

He turned back into the alley and at last found a crooked passageway between buildings that he hoped might lead him to a spot where there was no sentry, and from which he could find his way out of the village toward the south. The passage, after devious windings, led into a large, open court, but when Barney attempted to leave the court upon the opposite side he found the ubiquitous sentries upon guard there.

Evidently there would be no escape while the Austrians remained in the town. There was nothing to do, therefore, but hide until the happy moment of their departure arrived. He returned to the courtyard, and after a short search discovered a shed in one corner that had evidently been used to stable a horse, for there was straw at one end of it and a stall in the other. Barney sat down upon the straw to wait developments. Tired nature would be denied no longer. His eyes closed, his head drooped upon his breast. In three minutes from the time he entered the shed he was stretched full length upon the straw, fast asleep.

The chugging of a motor awakened him. It was broad daylight. Many sounds came from the courtyard without. It did not take Barney long to gather his scattered wits—in an instant he was wide awake. He glanced about. He was the only occupant of the shed. Rising, he approached a small window that looked out upon the court. All was life and movement. A dozen military cars either stood about or moved in and out of the wide gates at the opposite end of the enclosure. Officers and soldiers moved briskly through a doorway that led into a large building that flanked the court upon one side. While Barney slept the headquarters of an Austrian army corps had moved in and taken possession of the building, the back of which abutted upon the court where lay his modest little shed.

Barney took it all in at a single glance, but his eyes hung long and greedily upon the great, high-powered machines that chugged or purred about him.

Gad! If he could but be behind the wheel of such a car for an hour! The frontier could not be over fifty miles to the south, of that he was quite positive; and what would fifty miles be to one of those machines?

Barney sighed as a great, gray-painted car whizzed into the courtyard and pulled up before the doorway. Two officers jumped out and ran up the steps. The driver, a young man in a uniform not unlike that which Barney wore, drew the car around to the end of the courtyard close beside Barney's shed. Here he left it and entered the building into which his passengers had gone. By reaching through the window Barney could have touched the fender of the machine. A few seconds' start in that and it would take more than an Austrian army corps to stop him this side of the border. Thus mused Barney, knowing already that the mad scheme that had been born within his brain would be put to action before he was many minutes older.

There were many soldiers on guard about the courtyard. The greatest danger lay in arousing the suspicions of one of these should he chance to see Barney emerge from the shed and enter the car.

"The proper thing," thought Barney, "is to come from the building into which everyone seems to pass, and the only way to be seen coming out of it is to get into it; but how the devil am I to get into it?"

The longer he thought the more convinced he became that utter recklessness and boldness would be his only salvation. Briskly he walked from the shed out into the courtyard beneath the eyes of the sentries, the officers, the soldiers, and the military drivers. He moved straight among them toward the doorway of the headquarters as though bent upon important business—which, indeed, he was. At least it was quite the most important business to Barney Custer that that young gentleman could recall having ventured upon for some time.

No one paid the slightest attention to him. He had left his gun in the shed for he noticed that only the men on guard carried them. Without an instant's hesitation he ran briskly up the short flight of steps and entered the headquarters building. Inside was another sentry who barred his way questioningly. Evidently one must state one's business to this person before going farther. Barney, without any loss of time or composure, stepped up to the guard.

"Has General Kampf passed in this morning?" he asked blithely. Barney had never heard of any "General Kampf," nor had the sentry, since there was no such person in the Austrian army. But he did know, however, that there were altogether too many generals for any one soldier to know the names of them all.

"I do not know the general by sight," replied the sentry.

Here was a pretty mess, indeed. Doubtless the sergeant would know a great deal more than would be good for Barney Custer. The young man looked toward the door through which he had just entered. His sole object in coming into the spider's parlor had been to make it possible for him to come out again in full view of all the guards and officers and military

106

chauffeurs, that their suspicions might not be aroused when he put his contemplated coup to the test.

He glanced toward the door. Machines were whizzing in and out of the courtyard. Officers on foot were passing and repassing. The sentry in the hallway was on the point of calling his sergeant.

"Ah!" cried Barney. "There is the general now," and without waiting to cast even a parting glance at the guard he stepped quickly through the doorway and ran down the steps into the courtyard. Looking neither to right nor to left, and with a convincing air of self-confidence and important business, he walked directly to the big, gray machine that stood beside the little shed at the end of the courtyard.

To crank it and leap to the driver's seat required but a moment. The big car moved smoothly forward. A turn of the steering wheel brought it around headed toward the wide gates. Barney shifted to second speed, stepped on the accelerator and the cut-out simultaneously, and with a noise like the rattle of a machine gun, shot out of the courtyard.

None who saw his departure could have guessed from the manner of it that the young man at the wheel of the gray car was stealing the machine or that his life depended upon escape without detection. It was the very boldness of his act that crowned it with success.

Once in the street Barney turned toward the south. Cars were passing up and down in both directions, usually at high speed. Their numbers protected the fugitive. Momentarily he expected to be halted; but he passed out of the village without mishap and reached a country road which, except for a lane down its center along which automobiles were moving, was blocked with troops marching southward. Through this soldier-walled lane Barney drove for half an hour.

From a great distance, toward the southeast, he could hear the boom of cannon and the bursting of shells. Presently the road forked. The troops were moving along the road on the left toward the distant battle line. Not a man or machine was turning into the right fork, the road toward the south that Barney wished to take.

Could he successfully pass through the marching soldiers at his right? Among all those officers there surely would be one who would question the purpose and destination of this private soldier who drove alone in the direction of the nearby frontier.

The moment had come when he must stake everything on his ability to gain the open road beyond the plodding mass of troops. Diminishing the speed of the car Barney turned it in toward the marching men at the same time sounding his horn loudly. An infantry captain, marching beside his company, was directly in front of the car. He looked up at the American. Barney saluted and pointed toward the right-hand fork.

The captain turned and shouted a command to his men. Those who had not passed in front of the car halted. Barney shot through the little lane they had opened, which immediately closed up behind him. He was through! He was upon the open road! Ahead, as far as he could see, there was no sign of any living creature to bar his way, and the frontier could not be more than twenty-five miles away.

V

THE TRAITOR KING

In his castle at Lustadt, Leopold of Lutha paced nervously back and forth between his great desk and the window that overlooked the royal gardens. Upon the opposite side of the desk stood an old man—a tall, straight, old man with the bearing of a soldier and the head of a lion. His keen, gray eyes were upon the king, and sorrow was written upon his face. He was Ludwig von der Tann, chancellor of the kingdom of Lutha.

At last the king stopped his pacing and faced the old man, though he could not meet those eagle eyes squarely, try as he would. It was his inability to do so, possibly, that added to his anger. Weak himself, he feared this strong man and envied him his strength, which, in a weak nature, is but a step from hatred. There evidently had been a long pause in their conversation, yet the king's next words took up the thread of their argument where it had broken.

"You speak as though I had no right to do it," he snapped. "One might think that you were the king from the manner with which you upbraid and reproach me. I tell you, Prince von der Tann, that I shall stand it no longer."

The king approached the desk and pounded heavily upon its polished surface with his fist. The physical act of violence imparted to him a certain substitute for the moral courage which he lacked.

"I will tell you, sir, that I am king. It was not necessary that I consult you or any other man before pardoning Prince Peter and his associates. I have investigated the matter thoroughly and I am convinced that they have been taught a sufficient lesson and that hereafter they will be my most loyal subjects."

He hesitated. "Their presence here," he added, "may prove an antidote to the ambitions of others who lately have taken it upon themselves to rule Lutha for me."

There was no mistaking the king's meaning, but Prince Ludwig did not show by any change of expression that the shot had struck him in a vulnerable spot; nor, upon the other hand, did he ignore the insinuation. There was only sorrow in his voice when he replied.

"Sire," he said, "for some time I have been aware of the activity of those who would like to see Peter of Blentz returned to favor with your majesty. I have warned you, only to see that my motives were always misconstrued. There is a greater power at work, your majesty, than any of us—greater than Lutha itself. One that will stop at nothing in order to gain its ends. It cares naught for Peter of Blentz, naught for me, naught for you. It cares only for Lutha. For strategic purposes it must have Lutha. It will trample you under foot to gain its end, and then it will cast Peter of Blentz aside. You have insinuated, sire, that I am ambitious. I am. I am ambitious to maintain the integrity and freedom of Lutha.

"For three hundred years the Von der Tanns have labored and fought for the welfare of Lutha. It was a Von der Tann that put the first Rubinroth king upon the throne of Lutha. To the last they were loyal to the former dynasty while that dynasty was loyal to Lutha. Only when the king attempted to sell the freedom of his people to a powerful neighbor did the Von der Tanns rise against him.

"Sire! the Von der Tanns have always been loyal to the house of Rubinroth. And but a single thing rises superior within their breasts to that loyalty, and that is their loyalty to Lutha." He paused for an instant before concluding. "And I, sire, am a Von der Tann."

There could be no mistaking the old man's meaning. So long as Leopold was loyal to his people and their interests Ludwig von der Tann would be loyal to Leopold. The king was cowed. He was very much afraid of this grim old warrior. He chafed beneath his censure.

"You are always scolding me," he cried irritably. "I am getting tired of it. And now you threaten me. Do you call that loyalty? Do you call it loyalty to refuse to compel your daughter to keep her plighted troth? If you wish to prove your loyalty command the Princess Emma to fulfil the promise you made my father—command her to wed me at once."

Von der Tann looked the king straight in the eyes.

"I cannot do that," he said. "She has told me that she will kill herself rather than wed with your majesty. She is all I have left, sire. What good would be accomplished by robbing me of her if you could not gain her by the act? Win her confidence and love, sire. It may be done. Thus only may happiness result to you and to her."

"You see," exclaimed the king, "what your loyalty amounts to! I believe that you are saving her for the impostor—I have heard as much hinted at before this. Nor do I doubt that she would gladly connive with the fellow if she thought there was a chance of his seizing the throne."

Von der Tann paled. For the first time righteous indignation and anger got the better of him. He took a step toward the king.

"Stop!" he commanded. "No man, not even my king, may speak such words to a Von der Tann."

In an antechamber just outside the room a man sat near the door that led into the apartment where the king and his chancellor quarreled. He had been straining his ears to catch the conversation which he could hear rising and falling in the adjoining chamber, but till now he had been unsuccessful. Then came Prince Ludwig's last words booming loudly through the paneled door, and the man smiled. He was Count Zellerndorf, the Austrian minister to Lutha.

The king's outraged majesty goaded him to an angry retort.

"You forget yourself, Prince von der Tann," he cried. "Leave our presence. When we again desire to be insulted we shall send for you."

As the chancellor passed into the antechamber Count Zellerndorf rose and greeted him warmly, almost effusively. Von der Tann returned his salutations with courtesy but with no answering warmth. Then he passed on out of the palace.

"The old fox must have heard," he mused as he mounted his horse and turned his face toward Tann and the Old Forest.

When Count Zellerndorf of Austria entered the presence of Leopold of Lutha he found that young ruler much disturbed. He had resumed his restless pacing between desk and window, and as the Austrian entered he scarce paused to receive his salutation. Count Zellerndorf was a frequent visitor at the palace. There were few formalities between this astute diplomat and the young king; those had passed gradually away as their acquaintance and friendship ripened.

"Prince Ludwig appeared angry when he passed through the antechamber," ventured Zellerndorf. "Evidently your majesty found cause to rebuke him."

The king nodded and looked narrowly at the Austrian. "The Prince von der Tann insinuated that Austria's only wish in connection with Lutha is to seize her," he said.

Zellerndorf raised his hands in well-simulated horror.

"Your majesty!" he exclaimed. "It cannot be that the prince has gone to such lengths to turn you against your best friend, my emperor. If he has I can only attribute it to his own ambitions. I have hesitated to speak to you of this matter, your majesty, but now that the honor of my own ruler is questioned I must defend him.

"Bear with me then, should what I have to say wound you. I well know the confidence which the house of Von der Tann has enjoyed for centuries in Lutha; but I must brave your wrath in the interest of right. I must tell you that it is common gossip in Vienna that Von der Tann aspires to the throne of Lutha either for himself or for his daughter through the American impostor who once sat upon your throne for a few days. And let me tell you more.

"The American will never again menace you—he was arrested in Burgova as a spy and executed. He is dead; but not so are Von der Tann's ambitions. When he learns that he no longer may rely upon the strain of the Rubinroth blood that flowed in the veins of the American from his royal mother, the runaway Princess Victoria, there will remain to him only the other alternative of seizing the throne for himself. He is a very ambitious man, your majesty. Already he has caused it to become current gossip that he is the real power behind the throne of Lutha—that your majesty is but a figure-head, the puppet of Von der Tann."

Zellerndorf paused. He saw the flush of shame and anger that suffused the king's face, and then he shot the bolt that he had come to fire, but which he had not dared to hope would find its target so denuded of defense.

"Your majesty," he whispered, coming quite close to the king, "all Lutha is inclined to believe that you fear Prince von der Tann. Only a few of us know the truth to be the contrary. For the sake of your prestige you must take some step to counteract this belief and stamp it out for good and all. I have planned a way—hear it.

"Von der Tann's hatred of Peter of Blentz is well known. No man in Lutha believes that he would permit you to have any intercourse with Peter. I have brought from Blentz an invitation to your majesty to honor the Blentz prince with your presence as a guest for the ensuing week. Accept it, your majesty.

"Nothing could more conclusively prove to the most skeptical that you are still the king, and that Von der Tann, nor any other, may not dare to dictate to you. It will be the most splendid stroke of statesmanship that you could achieve at the present moment."

For an instant the king stood in thought. He still feared Peter of Blentz as the devil is reputed to fear holy water, though for converse reasons. Yet he was very angry with Von der Tann. It would indeed be an excellent way to teach the presumptuous chancellor his place.

Leopold almost smiled as he thought of the chagrin with which Prince Ludwig would receive the news that he had gone to Blentz as the guest of Peter. It was the last impetus that was required by his weak, vindictive nature to press it to a decision.

"Very well," he said, "I will go tomorrow."

It was late the following day that Prince von der Tann received in his castle in the Old Forest word that an Austrian army had crossed the Luthanian frontier—the neutrality of Lutha had been violated. The old chancellor set out immediately for Lustadt. At the palace he sought an interview with the king only to learn that Leopold had departed earlier in the day to visit Peter of Blentz.

There was but one thing to do and that was to follow the king to Blentz. Some action must be taken immediately—it would never do to let this breach of treaty pass unnoticed.

The Serbian minister who had sent word to the chancellor of the invasion by the Austrian troops was closeted with him for an hour after his arrival at the palace. It was clear to both these men that the hand of Zellerndorf was plainly in evidence in both the important moves that had occurred in Lutha within the past twenty-four hours—the luring of the king to Blentz and the entrance of Austrian soldiery into Lutha.

Following his interview with the Serbian minister Von der Tann rode toward Blentz with only his staff in attendance. It was long past midnight when the lights of the town appeared directly ahead of the little party. They rode at a trot along the road which passes through the village to wind upward again toward the ancient feudal castle that looks down from its hilltop upon the town.

At the edge of the village Von der Tann was thunderstruck by a challenge from a sentry posted in the road, nor was his dismay lessened when he discovered that the man was an Austrian.

"What is the meaning of this?" he cried angrily. "What are Austrian soldiers doing barring the roads of Lutha to the chancellor of Lutha?"

The sentry called an officer. The latter was extremely suave. He regretted the incident, but his orders were most positive—no one could be permitted to pass through the lines without an order from the general commanding. He would go at once to the general and see if he could procure the necessary order. Would the prince be so good as to await his return? Von der Tann turned on the young officer, his face purpling with rage.

"I will pass nowhere within the boundaries of Lutha," he said, "upon the order of an Austrian. You may tell your general that my only regret is that I have not with me tonight the necessary force to pass through his lines to my king—another time I shall not be so handicapped," and Ludwig, Prince von der Tann, wheeled his mount and spurred away in the direction of Lustadt, at his heels an extremely angry and revengeful staff.

VI

A TRAP IS SPRUNG

Long before Prince von der Tann reached Lustadt he had come to the conclusion that Leopold was in virtue a prisoner in Blentz. To prove his conclusion he directed one of his staff to return to Blentz and attempt to have audience with the king.

"Risk anything," he instructed the officer to whom he had entrusted the mission. "Submit, if necessary, to the humiliation of seeking an Austrian pass through the lines to the castle. See the king at any cost and deliver this message to him and to him alone and secretly. Tell him my fears, and that if I do not have word from him within twenty-four hours I shall assume that he is indeed a prisoner.

"I shall then direct the mobilization of the army and take such steps as seem fit to rescue him and drive the invaders from the soil of Lutha. If you do not return I shall understand that you are held prisoner by the Austrians and that my worst fears have been realized."

But Prince Ludwig was one who believed in being forehanded and so it happened that the orders for the mobilization of the army of Lutha were issued within fifteen minutes of his return to Lustadt. It would do no harm, thought the old man, with a grim smile, to get things well under way a day ahead of time. This accomplished, he summoned the Serbian minister, with what purpose and to what effect became historically evident several days later. When, after twenty-four hours' absence, his aide had not returned from Blentz, the chancellor had no regrets for his forehandedness.

In the castle of Peter of Blentz the king of Lutha was being entertained royally. He was told nothing of the attempt of his chancellor to see him, nor did he know that a messenger from Prince von der Tann was being held a prisoner in the camp of the Austrians in the village. He was surrounded by the creatures of Prince Peter and by Peter's staunch allies, the Austrian minister and the Austrian officers attached to the expeditionary force occupying the town. They told him that they had positive information that the Serbians already had crossed the frontier into Lutha, and that the presence of the Austrian troops was purely for the protection of Lutha.

It was not until the morning following the rebuff of Prince von der Tann that Peter of Blentz, Count Zellerndorf and Maenck heard of the occurrence. They were chagrined by the accident, for they were not ready to deliver their final stroke. The young officer of the guard had, of course, but followed his instructions—who would have thought that old Von der Tann would come to Blentz! That he suspected their motives seemed apparent, and now that his rebuff at the gates had aroused his ire and, doubtless, crystallized his suspicions, they might find in him a very ugly obstacle to the fruition of their plans.

With Von der Tann actively opposed to them, the value of having the king upon their side would be greatly minimized. The people and the army had every confidence in the old chancellor. Even if he opposed the king there was reason to believe that they might still side with him.

"What is to be done?" asked Zellerndorf. "Is there no way either to win or force Von der Tann to acquiescence?"

"I think we can accomplish it," said Prince Peter, after a moment of thought. "Let us see Leopold. His mind has been prepared to receive almost gratefully any insinuations against the

112

loyalty of Von der Tann. With proper evidence the king may easily be persuaded to order the chancellor's arrest—possibly his execution as well."

So they saw the king, only to meet a stubborn refusal upon the part of Leopold to accede to their suggestions. He still was madly in love with Von der Tann's daughter, and he knew that a blow delivered at her father would only tend to increase her bitterness toward him. The conspirators were nonplussed.

They had looked for a comparatively easy road to the consummation of their desires. What in the world could be the cause of the king's stubborn desire to protect the man they knew he feared, hated, and mistrusted with all the energy of his suspicious nature? It was the king himself who answered their unspoken question.

"I cannot believe in the disloyalty of Prince Ludwig," he said, "nor could I, even if I desired it, take such drastic steps as you suggest. Some day the Princess Emma, his daughter, will be my queen."

Count Zellerndorf was the first to grasp the possibilities that lay in the suggestion the king's words carried.

"Your majesty," he cried, "there is a way to unite all factions in Lutha. It would be better to insure the loyalty of Von der Tann through bonds of kinship than to antagonize him. Marry the Princess Emma at once.

"Wait, your majesty," he added, as Leopold raised an objecting hand. "I am well informed as to the strange obstinacy of the princess, but for the welfare of the state—yes, for the sake of your very throne, sire—you should exert your royal prerogatives and command the Princess Emma to carry out the terms of your betrothal."

"What do you mean, Zellerndorf?" asked the king.

"I mean, sire, that we should bring the princess here and compel her to marry you."

Leopold shook his head. "You do not know her," he said. "You do not know the Von der Tann nature—one cannot force a Von der Tann."

"Pardon, sire," urged Zellerndorf, "but I think it can be accomplished. If the Princess Emma knew that your majesty believed her father to be a traitor—that the order for his arrest and execution but awaited your signature—I doubt not that she would gladly become queen of Lutha, with her father's life and liberty as a wedding gift."

For several minutes no one spoke after Count Zellerndorf had ceased. Leopold sat looking at the toe of his boot. Peter of Blentz, Maenck, and the Austrian watched him intently. The possibilities of the plan were sinking deep into the minds of all four. At last the king rose. He was mumbling to himself as though unconscious of the presence of the others.

"She is a stubborn jade," he mumbled. "It would be an excellent lesson for her. She needs to be taught that I am her king," and then as though his conscience required a sop, "I shall be very good to her. Afterward she will be happy." He turned toward Zellerndorf. "You think it can be done?"

"Most assuredly, your majesty. We shall take immediate steps to fetch the Princess Emma to Blentz," and the Austrian rose and backed from the apartment lest the king change his mind. Prince Peter and Maenck followed him.

Princess Emma von der Tann sat in her boudoir in her father's castle in the Old Forest. Except for servants, she was alone in the fortress, for Prince von der Tann was in Lustadt. Her mind was occupied with memories of the young American who had entered her life under such strange circumstances two years before—memories that had been awakened by the return of Lieutenant Otto Butzow to Lutha. He had come directly to her father and had been attached to the prince's personal staff.

From him she had heard a great deal about Barney Custer, and the old interest, never a moment forgotten during these two years, was reawakened to all its former intensity.

Butzow had accompanied Prince Ludwig to Lustadt, but Princess Emma would not go with them. For two years she had not entered the capital, and much of that period had been spent in Paris. Only within the past fortnight had she returned to Lutha.

In the middle of the morning her reveries were interrupted by the entrance of a servant bearing a message. She had to read it twice before she could realize its purport; though it was plainly worded—the shock of it had stunned her. It was dated at Lustadt and signed by one of the palace functionaries:

Prince von der Tann has suffered a slight stroke. Do not be alarmed, but come at once. The two troopers who bear this message will act as your escort.

It required but a few minutes for the girl to change to her riding clothes, and when she ran down into the court she found her horse awaiting her in the hands of her groom, while close by two mounted troopers raised their hands to their helmets in salute.

A moment later the three clattered over the drawbridge and along the road that leads toward Lustadt. The escort rode a short distance behind the girl, and they were hard put to it to hold the mad pace which she set them.

A few miles from Tann the road forks. One branch leads toward the capital and the other winds over the hills in the direction of Blentz. The fork occurs within the boundaries of the Old Forest. Great trees overhang the winding road, casting a twilight shade even at high noon. It is a lonely spot, far from any habitation.

As the Princess Emma approached the fork she reined in her mount, for across the road to Lustadt a dozen horsemen barred her way. At first she thought nothing of it, turning her horse's head to the righthand side of the road to pass the party, all of whom were in uniform; but as she did so one of the men reined directly in her path. The act was obviously intentional.

The girl looked quickly up into the man's face, and her own went white. He who stopped her way was Captain Ernst Maenck. She had not seen the man for two years, but she had good cause to remember him as the governor of the castle of Blentz and the man who had attempted to take advantage of her helplessness when she had been a prisoner in Prince Peter's fortress. Now she looked straight into the fellow's eyes.

"Let me pass, please," she said coldly.

"I am sorry," replied Maenck with an evil smile; "but the king's orders are that you accompany me to Blentz—the king is there."

For answer the girl drove her spur into her mount's side. The animal leaped forward, striking Maenck's horse on the shoulder and half turning him aside, but the man clutched at the girl's bridle-rein, and, seizing it, brought her to a stop.

"You may as well come voluntarily, for come you must," he said. "It will be easier for you."

"I shall not come voluntarily," she replied. "If you take me to Blentz you will have to take me by force, and if my king is not sufficiently a gentleman to demand an accounting of you, I am at least more fortunate in the possession of a father who will."

"Your father will scarce wish to question the acts of his king," said Maenck—"his king and the husband of his daughter."

"What do you mean?" she cried.

"That before you are many hours older, your highness, you will be queen of Lutha."

The Princess Emma turned toward her tardy escort that had just arrived upon the scene.

"This person has stopped me," she said, "and will not permit me to continue toward Lustadt. Make a way for me; you are armed!"

Maenck smiled. "Both of them are my men," he explained.

The girl saw it all now—the whole scheme to lure her to Blentz. Even then, though, she could not believe the king had been one of the conspirators of the plot.

Weak as he was he was still a Rubinroth, and it was difficult for a Von der Tann to believe in the duplicity of a member of the house they had served so loyally for centuries. With bowed head the princess turned her horse into the road that led toward Blentz. Half the troopers preceded her, the balance following behind.

Maenck wondered at the promptness of her surrender.

"To be a queen—ah! that was the great temptation," he thought but he did not know what was passing in the girl's mind. She had seen that escape for the moment was impossible, and so had decided to bide her time until a more propitious chance should come. In silence she rode among her captors. The thought of being brought to Blentz alive was unbearable.

Somewhere along the road there would be an opportunity to escape. Her horse was fleet; with a short start he could easily outdistance these heavier cavalry animals and as a last resort she could—she must—find some way to end her life, rather than to be dragged to the altar beside Leopold of Lutha.

Since childhood Emma von der Tann had ridden these hilly roads. She knew every lane and bypath for miles around. She knew the short cuts, the gullies and ravines. She knew where one might, with a good jumper, save a wide detour, and as she rode toward Blentz she passed in review through her mind each of the many spots where a sudden break for liberty might have the best chance to succeed.

And at last she hit upon the place where a quick turn would take her from the main road into the roughest sort of going for one not familiar with the trail. Maenck and his soldiers had already partially relaxed their vigilance. The officer had come to the conclusion that his prisoner was resigned to her fate and that, after all, the fate of being forced to be queen did not appear so dark to her.

They had wound up a wooded hill and were half way up to the summit. The princess was riding close to the right-hand side of the road. Quite suddenly, and before a hand could be raised to stay her, she wheeled her mount between two trees, struck home her spur, and was gone into the wood upon the steep hillside.

With an oath, Maenck cried to his men to be after her. He himself spurred into the forest at the point where the girl had disappeared. So sudden had been her break for liberty and so quickly had the foliage swallowed her that there was something almost uncanny in it.

A hundred yards from the road the trees were further apart, and through them the pursuers caught a glimpse of their quarry. The girl was riding like mad along the rough, uneven hillside. Her mount, surefooted as a chamois, seemed in his element. But two of the horses of her pursuers were as swift, and under the cruel spurs of their riders were closing up on their fugitive. The girl urged her horse to greater speed, yet still the two behind closed in.

A hundred yards ahead lay a deep and narrow gully, hid by bushes that grew rankly along its verge. Straight toward this the Princess Emma von der Tann rode. Behind her came her pursuers—two quite close and the others trailing farther in the rear. The girl reined in a trifle, letting the troopers that were closest to her gain until they were but a few strides behind, then she put spur to her horse and drove him at topmost speed straight toward the gully. At the bushes she spoke a low word in his backlaid ears, raised him quickly with the bit, leaning forward as he rose in air. Like a bird that animal took the bushes and the gully beyond, while close behind him crashed the two luckless troopers.

Emma von der Tann cast a single backward glance over her shoulder, as her horse regained his stride upon the opposite side of the gully, to see her two foremost pursuers plunging headlong into it. Then she shook free her reins and gave her mount his head along a narrow trail that both had followed many times before.

Behind her, Maenck and the balance of his men came to a sudden stop at the edge of the gully. Below them one of the troopers was struggling to his feet. The other lay very still beneath his motionless horse. With an angry oath Maenck directed one of his men to remain and help the two who had plunged over the brink, then with the others he rode along the gully searching for a crossing.

Before they found one their captive was a mile ahead of them, and, barring accident, quite beyond recapture. She was making for a highway that would lead her to Lustadt. Ordinarily she had been wont to bear a little to the north-east at this point and strike back into the road that she had just left; but today she feared to do so lest she be cut off before she gained the north and south highroad which the other road crossed a little farther on.

To her right was a small farm across which she had never ridden, for she always had made it a point never to trespass upon fenced grounds. On the opposite side of the farm was a wood, and somewhere beyond that a small stream which the highroad crossed upon a little bridge. It was all new country to her, but it must be ventured.

She took the fence at the edge of the clearing and then reined in a moment to look behind her. A mile away she saw the head and shoulders of a horseman above some low bushes—the pursuers had found a way through the gully.

Turning once more to her flight the girl rode rapidly across the fields toward the wood. Here she found a high wire fence so close to thickly growing trees upon the opposite side that she dared not attempt to jump it—there was no point at which she would not have been raked from the saddle by overhanging boughs. Slipping to the ground she attacked the barrier with her bare hands, attempting to tear away the staples that held the wire in place. For several minutes she surged and tugged upon the unyielding metal strand. An occasional backward glance revealed to her horrified eyes the rapid approach of her enemies. One of them was far in advance of the others—in another moment he would be upon her.

With redoubled fury she turned again to the fence. A superhuman effort brought away a staple. One wire was down and an instant later two more. Standing with one foot upon the wires to keep them from tangling about her horse's legs, she pulled her mount across into the wood. The foremost horseman was close upon her as she finally succeeded in urging the animal across the fallen wires.

The girl sprang to her horse's side just as the man reached the fence. The wires, released from her weight, sprang up breast high against his horse. He leaped from the saddle the instant that the girl was swinging into her own. Then the fellow jumped the fence and caught her bridle.

She struck at him with her whip, lashing him across the head and face, but he clung tightly, dragged hither and thither by the frightened horse, until at last he managed to reach the girl's arm and drag her to the ground.

Almost at the same instant a man, unkempt and disheveled, sprang from behind a tree and with a single blow stretched the trooper unconscious upon the ground.

VII

BARNEY TO THE RESCUE

As Barney Custer raced along the Austrian highroad toward the frontier and Lutha, his spirits rose to a pitch of buoyancy to which they had been strangers for the past several days. For the first time in many hours it seemed possible to Barney to entertain reasonable hopes of escape from the extremely dangerous predicament into which he had gotten himself.

He was even humming a gay little tune as he drove into a tiny hamlet through which the road wound. No sign of military appeared to fill him with apprehension. He was very hungry and the odor of cooking fell gratefully upon his nostrils. He drew up before the single inn, and presently, washed and brushed, was sitting before the first meal he had seen for two days. In the enjoyment of the food he almost forgot the dangers he had passed through, or that other dangers might be lying in wait for him at his elbow.

From the landlord he learned that the frontier lay but three miles to the south of the hamlet. Three miles! Three miles to Lutha! What if there was a price upon his head in that kingdom? It was HER home. It had been his mother's birthplace. He loved it.

Further, he must enter there and reach the ear of old Prince von der Tann. Once more he must save the king who had shown such scant gratitude upon another occasion.

For Leopold, Barney Custer did not give the snap of his fingers; but what Leopold, the king, stood for in the lives and sentiments of the Luthanians—of the Von der Tanns—was very dear to the American because it was dear to a trim, young girl and to a rugged, leonine, old man, of both of whom Barney was inordinately fond. And possibly, too, it was dear to him because of the royal blood his mother had bequeathed him.

His meal disposed of to the last morsel, and paid for, Barney entered the stolen car and resumed his journey toward Lutha. That he could remain there he knew to be impossible, but in delivering his news to Prince Ludwig he might have an opportunity to see the Princess Emma once again—it would be worth risking his life for, of that he was perfectly satisfied. And then he could go across into Serbia with the new credentials that he had no doubt Prince von der Tann would furnish him for the asking to replace those the Austrians had confiscated.

At the frontier Barney was halted by an Austrian customs officer; but when the latter recognized the military car and the Austrian uniform of the driver he waved him through without comment. Upon the other side the American expected possible difficulty with the Luthanian customs officer, but to his surprise he found the little building deserted, and none to bar his way. At last he was in Lutha—by noon on the following day he should be at Tann.

To reach the Old Forest by the best roads it was necessary to bear a little to the southeast, passing through Tafelberg and striking the north and south highway between that point and Lustadt, to which he could hold until reaching the east and west road that runs through both Tann and Blentz on its way across the kingdom.

The temptation to stop for a few minutes in Tafelberg for a visit with his old friend Herr Kramer was strong, but fear that he might be recognized by others, who would not guard his secret so well as the shopkeeper of Tafelberg would, decided him to keep on his way. So he flew through the familiar main street of the quaint old village at a speed that was little, if any, less, than fifty miles an hour.

On he raced toward the south, his speed often necessarily diminished upon the winding mountain roads, but for the most part clinging to a reckless mileage that caused the few natives he encountered to flee to the safety of the bordering fields, there to stand in open-mouthed awe.

Halfway between Tafelberg and the crossroad into which he purposed turning to the west toward Tann there is an S-curve where the bases of two small hills meet. The road here is narrow and treacherous—fifteen miles an hour is almost a reckless speed at which to travel around the curves of the S. Beyond are open fields upon either side of the road.

Barney took the turns carefully and had just emerged into the last leg of the S when he saw, to his consternation, a half-dozen Austrian infantrymen lolling beside the road. An officer stood near them talking with a sergeant. To turn back in that narrow road was impossible. He could only go ahead and trust to his uniform and the military car to carry him safely through. Before he reached the group of soldiers the fields upon either hand came into view.

118

They were dotted with tents, wagons, motor-vans and artillery. What did it mean? What was this Austrian army doing in Lutha?

Already the officer had seen him. This was doubtless an outpost, however clumsily placed it might be for strategic purposes. To pass it was Barney's only hope. He had passed through one Austrian army—why not another? He approached the outpost at a moderate rate of speed—to tear toward it at the rate his heart desired would be to awaken not suspicion only but positive conviction that his purposes and motives were ulterior.

The officer stepped toward the road as though to halt him. Barney pretended to be fussing with some refractory piece of controlling mechanism beneath the cowl—apparently he did not see the officer. He was just opposite him when the latter shouted to him. Barney straightened up quickly and saluted, but did not stop.

"Halt!" cried the officer.

Barney pointed down the road in the direction in which he was headed.

"Halt!" repeated the officer, running to the car.

Barney glanced ahead. Two hundred yards farther on was another post—beyond that he saw no soldiers. He turned and shouted a volley of intentionally unintelligible jargon at the officer, continuing to point ahead of him.

He hoped to confuse the man for the few seconds necessary for him to reach the last post. If the soldiers there saw that he had been permitted to pass through the first they doubtless would not hinder his further passage. That they were watching him Barney could see.

He had passed the officer now. There was no necessity for dalliance. He pressed the accelerator down a trifle. The car moved forward at increased speed. A final angry shout broke from the officer behind him, followed by a quick command. Barney did not have to wait long to learn the tenor of the order, for almost immediately a shot sounded from behind and a bullet whirred above his head. Another shot and another followed.

Barney was pressing the accelerator downward to the limit. The car responded nobly—there was no sputtering, no choking. Just a rapid rush of increasing momentum as the machine gained headway by leaps and bounds.

The bullets were ripping the air all about him. Just ahead the second outpost stood directly in the center of the road. There were three soldiers and they were taking deliberate aim, as carefully as though upon the rifle range. It seemed to Barney that they couldn't miss him. He swerved the car suddenly from one side of the road to the other. At the rate that it was going the move was fraught with but little less danger than the supine facing of the leveled guns ahead.

The three rifles spoke almost simultaneously. The glass of the windshield shattered in Barney's face. There was a hole in the left-hand front fender that had not been there before.

"Rotten shooting," commented Barney Custer, of Beatrice.

The soldiers still stood in the center of the road firing at the swaying car as, lurching from side to side, it bore down upon them. Barney sounded the raucous military horn; but the

119

soldiers seemed unconscious of their danger—they still stood there pumping lead toward the onrushing Juggernaut. At the last instant they attempted to rush from its path; but they were too late.

At over sixty miles an hour the huge, gray monster bore down upon them. One of them fell beneath the wheels—the two others were thrown high in air as the bumper struck them. The body of the man who had fallen beneath the wheels threw the car half way across the road—only iron nerve and strong arms held it from the ditch upon the opposite side.

Barney Custer had never been nearer death than at that moment—not even when he faced the firing squad before the factory wall in Burgova. He had done that without a tremor—he had heard the bullets of the outpost whistling about his head a moment before, with a smile upon his lips—he had faced the leveled rifles of the three he had ridden down and he had not quailed. But now, his machine in the center of the road again, he shook like a leaf, still in the grip of the sickening nausea of that awful moment when the mighty, insensate monster beneath him had reeled drunkenly in its mad flight, swerving toward the ditch and destruction.

For a few minutes he held to his rapid pace before he looked around, and then it was to see two cars climbing into the road from the encampment in the field and heading toward him in pursuit. Barney grinned. Once more he was master of his nerves. They'd have a merry chase, he thought, and again he accelerated the speed of the car. Once before he had had it up to seventy-five miles, and for a moment, when he had had no opportunity to even glance at the speedometer, much higher. Now he was to find the maximum limit of the possibilities of the brave car he had come to look upon with real affection.

The road ahead was comparatively straight and level. Behind him came the enemy. Barney watched the road rushing rapidly out of sight beneath the gray fenders. He glanced occasionally at the speedometer. Seventy-five miles an hour. Seventy-seven! "Going some," murmured Barney as he saw the needle vibrate up to eighty. Gradually he nursed her up and up to greater speed.

Eighty-five! The trees were racing by him in an indistinct blur of green. The fences were thin, wavering lines—the road a white-gray ribbon, ironed by the terrific speed to smooth unwrinkledness. He could not take his eyes from the business of steering to glance behind; but presently there broke faintly through the whir of the wind beating against his ears the faint report of a gun. He was being fired upon again. He pressed down still further upon the accelerator. The car answered to the pressure. The needle rose steadily until it reached ninety miles an hour—and topped it.

Then from somewhere in the radiator hose a hissing and a spurt of steam. Barney was dumbfounded. He had filled the cooling system at the inn where he had eaten. It had been working perfectly before and since. What could have happened? There could be but a single explanation. A bullet from the gun of one of the three men who had attempted to stop him at the second outpost had penetrated the radiator, and had slowly drained it.

Barney knew that the end was near, since the usefulness of the car in furthering his escape was over. At the speed he was going it would be but a short time before the superheated pistons expanding in their cylinders would tear the motor to pieces. Barney felt that he would be lucky if he himself were not killed when it happened.

He reduced his speed and glanced behind. His pursuers had not gained upon him, but they still were coming. A bend in the road shut them from his view. A little way ahead the road crossed over a river upon a wooden bridge. On the opposite side and to the right of the road was a wood. It seemed to offer the most likely possibilities of concealment in the vicinity. If he could but throw his pursuers off the trail for a while he might succeed in escaping through the wood, eventually reaching Tann on foot. He had a rather hazy idea of the exact direction of the town and castle, but that he could find them eventually he was sure.

The sight of the river and the bridge he was nearing suggested a plan, and the ominous grating of the overheated motor warned him that whatever he was to do he must do at once. As he neared the bridge he reduced the speed of the car to fifteen miles an hour, and set the hand throttle to hold it there. Still gripping the steering wheel with one hand, he climbed over the left-hand door to the running board. As the front wheels of the car ran up onto the bridge Barney gave the steering wheel a sudden turn to the right, and jumped.

The car veered toward the wooden handrail, there was a splintering of stanchions, as, with a crash, the big machine plunged through them headforemost into the river. Without waiting to give even a glance at his handiwork Barney Custer ran across the bridge, leaped the fence upon the right-hand side and plunged into the shelter of the wood.

Then he turned to look back up the road in the direction from which his pursuers were coming. They were not in sight—they had not seen his ruse. The water in the river was of sufficient depth to completely cover the car—no sign of it appeared above the surface.

Barney turned into the wood smiling. His scheme had worked well. The occupants of the two cars following him might not note the broken handrail, or, if they did, might not connect it with Barney in any way. In this event they would continue in the direction of Lustadt, wondering what in the world had become of their quarry. Or, if they guessed that his car had gone over into the river, they would doubtless believe that its driver had gone with it. In either event Barney would be given ample time to find his way to Tann.

He wished that he might find other clothes, since if he were dressed otherwise there would be no reason to imagine that his pursuers would recognize him should they come upon him. None of them could possibly have gained a sufficiently good look at his features to recognize them again.

The Austrian uniform, however, would convict him, or at least lay him under suspicion, and in Barney's present case, suspicion was as good as conviction were he to fall into the hands of the Austrians. The garb had served its purpose well in aiding in his escape from Austria, but now it was more of a menace than an asset.

For a week Barney Custer wandered through the woods and mountains of Lutha. He did not dare approach or question any human being. Several times he had seen Austrian cavalry that seemed to be scouring the country for some purpose that the American could easily believe was closely connected with himself. At least he did not feel disposed to stop them, as they cantered past his hiding place, to inquire the nature of their business.

Such farmhouses as he came upon he gave a wide berth except at night, and then he only approached them stealthily for such provender as he might filch. Before the week was up he had become an expert chicken thief, being able to rob a roost as quietly as the most finished carpetbagger on the sunny side of Mason and Dixon's line.

A careless housewife, leaving her lord and master's rough shirt and trousers hanging upon the line overnight, had made possible for Barney the coveted change in raiment. Now he was barged as a Luthanian peasant. He was hatless, since the lady had failed to hang out her mate's woolen cap, and Barney had not dared retain a single vestige of the damning Austrian uniform.

What the peasant woman thought when she discovered the empty line the following morning Barney could only guess, but he was morally certain that her grief was more than tempered by the gold piece he had wrapped in a bit of cloth torn from the soldier's coat he had worn, which he pinned on the line where the shirt and pants had been.

It was somewhere near noon upon the seventh day that Barney skirting a little stream, followed through the concealing shade of a forest toward the west. In his peasant dress he now felt safer to approach a farmhouse and inquire his way to Tann, for he had come a sufficient distance from the spot where he had stolen his new clothes to hope that they would not be recognized or that the news of their theft had not preceded him.

As he walked he heard the sound of the feet of a horse galloping over a dry field—muffled, rapid thud approaching closer upon his right hand. Barney remained motionless. He was sure that the rider would not enter the wood which, with its low-hanging boughs and thick underbrush, was ill adapted to equestrianism.

Closer and closer came the sound until it ceased suddenly scarce a hundred yards from where the American hid. He waited in silence to discover what would happen next. Would the rider enter the wood on foot? What was his purpose? Was it another Austrian who had by some miracle discovered the whereabouts of the fugitive? Barney could scarce believe it possible.

Presently he heard another horse approaching at the same mad gallop. He heard the sound of rapid, almost frantic efforts of some nature where the first horse had come to a stop. He heard a voice urging the animal forward—pleading, threatening. A woman's voice. Barney's excitement became intense in sympathy with the subdued excitement of the woman whom he could not as yet see.

A moment later the second rider came to a stop at the same point at which the first had reined in. A man's voice rose roughly. "Halt!" it cried. "In the name of the king, halt!" The American could no longer resist the temptation to see what was going on so close to him "in the name of the king."

He advanced from behind his tree until he saw the two figures—a man's and a woman's. Some bushes intervened—he could not get a clear view of them, yet there was something about the figure of the woman, whose back was toward him as she struggled to mount her frightened horse, that caused him to leap rapidly toward her. He rounded a tree a few paces from her just as the man—a trooper in the uniform of the house of Blentz—caught her arm and dragged her from the saddle. At the same instant Barney recognized the girl—it was Princess Emma.

Before either the trooper or the princess were aware of his presence he had leaped to the man's side and dealt him a blow that stretched him at full length upon the ground—stunned.

VIII

AN ADVENTUROUS DAY

For an instant the two stood looking at one another. The girl's eyes were wide with incredulity, with hope, with fear. She was the first to break the silence.

"Who are you?" she breathed in a half whisper.

"I don't wonder that you ask," returned the man. "I must look like a scarecrow. I'm Barney Custer. Don't you remember me now? Who did you think I was?"

The girl took a step toward him. Her eyes lighted with relief.

"Captain Maenck told me that you were dead," she said, "that you had been shot as a spy in Austria, and then there is that uncanny resemblance to the king—since he has shaved his beard it is infinitely more remarkable. I thought you might be he. He has been at Blentz and I knew that it was quite possible that he had discovered treachery upon the part of Prince Peter. In which case he might have escaped in disguise. I really wasn't sure that you were not he until you spoke."

Barney stooped and removed the bandoleer of cartridges from the fallen trooper, as well as his revolver and carbine. Then he took the girl's hand and together they turned into the wood. Behind them came the sound of pursuit. They heard the loud words of Maenck as he ordered his three remaining men into the wood on foot. As he advanced, Barney looked to the magazine of his carbine and the cylinder of his revolver.

"Why were they pursuing you?" he asked.

"They were taking me to Blentz to force me to wed Leopold," she replied. "They told me that my father's life depended upon my consenting; but I should not have done so. The honor of my house is more precious than the life of any of its members. I escaped them a few miles back, and they were following to overtake me."

A noise behind them caused Barney to turn. One of the troopers had come into view. He carried his carbine in his hands and at sight of the man with the fugitive girl he raised it to his shoulder; but as the American turned toward him his eyes went wide and his jaw dropped.

Instantly Barney knew that the fellow had noted his resemblance to the king. Barney's body was concealed from the view of the other by a bush which grew between them, so the man saw only the face of the American. The fellow turned and shouted to Maenck: "The king is with her."

"Nonsense," came the reply from farther back in the wood. "If there is a man with her and he will not surrender, shoot him." At the words Barney and the girl turned once more to their flight. From behind came the command to halt—"Halt! or I fire." Just ahead Barney saw the river.

They were sure to be taken there if he was unable to gain the time necessary to make good a crossing. Upon the opposite side was a continuation of the wood. Behind them the leading trooper was crashing through the underbrush in renewed pursuit. He came in sight of them again, just as they reached the river bank. Once more his carbine was leveled. Barney pushed the girl to her knees behind a bush. Then he wheeled and fired, so quickly that the man with the already leveled gun had no time to anticipate his act.

With a cry the fellow threw his hands above his head, staggered forward and plunged full length upon his face. Barney gathered the princess in his arms and plunged into the shallow stream. The girl held his carbine as he stumbled over the rocky bottom. The water deepened rapidly—the opposite shore seemed a long way off and behind there were three more enemies in hot pursuit.

Under ordinary circumstances Barney could have found it in his heart to wish the little Luthanian river as broad as the Mississippi, for only under such circumstances as these could he ever hope to hold the Princess Emma in his arms. Two years before she had told him that she loved him; but at the same time she had given him to understand that their love was hopeless. She might refuse to wed the king; but that she should ever wed another while the king lived was impossible, unless Leopold saw fit to release her from her betrothal to him and sanction her marriage to another. That he ever would do this was to those who knew him not even remotely possible.

He loved Emma von der Tann and he hated Barney Custer—hated him with a jealous hatred that was almost fanatic in its intensity. And even that the Princess Emma von der Tann would wed him were she free to wed was a question that was not at all clear in the mind of Barney Custer. He knew something of the traditions of this noble family—of the pride of caste, of the fetish of blood that inexorably dictated the ordering of their lives.

The girl had just said that the honor of her house was more precious than the life of any of its members. How much more precious would it be to her than her own material happiness! Barney Custer sighed and struggled through the swirling waters that were now above his hips. If he pressed the lithe form closer to him than necessity demanded, who may blame him?

The girl, whose face was toward the bank they had just quitted, gave no evidence of displeasure if she noted the fierce pressure of his muscles. Her eyes were riveted upon the wood behind. Presently a man emerged. He called to them in a loud and threatening tone.

Barney redoubled his Herculean efforts to gain the opposite bank. He was in midstream now and the water had risen to his waist. The girl saw Maenck and the other trooper emerge from the underbrush beside the first. Maenck was crazed with anger. He shook his fist and screamed aloud his threatening commands to halt, and then, of a sudden, gave an order to one of the men at his side. Immediately the fellow raised his carbine and fired at the escaping couple.

The bullet struck the water behind them. At the sound of the report the girl raised the gun she held and leveled it at the group behind her. She pulled the trigger. There was a sharp report, and one of the troopers fell. Then she fired again, quickly, and again and again. She did not score another hit, but she had the satisfaction of seeing Maenck and the last of his troopers dodge back to the safety of protecting trees.

"The cowards!" muttered Barney as the enemy's shot announced his sinister intention; "they might have hit your highness."

The girl did not reply until she had ceased firing.

"Captain Maenck is notoriously a coward," she said. "He is hiding behind a tree now with one of his men—I hit the other."

"You hit one of them!" exclaimed Barney enthusiastically.

"Yes," said the girl. "I have shot a man. I often wondered what the sensation must be to have done such a thing. I should feel terribly, but I don't. They were firing at you, trying to shoot you in the back while you were defenseless. I am not sorry—I cannot be; but I only wish that it had been Captain Maenck."

In a short time Barney reached the bank and, helping the girl up, climbed to her side. A couple of shots followed them as they left the river, but did not fall dangerously near. Barney took the carbine and replied, then both of them disappeared into the wood.

For the balance of the day they tramped on in the direction of Lustadt, making but little progress owing to the fear of apprehension. They did not dare utilize the high road, for they were still too close to Blentz. Their only hope lay in reaching the protection of Prince von der Tann before they should be recaptured by the king's emissaries. At dusk they came to the outskirts of a town. Here they hid until darkness settled, for Barney had determined to enter the place after dark and hire horses.

The American marveled at the bravery and endurance of the girl. He had always supposed that a princess was so carefully guarded from fatigue and privation all her life that the least exertion would prove her undoing; but no hardy peasant girl could have endured more bravely the hardships and dangers through which the Princess Emma had passed since the sun rose that morning.

At last darkness came, and with it they approached and entered the village. They kept to unlighted side streets until they met a villager, of whom they inquired their way to some private house where they might obtain refreshments. The fellow scrutinized them with evident suspicion.

"There is an inn yonder," he said, pointing toward the main street. "You can obtain food there. Why should respectable folk want to go elsewhere than to the public inn? And if you are afraid to go there you must have very good reasons for not wanting to be seen, and—" he stopped short as though assailed by an idea. "Wait," he cried, excitedly, "I will go and see if I can find a place for you. Wait right here," and off he ran toward the inn.

"I don't like the looks of that," said Barney, after the man had left them. "He's gone to report us to someone. Come, we'd better get out of here before he comes back."

The two turned up a side street away from the inn. They had gone but a short distance when they heard the sound of voices and the thud of horses' feet behind them. The horses were coming at a walk and with them were several men on foot. Barney took the princess' hand and drew her up a hedge bordered driveway that led into private grounds. In the shadows of the hedge they waited for the party behind them to pass. It might be no one searching for them, but it was just as well to be on the safe side—they were still near Blentz. Before the men reached their hiding place a motor car followed and caught up with them, and as the party came opposite the driveway Barney and the princess overheard a portion of their conversation.

"Some of you go back and search the street behind the inn—they may not have come this way." The speaker was in the motor car. "We will follow along this road for a bit and then turn into the Lustadt highway. If you don't find them go back along the road toward Tann."

In her excitement the Princess Emma had not noticed that Barney Custer still held her hand in his. Now he pressed it. "It is Maenck's voice," he whispered. "Every road will be guarded."

For a moment he was silent, thinking. The searching party had passed on. They could still hear the purring of the motor as Maenck's car moved slowly up the street.

"This is a driveway," murmured Barney. "People who build driveways into their grounds usually have something to drive. Whatever it is it should be at the other end of the driveway. Let's see if it will carry two."

Still in the shadow of the hedge they moved cautiously toward the upper end of the private road until presently they saw a building looming in their path.

"A garage?" whispered Barney.

"Or a barn," suggested the princess.

"In either event it should contain something that can go," returned the American. "Let us hope that it can go like—like—ah—the wind."

"And carry two," supplemented the princess.

"Wait here," said Barney. "If I get caught, run. Whatever happens you mustn't be caught."

Princess Emma dropped back close to the hedge and Barney approached the building, which proved to be a private garage. The doors were locked, as also were the three windows. Barney passed entirely around the structure halting at last upon the darkest side. Here was a window. Barney tried to loosen the catch with the blade of his pocket knife, but it wouldn't unfasten. His endeavors resulted only in snapping short the blade of his knife. For a moment he stood contemplating the baffling window. He dared not break the glass for fear of arousing the inmates of the house which, though he could not see it, might be close at hand.

Presently he recalled a scene he had witnessed on State Street in Chicago several years before—a crowd standing before the window of a jeweler's shop inspecting a neat little hole that a thief had cut in the glass with a diamond and through which he had inserted his hand and brought forth several hundred dollars worth of loot. But Barney Custer wore no diamond—he would as soon have worn a celluloid collar. But women wore diamonds. Doubtless the Princess Emma had one. He ran quickly to her side.

"Have you a diamond ring?" he whispered.

"Gracious!" she exclaimed, "you are progressing rapidly," and slipped a solitaire from her finger to his hand.

"Thanks," said Barney. "I need the practice; but wait and you'll see that a diamond may be infinitely more valuable than even the broker claims," and he was gone again into the shadows of the garage. Here upon the window pane he scratched a rough deep circle, close to the catch. A quick blow sent the glass clattering to the floor within. For a minute Barney stood

126

listening for any sign that the noise had attracted attention, but hearing nothing he ran his hand through the hole that he had made and unlatched the frame. A moment later he had crawled within.

Before him, in the darkness, stood a roadster. He ran his hand over the pedals and levers, breathing a sigh of relief as his touch revealed the familiar control of a standard make. Then he went to the double doors. They opened easily and silently.

Once outside he hastened to the side of the waiting girl.

"It's a machine," he whispered. "We must both be in it when it leaves the garage—it's the through express for Lustadt and makes no stops for passengers or freight."

He led her back to the garage and helped her into the seat beside him. As silently as possible he ran the machine into the driveway. A hundred yards to the left, half hidden by intervening trees and shrubbery, rose the dark bulk of a house. A subdued light shone through the drawn blinds of several windows—the only sign of life about the premises until the car had cleared the garage and was moving slowly down the driveway. Then a door opened in the house letting out a flood of light in which the figure of a man was silhouetted. A voice broke the silence.

"Who are you? What are you doing there? Come back!"

The man in the doorway called excitedly, "Friedrich! Come! Come quickly! Someone is stealing the automobile," and the speaker came running toward the driveway at top speed. Behind him came Friedrich. Both were shouting, waving their arms and threatening. Their combined din might have aroused the dead.

Barney sought speed—silence now was useless. He turned to the left into the street away from the center of the town. In this direction had gone the automobile with Maenck, but by taking the first righthand turn Barney hoped to elude the captain. In a moment Friedrich and the other were hopelessly distanced. It was with a sigh of relief that the American turned the car into the dark shadows beneath the overarching trees of the first cross street.

He was running without lights along an unknown way; and beside him was the most precious burden that Barney Custer might ever expect to carry. Under these circumstances his speed was greatly reduced from what he would have wished, but at that he was forced to accept grave risks. The road might end abruptly at the brink of a ravine—it might swerve perilously close to a stone quarry—or plunge headlong into a pond or river. Barney shuddered at the possibilities; but nothing of the sort happened. The street ran straight out of the town into a country road, rather heavy with sand. In the open the possibilities of speed were increased, for the night, though moonless, was clear, and the road visible for some distance ahead.

The fugitives were congratulating themselves upon the excellent chance they now had to reach Lustadt. There was only Maenck and his companion ahead of them in the other car, and as there were several roads by which one might reach the main highway the chances were fair that Prince Peter's aide would miss them completely.

Already escape seemed assured when the pounding of horses' hoofs upon the roadway behind them arose to blast their new found hope. Barney increased the speed of the car. It leaped ahead in response to his foot; but the road was heavy, and the sides of the ruts gripping the tires retarded the speed. For a mile they held the lead of the galloping horsemen. The shouts of their pursuers fell clearly upon their ears, and the Princess Emma, turning in her seat, could easily see the four who followed. At last the car began to draw away—the distance between it and the riders grew gradually greater.

"I believe we are going to make it," whispered the girl, her voice tense with excitement. "If you could only go a little faster, Mr. Custer, I'm sure that we will."

"She's reached her limit in this sand," replied the man, "and there's a grade just ahead—we may find better going beyond, but they're bound to gain on us before we reach the top."

The girl strained her eyes into the night before them. On the right of the road stood an ancient ruin—grim and forbidding. As her eyes rested upon it she gave a little exclamation of relief.

"I know where we are now," she cried. "The hill ahead is sandy, and there is a quarter of a mile of sand beyond, but then we strike the Lustadt highway, and if we can reach it ahead of them their horses will have to go ninety miles an hour to catch us—provided this car possesses any such speed possibilities."

"If it can go forty we are safe enough," replied Barney; "but we'll give it a chance to go as fast as it can—the farther we are from the vicinity of Blentz the safer I shall feel for the welfare of your highness."

A shot rang behind them, and a bullet whistled high above their heads. The princess seized the carbine that rested on the seat between them.

"Shall I?" she asked, turning its muzzle back over the lowered top.

"Better not," answered the man. "They are only trying to frighten us into surrendering—that shot was much too high to have been aimed at us—they are shooting over our heads purposely. If they deliberately attempt to pot us later, then go for them, but to do it now would only draw their fire upon us. I doubt if they wish to harm your highness, but they certainly would fire to hit in self-defense."

The girl lowered the firearm. "I am becoming perfectly bloodthirsty," she said, "but it makes me furious to be hunted like a wild animal in my native land, and by the command of my king, at that. And to think that you who placed him upon his throne, you who have risked your life many times for him, will find no protection at his hands should you be captured is maddening. Ach, Gott, if I were a man!"

"I thank God that you are not, your highness," returned Barney fervently.

Gently she laid her hand upon his where it gripped the steering wheel.

"No," she said, "I was wrong—I do not need to be a man while there still be such men as you, my friend; but I would that I were not the unhappy woman whom Fate had bound to an ingrate king—to a miserable coward!"

They had reached the grade at last, and the motor was straining to the Herculean task imposed upon it.

Grinding and grating in second speed the car toiled upward through the clinging sand. The pace was snail-like. Behind, the horsemen were gaining rapidly. The labored breathing of their mounts was audible even above the noise of the motor, so close were they. The top of the ascent lay but a few yards ahead, and the pursuers were but a few yards behind.

"Halt!" came from behind, and then a shot. The ping of the bullet and the scream of the ricochet warned the man and the girl that those behind them were becoming desperate—the bullet had struck one of the rear fenders. Without again asking assent the princess turned and, kneeling upon the cushion of the seat, fired at the nearest horseman. The horse stumbled and plunged to his knees. Another, just behind, ran upon him, and the two rolled over together with their riders. Two more shots were fired by the remaining horsemen and answered by the girl in the automobile, and then the car topped the hill, shot into high, and with renewed speed forged into the last quarter-mile of heavy going toward the good road ahead; but now the grade was slightly downward and all the advantage was upon the side of the fugitives.

However, their margin would be but scant when they reached the highway, for behind them the remaining troopers were spurring their jaded horses to a final spurt of speed. At last the white ribbon of the main road became visible. To the right they saw the headlights of a machine. It was Maenck probably, doubtless attracted their way by the shooting.

But the machine was a mile away and could not possibly reach the intersection of the two roads before they had turned to the left toward Lustadt. Then the incident would resolve itself into a simple test of speed between the two cars—and the ability and nerve of the drivers. Barney hadn't the slightest doubt now as to the outcome. His borrowed car was a good one, in good condition. And in the matter of driving he rather prided himself that he needn't take his hat off to anyone when it came to ability and nerve.

They were only about fifty feet from the highway. The girl touched his hand again. "We're safe," she cried, her voice vibrant with excitement, "we're safe at last." From beneath the bonnet, as though in answer to her statement, came a sickly, sucking sputter. The momentum of the car diminished. The throbbing of the engine ceased. They sat in silence as the machine coasted toward the highway and came to a dead stop, with its front wheels upon the road to safety. The girl turned toward Barney with an exclamation of surprise and interrogation.

"The jig's up," he groaned; "we're out of gasoline!"

IX

THE CAPTURE

The capture of Princess Emma von der Tann and Barney Custer was a relatively simple matter. Open fields spread in all directions about the crossroads at which their car had come to its humiliating stop. There was no cover. To have sought escape by flight, thus in the open, would have been to expose the princess to the fire of the troopers. Barney could not do this. He preferred to surrender and trust to chance to open the way to escape later.

When Captain Ernst Maenck drove up he found the prisoners disarmed, standing beside the now-useless car. He alighted from his own machine and with a low bow saluted the princess, an ironical smile upon his thin lips. Then he turned his attention toward her companion.

"Who are you?" he demanded gruffly. In the darkness he failed to recognize the American whom he thought dead in Austria.

"A servant of the house of Von der Tann," replied Barney.

"You deserve shooting," growled the officer, "but we'll leave that to Prince Peter and the king. When I tell them the trouble you have caused us—well, God help you."

The journey to Blentz was a short one. They had been much nearer that grim fortress than either had guessed. At the outskirts of the town they were challenged by Austrian sentries, through which Maenck passed with ease after the sentinel had summoned an officer. From this man Maenck received the password that would carry them through the line of outposts between the town and the castle—"Slankamen." Barney, who overheard the word, made a mental note of it.

At last they reached the dreary castle of Peter of Blentz. In the courtyard Austrian soldiers mingled with the men of the bodyguard of the king of Lutha. Within, the king's officers fraternized with the officers of the emperor. Maenck led his prisoners to the great hall which was filled with officers and officials of both Austria and Lutha.

The king was not there. Maenck learned that he had retired to his apartments a few minutes earlier in company with Prince Peter of Blentz and Von Coblich. He sent a servant to announce his return with the Princess von der Tann and a man who had attempted to prevent her being brought to Blentz.

Barney had, as far as possible, kept his face averted from Maenck since they had entered the lighted castle. He hoped to escape recognition, for he knew that if his identity were guessed it might go hard with the princess. As for himself, it might go even harder, but of that he gave scarcely a thought—the safety of the princess was paramount.

After a few minutes of waiting the servant returned with the king's command to fetch the prisoners to his apartments. The face of the Princess Emma was haggard. For the first time Barney saw signs of fear upon her countenance. With leaden steps they accompanied their guard up the winding stairway to the tower rooms that had been furnished for the king. They were the same in which Emma von der Tann had been imprisoned two years before.

On either side of the doorway stood a soldier of the king's bodyguard. As Captain Maenck approached they saluted. A servant opened the door and they passed into the room. Before them were Peter of Blentz and Von Coblich standing beside a table at which Leopold of Lutha was sitting. The eyes of the three men were upon the doorway as the little party entered. The king's face was flushed with wine. He rose as his eyes rested upon the face of the princess.

"Greetings, your highness," he cried with an attempt at cordiality.

The girl looked straight into his eyes, coldly, and then bent her knee in formal curtsy. The king was about to speak again when his eyes wandered to the face of the American. Instantly his own went white and then scarlet. The eyes of Peter of Blentz followed those of the king, widening in astonishment as they rested upon the features of Barney Custer.

"You told me he was dead," shouted the king. "What is the meaning of this, Captain Maenck?"

Maenck looked at his male prisoner and staggered back as though struck between the eyes.

"Mein Gott," he exclaimed, "the impostor!"

"You told me he was dead," repeated the king accusingly.

"As God is my judge, your majesty," cried Peter of Blentz, "this man was shot by an Austrian firing squad in Burgova over a week ago."

"Sire," exclaimed Maenck, "this is the first sight I have had of the prisoners except in the darkness of the night; until this instant I had not the remotest suspicion of his identity. He told me that he was a servant of the house of Von der Tann."

"I told you the truth, then," interjected Barney.

"Silence, you ingrate!" cried the king.

"Ingrate?" repeated Barney. "You have the effrontery to call me an ingrate? You miserable puppy."

A silence, menacing in its intensity, fell upon the little assemblage. The king trembled. His rage choked him. The others looked as though they scarce could believe the testimony of their own ears. All there, with the possible exception of the king, knew that he deserved even more degrading appellations; but they were Europeans, and to Europeans a king is a king— that they can never forget. It had been the inherent suggestion of kingship that had bent the knee of the Princess Emma before the man she despised.

But to the American a king was only what he made himself. In this instance he was not even a man in the estimation of Barney Custer. Maenck took a step toward the prisoner—a menacing step, for his hand had gone to his sword. Barney met him with a level look from between narrowed lids. Maenck hesitated, for he was a great coward. Peter of Blentz spoke:

"Sire," he said, "the fellow knows that he is already as good as dead, and so in his bravado he dares affront you. He has been convicted of spying by the Austrians. He is still a spy. It is unnecessary to repeat the formality of a trial."

Leopold at last found his voice, though it trembled and broke as he spoke.

"Carry out the sentence of the Austrian court in the morning," he said. "A volley now might arouse the garrison in the town and be misconstrued."

Maenck ordered Barney escorted from the apartment, then he turned toward the king.

"And the other prisoner, sire?" he inquired.

"There is no other prisoner," he said. "Her highness, the Princess von der Tann, is a guest of Prince Peter. She will be escorted to her apartment at once."

"Her highness, the Princess von der Tann, is not a guest of Prince Peter." The girl's voice was low and cold. "If Mr. Custer is a prisoner, her highness, too, is a prisoner. If he is to be shot, she demands a like fate. To die by the side of a MAN would be infinitely preferable to living by the side of your majesty."

Once again Leopold of Lutha reddened. For a moment he paced the room angrily to hide his emotion. Then he turned once to Maenck.

"Escort the prisoner to the north tower," he commanded, "and this insolent girl to the chambers next to ours. Tomorrow we shall talk with her again."

Outside the room Barney turned for a last look at the princess as he was being led in one direction and she in another. A smile of encouragement was on his lips and cold hopelessness in his heart. She answered the smile and her lips formed a silent "good-bye." They formed something else, too—three words which he was sure he could not have mistaken, and then they parted, he for the death chamber and she for what fate she could but guess.

As his guard halted before a door at the far end of a long corridor Barney Custer sensed a sudden familiarity in his surroundings. He was conscious of that sensation which is common to all of us—of having lived through a scene at some former time, to each minutest detail.

As the door opened and he was pushed into the room he realized that there was excellent foundation for the impression—he immediately recognized the apartment as the same in which he had once before been imprisoned. At that time he had been mistaken for the mad king who had escaped from the clutches of Peter of Blentz. The same king was now visiting as a guest the fortress in which he had spent ten bitter years as a prisoner.

"Say your prayers, my friend," admonished Maenck, as he was about to leave him alone, "for at dawn you die—and this time the firing squad will make a better job of it."

Barney did not answer him, and the captain departed, locking the door after him and leaving two men on guard in the corridor. Alone, Barney looked about the room. It was in no wise changed since his former visit to it. He recalled the incidents of the hour of his imprisonment here, thought of old Joseph who had aided his escape, looked at the paneled fireplace, whose secret, it was evident, not even the master of Blentz was familiar with—and grinned.

"'For at dawn you die!'" he repeated to himself, still smiling broadly. Then he crossed quickly to the fireplace, running his fingers along the edge of one of the large tiled panels that hid the entrance to the well-like shaft that rose from the cellars beneath to the towers above and which opened through similar concealed exits upon each floor. If the floor above should be untenanted he might be able to reach it as he and Joseph had done two years ago when they opened the secret panel in the fireplace and climbed a hidden ladder to the room overhead; and then by vacant corridors reached the far end of the castle above the suite in which the princess had been confined and near which Barney had every reason to believe she was now imprisoned.

Carefully Barney's fingers traversed the edges of the panel. No hidden latch rewarded his search. Again and again he examined the perfectly fitted joints until he was convinced either that there was no latch there or that it was hid beyond possibility of discovery. With each succeeding minute the American's heart and hopes sank lower and lower. Two years had elapsed since he had seen the secret portal swing to the touch of Joseph's fingers. One may forget much in two years; but that he was at work upon the right panel Barney was positive. However, it would do no harm to examine its mate which resembled it in minutest detail.

Almost indifferently Barney turned his attention to the other panel. He ran his fingers over it, his eyes following them. What was that? A finger-print? Upon the left side half way up a tiny smudge was visible. Barney examined it more carefully. A round, white figure of the conventional design that was burned into the tile bore the telltale smudge.

Otherwise it differed apparently in no way from the numerous other round, white figures that were repeated many times in the scheme of decoration. Barney placed his thumb exactly over the mark that another thumb had left there and pushed. The figure sank into the panel beneath the pressure. Barney pushed harder, breathless with suspense. The panel swung in at his effort. The American could have whooped with delight.

A moment more and he stood upon the opposite side of the secret door in utter darkness, for he had quickly closed it after him. To strike a match was but the matter of a moment. The wavering light revealed the top of the ladder that led downward and the foot of another leading aloft. He struck still more matches in search of the rope. It was not there, but his quest revealed the fact that the well at this point was much larger than he had imagined—it broadened into a small chamber.

The light of many matches finally led him to the discovery of a passageway directly behind the fireplace. It was narrow, and after spanning the chimney descended by a few rough steps to a slightly lower level. It led toward the opposite end of the castle. Could it be possible that it connected directly with the apartments in the farther tower—in the tower where the king was and the Princess Emma? Barney could scarce hope for any such good luck, but at least it was worth investigating—it must lead somewhere.

He followed it warily, feeling his way with hands and feet and occasionally striking a match. It was evident that the corridor lay in the thick wall of the castle, midway between the bottoms of the windows of the second floor and the tops of those upon the first—this would account for the slightly lower level of the passage from the floor of the second story.

Barney had traversed some distance in the darkness along the forgotten corridor when the sound of voices came to him from beyond the wall at his right. He stopped, motionless, pressing his ear against the side wall. As he did so he became aware of the fact that at this point the wall was of wood—a large panel of hardwood. Now he could hear even the words of the speaker upon the opposite side.

"Fetch her here, captain, and I will talk with her alone." The voice was the king's. "And, captain, you might remove the guard from before the door temporarily. I shall not require them, nor do I wish them to overhear my conversation with the princess."

Barney could hear the officer acknowledge the commands of the king, and then he heard a door close. The man had gone to fetch the princess. The American struck a match and examined the panel before him. It reached to the top of the passageway and was some three feet in width.

At one side were three hinges, and at the other an ancient spring lock. For an instant Barney stood in indecision. What should he do? His entry into the apartments of the king would result in alarming the entire fortress. Were he sure the king was alone it might be accomplished. Should he enter now or wait until the Princess Emma had been brought to the king?

With the question came the answer—a bold and daring scheme. His fingers sought the lock. Very gently, he unlatched it and pushed outward upon the panel. Suddenly the great doorway gave beneath his touch. It opened a crack letting a flood of light into his dark cell that almost blinded him.

For a moment he could see nothing, and then out of the glaring blur grew the figure of a man sitting at a table—with his back toward the panel.

It was the king, and he was alone. Noiselessly Barney Custer entered the apartment, closing the panel after him. At his back now was the great oil painting of the Blentz princess that had hid the secret entrance to the room. He crossed the thick rugs until he stood behind the king. Then he clapped one hand over the mouth of the monarch of Lutha and threw the other arm about his neck.

"Make the slightest outcry and I shall kill you," he whispered in the ear of the terrified man.

Across the room Barney saw a revolver lying upon a small table. He raised the king to his feet and, turning his back toward the weapon dragged him across the apartment until the table was within easy reach. Then he snatched up the revolver and swung the king around into a chair facing him, the muzzle of the gun pressed against his face.

"Silence," he whispered.

The king, white and trembling, gasped as his eyes fell upon the face of the American.

"You?" His voice was barely audible.

"Take off your clothes—every stitch of them—and if any one asks for admittance, deny them. Quick, now," as the king hesitated. "My life is forfeited unless I can escape. If I am apprehended I shall see that you pay for my recapture with your life—if any one enters this room without my sanction they will enter it to find a dead king upon the floor; do you understand?"

The king made no reply other than to commence divesting himself of his clothing. Barney followed his example, but not before he had crossed to the door that opened into the main corridor and shot the bolt upon the inside. When both men had removed their clothing Barney pointed to the little pile of soiled peasant garb that he had worn.

"Put those on," he commanded.

The king hesitated, drawing back in disgust. Barney paused, half-way into the royal union suit, and leveled the revolver at Leopold. The king picked up one of the garments gingerly between the tips of his thumb and finger.

"Hurry!" admonished the American, drawing the silk half-hose of the ruler of Lutha over his foot. "If you don't hurry," he added, "someone may interrupt us, and you know what the result would be—to you."

Scowling, Leopold donned the rough garments. Barney, fully clothed in the uniform the king had been wearing, stepped across the apartment to where the king's sword and helmet lay upon the side table that had also borne the revolver. He placed the helmet upon his head and buckled the sword-belt about his waist, then he faced the king, behind whom was a cheval glass. In it Barney saw his image. The king was looking at the American, his eyes wide and his jaw dropped. Barney did not wonder at his consternation. He himself was dumbfounded by the likeness which he bore to the king. It was positively uncanny. He approached Leopold.

"Remove your rings," he said, holding out his hand. The king did as he was bid, and Barney slipped the two baubles upon his fingers. One of them was the royal ring of the kings of Lutha.

The American now blindfolded the king and led him toward the panel which had given him ingress to the room. Through it the two men passed, Barney closing the panel after them. Then he conducted the king back along the dark passageway to the room which the American had but recently quitted. At the back of the panel which led into his former prison Barney halted and listened. No sound came from beyond the partition. Gently Barney opened the secret door a trifle—just enough to permit him a quick survey of the interior of the apartment. It was empty. A smile crossed his face as he thought of the difficulty Leopold might encounter the following morning in convincing his jailers that he was not the American.

Then he recalled his reflection in the cheval glass and frowned. Could Leopold convince them? He doubted it—and what then? The American was sentenced to be shot at dawn. They would shoot the king instead. Then there would be none to whom to return the kingship. What would he do with it? The temptation was great. Again a throne lay within his grasp—a throne and the woman he loved. None might ever know unless he chose to tell—his resemblance to Leopold was too perfect. It defied detection.

With an exclamation of impatience he wheeled about and dragged the frightened monarch back to the room from which he had stolen him. As he entered he heard a knock at the door.

"Do not disturb me now," he called. "Come again in half an hour."

"But it is Her Highness, Princess Emma, sire," came a voice from beyond the door. "You summoned her."

"She may return to her apartments," replied Barney.

All the time he kept his revolver leveled at the king, from his eyes he had removed the blind after they had entered the apartment. He crossed to the table where the king had been sitting when he surprised him, motioning the ragged ruler to follow and be seated.

"Take that pen," he said, "and write a full pardon for Mr. Bernard Custer, and an order requiring that he be furnished with money and set at liberty at dawn."

The king did as he was bid. For a moment the American stood looking at him before he spoke again.

"You do not deserve what I am going to do for you," he said. "And Lutha deserves a better king than the one my act will give her; but I am neither a thief nor a murderer, and so I must forbear leaving you to your just deserts and return your throne to you. I shall do so after I have insured my own safety and done what I can for Lutha—what you are too little a man and king to do yourself.

"So soon as they liberate you in the morning, make the best of your way to Brosnov, on the Serbian frontier. Await me there. When I can, I shall come. Again we may exchange clothing and you can return to Lustadt. I shall cross over into Siberia out of your reach, for I know you too well to believe that any sense of honor or gratitude would prevent you signing my death-warrant at the first opportunity. Now, come!"

Once again Barney led the blindfolded king through the dark corridor to the room in the opposite tower—to the prison of the American. At the open panel he shoved him into the apartment. Then he drew the door quietly to, leaving the king upon the inside, and retraced his steps to the royal apartments. Crossing to the center table, he touched an electric button. A moment later an officer knocked at the door, which, in the meantime, Barney had unbolted.

"Enter!" said the American. He stood with his back toward the door until he heard it close behind the officer. When he turned he was apparently examining his revolver. If the officer suspected his identity, it was just as well to be prepared. Slowly he raised his eyes to the newcomer, who stood stiffly at salute. The officer looked him full in the face.

"I answered your majesty's summons," said the man.

"Oh, yes!" returned the American. "You may fetch the Princess Emma."

The officer saluted once more and backed out of the apartment. Barney walked to the table and sat down. A tin box of cigarettes lay beside the lamp. Barney lighted one of them. The king had good taste in the selection of tobacco, he thought. Well, a man must need have some redeeming characteristics.

Outside, in the corridor, he heard voices, and again the knock at the door. He bade them enter. As the door opened Emma von der Tann, her head thrown back and a flush of anger on her face, entered the room. Behind her was the officer who had been despatched to bring her. Barney nodded to the latter.

"You may go," he said. He drew a chair from the table and asked the princess to be seated. She ignored his request.

"What do you wish of me?" she asked. She was looking straight into his eyes. The officer had withdrawn and closed the door after him. They were alone, with nothing to fear; yet she did not recognize him.

"You are the king," she continued in cold, level tones, "but if you are also a gentleman, you will at once order me returned to my father at Lustadt, and with me the man to whom you owe so much. I do not expect it of you, but I wish to give you the chance.

"I shall not go without him. I am betrothed to you; but until tonight I should rather have died than wed you. Now I am ready to compromise. If you will set Mr. Custer at liberty in Serbia and return me unharmed to my father, I will fulfill my part of our betrothal."

Barney Custer looked straight into the girl's face for a long moment. A half smile played upon his lips at the thought of her surprise when she learned the truth, when suddenly it dawned upon him that she and he were both much safer if no one, not even her loyal self, guessed that he was other than the king. It is not difficult to live a part, but often it is difficult to act one. Some little word or look, were she to know that he was Barney Custer, might betray them; no, it was better to leave her in ignorance, though his conscience pricked him for the disloyalty that his act implied.

It seemed a poor return for her courage and loyalty to him that her statement to the man she thought king had revealed. He marveled that a Von der Tann could have spoken those words—a Von der Tann who but the day before had refused to save her father's life at the loss of the family honor. It seemed incredible to the American that he had won such love from such a woman. Again came the mighty temptation to keep the crown and the girl both; but with a straightening of his broad shoulders he threw it from him.

She was promised to the king, and while he masqueraded in the king's clothes, he at least would act the part that a king should. He drew a folded paper from his inside pocket and handed it to the girl.

"Here is the American's pardon," he said, "drawn up and signed by the king's own hand."

She opened it and, glancing through it hurriedly, looked up at the man before her with a questioning expression in her eyes.

"You came, then," she said, "to a realization of the enormity of your ingratitude?"

The man shrugged.

"He will never die at my command," he said.

"I thank your majesty," she said simply. "As a Von der Tann, I have tried to believe that a Rubinroth could not be guilty of such baseness. And now, tell me what your answer is to my proposition."

"We shall return to Lustadt tonight," he replied. "I fear the purpose of Prince Peter. In fact, it may be difficult—even impossible—for us to leave Blentz; but we can at least make the attempt."

"Can we not take Mr. Custer with us?" she asked. "Prince Peter may disregard your majesty's commands and, after you are gone, have him shot. Do not forget that he kept the crown from Peter of Blentz—it is certain that Prince Peter will never forget it."

"I give you my word, your highness, that I know positively that if I leave Blentz tonight Prince Peter will not have Mr. Custer shot in the morning, and it will so greatly jeopardize his own plans if we attempt to release the prisoner that in all probability we ourselves will be unable to escape."

She looked at him thoughtfully for a moment.

"You give me your word that he will be safe?" she asked.

"My royal word," he replied.

"Very well, let us leave at once."

Barney touched the bell once more, and presently an officer of the Blentz faction answered the summons. As the man closed the door and approached, saluting, Barney stepped close to him.

"We are leaving for Tann tonight," he said, "at once. You will conduct us from the castle and procure horses for us. All the time I shall walk at your elbow, and in my hand I shall carry this," and he displayed the king's revolver. "At the first indication of defection upon your part I shall kill you. Do you perfectly understand me?"

"But, your majesty," exclaimed the officer, "why is it necessary that you leave thus surreptitiously? May not the king go and come in his own kingdom as he desires? Let me announce your wishes to Prince Peter that he may furnish you with a proper escort. Doubtless he will wish to accompany you himself, sire."

"You will do precisely what I say without further comment," snapped Barney. "Now get a—" He had been about to say: "Now get a move on you," when it occurred to him that this was not precisely the sort of language that kings were supposed to use to their inferiors. So he changed it. "Now get a couple of horses for her highness and myself, as well as your own, for you will accompany us to Tann."

The officer looked at the weapon in the king's hand. He measured the distance between himself and the king. He well knew the reputed cowardice of Leopold. Could he make the leap and strike up the king's hand before the timorous monarch found even the courage of the cornered rat to fire at him? Then his eyes sought the face of the king, searching for the signs of nervous terror that would make his conquest an easy one; but what he saw in the eyes that bored straight into his brought his own to the floor at the king's feet.

What new force animated Leopold of Lutha? Those were not the eyes of a coward. No fear was reflected in their steely glitter. The officer mumbled an apology, saluted, and turned toward the door. At his elbow walked the impostor; a cavalry cape that had belonged to the king now covered his shoulders and hid the weapon that pressed its hard warning now and again into the short-ribs of the Blentz officer. Just behind the American came the Princess Emma von der Tann.

The three passed through the deserted corridors of the sleeping castle, taking a route at Barney's suggestion that led them to the stable courtyard without necessitating traversing the main corridors or the great hall or the guardroom, in all of which there still were Austrian and Blentz soldiers, whose duties or pleasures had kept them from their blankets.

At the stables a sleepy groom answered the summons of the officer, whom Barney had warned not to divulge the identity of himself or the princess. He left the princess in the shadows outside the building. After what seemed an eternity to the American, three horses were led into the courtyard, saddled, and bridled. The party mounted and approached the gates. Here, Barney knew, might be encountered the most serious obstacle in their path. He rode close to the side of their unwilling conductor. Leaning forward in his saddle, he whispered in the man's ear.

"Failure to pass us through the gates," he said, "will be the signal for your death."

The man reined in his mount and turned toward the American.

"I doubt if they will pass even me without a written order from Prince Peter," he said. "If they refuse, you must reveal your identity. The guard is composed of Luthanians—I doubt if they will dare refuse your majesty."

Then they rode on up to the gates. A soldier stepped from the sentry box and challenged them.

"Lower the drawbridge," ordered the officer. "It is Captain Krantzwort on a mission for the king."

The soldier approached, raising a lantern, which he had brought from the sentry box, and inspected the captain's face. He seemed ill at ease. In the light of the lantern, the American saw that he was scarce more than a boy—doubtless a recruit. He saw the expression of fear and awe with which he regarded the officer, and it occurred to him that the effect of the king's presence upon him would be absolutely overpowering. Still the soldier hesitated.

"My orders are very strict, sir," he said. "I am to let no one leave without a written order from Prince Peter. If the sergeant or the lieutenant were here they would know what to do; but they are both at the castle—only two other soldiers are at the gates with me. Wait, and I will send one of them for the lieutenant."

"No," interposed the American. "You will send for no one, my man. Come closer—look at my face."

The soldier approached, holding his lantern above his head. As its feeble rays fell upon the face and uniform of the man on horseback, the sentry gave a little gasp of astonishment.

"Now, lower the drawbridge," said Barney Custer, "it is your king's command."

Quickly the fellow hastened to obey the order. The chains creaked and the windlass groaned as the heavy planking sank to place across the moat.

As Barney passed the soldier he handed him the pardon Leopold had written for the American.

"Give this to your lieutenant," he said, "and tell him to hand it to Prince Peter before dawn tomorrow. Do not fail."

A moment later the three were riding down the winding road toward Blentz. Barney had no further need of the officer who rode with them. He would be glad to be rid of him, for he anticipated that the fellow might find ample opportunity to betray them as they passed through the Austrian lines, which they must do to reach Lustadt.

He had told the captain that they were going to Tann in order that, should the man find opportunity to institute pursuit, he might be thrown off the track. The Austrian sentries were no great distance ahead when Barney ordered a halt.

"Dismount," he directed the captain, leaping to the ground himself at the same time. "Put your hands behind your back."

The officer did as he was bid, and Barney bound his wrists securely with a strap and buckle that he had removed from the cantle of his saddle as he rode. Then he led him off the road among some weeds and compelled him to lie down, after which he bound his ankles together and stuffed a gag in his mouth, securing it in place with a bit of stick and the chinstrap from the man's helmet. The threat of the revolver kept Captain Krantzwort silent and obedient throughout the hasty operations.

"Good-bye, captain," whispered Barney, "and let me suggest that you devote the time until your discovery and release in pondering the value of winning your king's confidence in the future. Had you chosen your associates more carefully in the past, this need not have occurred."

Barney unsaddled the captain's horse and turned him loose, then he remounted and, with the princess at his side, rode down toward Blentz.

X

A NEW KING IN LUTHA

As the two riders approached the edge of the village of Blentz a sentry barred their way. To his challenge the American replied that they were "friends from the castle."

"Advance," directed the sentry, "and give the countersign."

Barney rode to the fellow's side, and leaning from the saddle whispered in his ear the word "Slankamen."

Would it pass them out as it had passed Maenck in? Barney scarcely breathed as he awaited the result of his experiment. The soldier brought his rifle to present and directed them to pass. With a sigh of relief that was almost audible the two rode into the village and the Austrian lines.

Once within they met with no further obstacle until they reached the last line of sentries upon the far side of the town. It was with more confidence that Barney gave the countersign here, nor was he surprised that the soldier passed them readily; and now they were upon the highroad to Lustadt, with nothing more to bar their way.

For hours they rode on in silence. Barney wanted to talk with his companion, but as king he found nothing to say to her. The girl's mind was filled with morbid reflections of the past few hours and dumb terror for the future. She would keep her promise to the king; but after— life would not be worth the living; why should she live? She glanced at the man beside her in the light of the coming dawn. Ah, why was he so like her American in outward appearances only? Their own mothers could scarce have distinguished them, and yet in character no two men could have differed more widely. The man turned to her.

"We are almost there," he said. "You must be very tired."

The words reflected a consideration that had never been a characteristic of Leopold. The girl began to wonder if there might not possibly be a vein of nobility in the man, after all, that she had never discovered. Since she had entered his apartments at Blentz he had been in every way a different man from the Leopold she had known of old. The boldness of his escape from Blentz supposed a courage that the king had never given the slightest indication of in the past. Could it be that he was making a genuine effort to become a man—to win her respect?

They were approaching Lustadt as the sun rose. A troop of horse was just emerging from the north gate. As it neared them they saw that the cavalrymen wore the uniforms of the Royal Horse Guard. At their head rode a lieutenant. As his eyes fell upon the face of the princess and her companion, he brought his troopers to a halt, and, with incredulity plain upon his countenance, advanced to meet them, his hand raised in salute to the king. It was Butzow.

Now Barney was sure that he would be recognized. For two years he and the Luthanian officer had been inseparable. Surely Butzow would penetrate his disguise. He returned his friend's salute, looked him full in the eyes, and asked where he was riding.

"To Blentz, your majesty," replied Butzow, "to demand an audience. I bear important word from Prince von der Tann. He has learned the Austrians are moving an entire army corps into Lutha, together with siege howitzers. Serbia has demanded that all Austrian troops be withdrawn from Luthanian territory at once, and has offered to assist your majesty in maintaining your neutrality by force, if necessary."

As Butzow spoke his eyes were often upon the Princess Emma, and it was quite evident that he was much puzzled to account for her presence with the king. She was supposed to be at Tann, and Butzow knew well enough her estimate of Leopold to know that she would not be in his company of her own volition. His expression as he addressed the man he supposed to be his king was far from deferential. Barney could scarce repress a smile.

"We will ride at once to the palace," he said. "At the gate you may instruct one of your sergeants to telephone to Prince von der Tann that the king is returning and will grant him audience immediately. You and your detachment will act as our escort."

Butzow saluted and turned to his troopers, giving the necessary commands that brought them about in the wake of the pseudo-king. Once again Barney Custer, of Beatrice, rode into Lustadt as king of Lutha. The few people upon the streets turned to look at him as he passed, but there was little demonstration of love or enthusiasm.

Leopold had awakened no emotions of this sort in the hearts of his subjects. Some there were who still remembered the gallant actions of their ruler on the field of battle when his forces had defeated those of the regent, upon that other occasion when this same American had sat upon the throne of Lutha for two days and had led the little army to victory; but since then the true king had been with them daily in his true colors. Arrogance, haughtiness, and petty tyranny had marked his reign. Taxes had gone even higher than under the corrupt influence of the Blentz regime. The king's days were spent in bed; his nights in dissipation. Old Ludwig von der Tann seemed Lutha's only friend at court. Him the people loved and trusted.

It was the old chancellor who met them as they entered the palace—the Princess Emma, Lieutenant Butzow, and the false king. As the old man's eyes fell upon his daughter, he gave an exclamation of surprise and of incredulity. He looked from her to the American.

"What is the meaning of this, your majesty?" he cried in a voice hoarse with emotion. "What does her highness in your company?"

There was neither fear nor respect in Prince Ludwig's tone—only anger. He was demanding an accounting from Leopold, the man; not from Leopold, the king. Barney raised his hand.

"Wait," he said, "before you judge. The princess was brought to Blentz by Prince Peter. She will tell you that I have aided her to escape and that I have accorded her only such treatment as a woman has a right to expect from a king."

The girl inclined her head.

"His majesty has been most kind," she said. "He has treated me with every consideration and respect, and I am convinced that he was not a willing party to my arrest and forcible detention at Blentz; or," she added, "if he was, he regretted his action later and has made full reparation by bringing me to Lustadt."

Prince von der Tann found difficulty in hiding his surprise at this evidence of chivalry in the cowardly king. But for his daughter's testimony he could not have believed it possible that it lay within the nature of Leopold of Lutha to have done what he had done within the past few hours.

He bowed low before the man who wore the king's uniform. The American extended his hand, and Von der Tann, taking it in his own, raised it to his lips.

"And now," said Barney briskly, "let us go to my apartments and get to work. Your highness"—and he turned toward the Princess Emma—"must be greatly fatigued. Lieutenant Butzow, you will see that a suite is prepared for her highness. Afterward you may call upon Count Zellerndorf, whom I understand returned to Lustadt yesterday, and notify him that I will receive him in an hour. Inform the Serbian minister that I desire his presence at the palace immediately. Lose no time, lieutenant, and be sure to impress upon the Serbian minister that immediately means immediately."

Butzow saluted and the Princess Emma curtsied, as the king turned and, slipping his arm through that of Prince Ludwig, walked away in the direction of the royal apartments. Once at the king's desk Barney turned toward the chancellor. In his mind was the determination to save Lutha if Lutha could be saved. He had been forced to place the king in a position where he would be helpless, though that he would have been equally as helpless upon his throne the American did not doubt for an instant. However, the course of events had placed within his hands the power to serve not only Lutha but the house of Von der Tann as well. He would do in the king's place what the king should have done if the king had been a man.

"Now, Prince Ludwig," he said, "tell me just what conditions we must face. Remember that I have been at Blentz and that there the King of Lutha is not apt to learn all that transpires in Lustadt."

"Sire," replied the chancellor, "we face a grave crisis. Not only is there within Lutha the small force of Austrian troops that surround Blentz, but now an entire army corps has crossed the border. Unquestionably they are marching on Lustadt. The emperor is going to take no chances. He sent the first force into Lutha to compel Serbian intervention and draw Serbian troops from the Austro-Serbian battle line. Serbia has withheld her forces at my request, but she will not withhold them for long. We must make a declaration at once. If we declare against Austria we are faced by the menace of the Austrian troops already within our boundaries, but we shall have Serbia to help us.

"A Serbian army corps is on the frontier at this moment awaiting word from Lutha. If it is adverse to Austria that army corps will cross the border and march to our assistance. If it is favorable to Austria it will none the less cross into Lutha, but as enemies instead of allies. Serbia has acted honorably toward Lutha. She has not violated our neutrality. She has no desire to increase her possessions in this direction.

"On the other hand, Austria has violated her treaty with us. She has marched troops into our country and occupied the town of Blentz. Constantly in the past she has incited internal discord. She is openly championing the Blentz cause, which at last I trust your majesty has discovered is inimical to your interests.

"If Austria is victorious in her war with Serbia, she will find some pretext to hold Lutha whether Lutha takes her stand either for or against her. And most certainly is this true if it occurs that Austrian troops are still within the boundaries of Lutha when peace is negotiated. Not only our honor but our very existence demands that there be no Austrian troops in Lutha at the close of this war. If we cannot force them across the border we can at least make such an effort as will win us the respect of the world and a voice in the peace negotiations.

"If we must bow to the surrender of our national integrity, let us do so only after we have exhausted every resource of the country in our country's defense. In the past your majesty has not appeared to realize the menace of your most powerful neighbor. I beg of you, sire, to trust me. Believe that I have only the interests of Lutha at heart, and let us work together for the salvation of our country and your majesty's throne."

Barney laid his hand upon the old man's shoulder. It seemed a shame to carry the deception further, but the American well knew that only so could he accomplish aught for Lutha or the Von der Tanns. Once the old chancellor suspected the truth as to his identity he would be the first to denounce him.

"I think that you and I can work together, Prince Ludwig," he said. "I have sent for the Serbian and Austrian ministers. The former should be here immediately."

Nor did they have long to wait before the tall Slav was announced. Barney lost no time in getting down to business. He asked no questions. What Von der Tann had told him, what he had seen with his own eyes since he had entered Lutha, and what he had overheard in the inn at Burgova was sufficient evidence that the fate of Lutha hung upon the prompt and energetic decisions of the man who sat upon Lutha's throne for the next few days.

Had Leopold been the present incumbent Lutha would have been lost, for that he would play directly into the hands of Austria was not to be questioned. Were Von der Tann to seize the reins of government a state of revolution would exist that would divide the state into two bitter factions, weaken its defense, and give Austria what she most desired—a plausible pretext for intervention.

Lutha's only hope lay in united defense of her liberties under the leadership of the one man whom all acknowledged king—Leopold. Very well, Barney Custer, of Beatrice, would be Leopold for a few days, since the real Leopold had proven himself incompetent to meet the emergency.

General Petko, the Serbian minister to Lutha, brought to the audience the memory of a series of unpleasant encounters with the king. Leopold had never exerted himself to hide his pro-Austrian sentiments. Austria was a powerful country—Serbia, a relatively weak neighbor. Leopold, being a royal snob, had courted the favor of the emperor and turned up his nose at Serbia. The general was prepared for a repetition of the veiled affronts that Leopold delighted in according him; but this time he brought with him a reply that for two years he had been living in the hope of some day being able to deliver to the young monarch he so cordially despised.

It was an ultimatum from his government—an ultimatum couched in terms from which all diplomatic suavity had been stripped. If Barney Custer, of Beatrice, could have read it he

143

would have smiled, for in plain American it might have been described as announcing to Leopold precisely "where he got off." But Barney did not have the opportunity to read it, since that ultimatum was never delivered.

Barney took the wind all out of it by his first words. "Your excellency may wonder why it is that we have summoned you at such an early hour," he said.

General Petko inclined his head in deferential acknowledgment of the truth of the inference.

"It is because we have learned from our chancellor," continued the American, "that Serbia has mobilized an entire army corps upon the Luthanian frontier. Am I correctly informed?"

General Petko squared his shoulders and bowed in assent. At the same time he reached into his breast-pocket for the ultimatum.

"Good!" exclaimed Barney, and then he leaned close to the ear of the Serbian. "How long will it take to move that army corps to Lustadt?"

General Petko gasped and returned the ultimatum to his pocket.

"Sire!" he cried, his face lighting with incredulity. "You mean—"

"I mean," said the American, "that if Serbia will loan Lutha an army corps until the Austrians have evacuated Luthanian territory, Lutha will loan Serbia an army corps until such time as peace is declared between Serbia and Austria. Other than this neither government will incur any obligations to the other.

"We may not need your help, but it will do us no harm to have them well on the way toward Lustadt as quickly as possible. Count Zellerndorf will be here in a few minutes. We shall, through him, give Austria twenty-four hours to withdraw all her troops beyond our frontiers. The army of Lutha is mobilized before Lustadt. It is not a large army, but with the help of Serbia it should be able to drive the Austrians from the country, provided they do not leave of their own accord."

General Petko smiled. So did the American and the chancellor. Each knew that Austria would not withdraw her army from Lutha.

"With your majesty's permission I will withdraw," said the Serbian, "and transmit Lutha's proposition to my government; but I may say that your majesty need have no apprehension but that a Serbian army corps will be crossing into Lutha before noon today."

"And now, Prince Ludwig," said the American after the Serbian had bowed himself out of the apartment, "I suggest that you take immediate steps to entrench a strong force north of Lustadt along the road to Blentz."

Von der Tann smiled as he replied. "It is already done, sire," he said.

"But I passed in along the road this morning," said Barney, "and saw nothing of such preparations."

"The trenches and the soldiers were there, nevertheless, sire," replied the old man, "only a little gap was left on either side of the highway that those who came and went might not

144

suspect our plans and carry word of them to the Austrians. A few hours will complete the link across the road."

"Good! Let it be completed at once. Here is Count Zellerndorf now," as the minister was announced.

Von der Tann bowed himself out as the Austrian entered the king's presence. For the first time in two years the chancellor felt that the destiny of Lutha was safe in the hands of her king. What had caused the metamorphosis in Leopold he could not guess. He did not seem to be the same man that had whined and growled at their last audience a week before.

The Austrian minister entered the king's presence with an expression of ill-concealed surprise upon his face. Two days before he had left Leopold safely ensconced at Blentz, where he was to have remained indefinitely. He glanced hurriedly about the room in search of Prince Peter or another of the conspirators who should have been with the king. He saw no one. The king was speaking. The Austrian's eyes went wider, not only at the words, but at the tone of voice.

"Count Zellerndorf," said the American, "you were doubtless aware of the embarrassment under which the king of Lutha was compelled at Blentz to witness the entry of a foreign army within his domain. But we are not now at Blentz. We have summoned you that you may receive from us, and transmit to your emperor, the expression of our surprise and dismay at the unwarranted violation of Luthanian neutrality."

"But, your majesty—" interrupted the Austrian.

"But nothing, your excellency," snapped the American. "The moment for diplomacy is passed; the time for action has come. You will oblige us by transmitting to your government at once a request that every Austrian soldier now in Lutha be withdrawn by noon tomorrow."

Zellerndorf looked his astonishment.

"Are you mad, sire?" he cried. "It will mean war!"

"It is what Austria has been looking for," snapped the American, "and what people look for they usually get, especially if they chance to be looking for trouble. When can you expect a reply from Vienna?"

"By noon, your majesty," replied the Austrian, "but are you irretrievably bound to your present policy? Remember the power of Austria, sire. Think of your throne. Think—"

"We have thought of everything," interrupted Barney. "A throne means less to us than you may imagine, count; but the honor of Lutha means a great deal."

XI

THE BATTLE

At five o'clock that afternoon the sidewalks bordering Margaretha Street were crowded with promenaders. The little tables before the cafes were filled. Nearly everyone spoke of the great war and of the peril which menaced Lutha. Upon many a lip was open disgust at the supine attitude of Leopold of Lutha in the face of an Austrian invasion of his country. Discontent was open. It was ripening to something worse for Leopold than an Austrian invasion.

Presently a sergeant of the Royal Horse Guards cantered down the street from the palace. He stopped here and there, and, dismounting, tacked placards in conspicuous places. At the notice, and in each instance cheers and shouting followed the sergeant as he rode on to the next stop.

Now, at each point men and women were gathered, eagerly awaiting an explanation of the jubilation farther up the street. Those whom the sergeant passed called to him for an explanation, and not receiving it, followed in a quickly growing mob that filled Margaretha Street from wall to wall. When he dismounted he had almost to fight his way to the post or door upon which he was to tack the next placard. The crowd surged about him in its anxiety to read what the placard bore, and then, between the cheering and yelling, those in the front passed back to the crowd the tidings that filled them with so great rejoicing.

"Leopold has declared war on Austria!" "The king calls for volunteers!" "Long live the king!"

The battle of Lustadt has passed into history. Outside of the little kingdom of Lutha it received but passing notice by the world at large, whose attention was riveted upon the great conflicts along the banks of the Meuse, the Marne, and the Aisne. But in Lutha! Ah, it will be told and retold, handed down from mouth to mouth and from generation to generation to the end of time.

How the cavalry that the king sent north toward Blentz met the advancing Austrian army. How, fighting, they fell back upon the infantry which lay, a thin line that stretched east and west across the north of Lustadt, in its first line of trenches. A pitifully weak line it was, numerically, in comparison with the forces of the invaders; but it stood its ground heroically, and from the heights to the north of the city the fire from the forts helped to hold the enemy in check for many hours.

And then the enemy succeeded in bringing up their heavy artillery to the ridge that lies three miles north of the forts. Shells were bursting in the trenches, the forts, and the city. To the south a stream of terror-stricken refugees was pouring out of Lustadt along the King's Road. Rich and poor, animated by a common impulse, filled the narrow street that led to the city's southern gate. Carts drawn by dogs, laden donkeys, French limousines, victorias, wheelbarrows—every conceivable wheeled vehicle and beast of burden—were jammed in a seemingly inextricable tangle in the mad rush for safety.

Rumor passed back and forth through the fleeing thousands. Now came word that Fort No. 2 had been silenced by the Austrian guns. Immediately followed news that the Luthanian line was falling back upon the city. Fear turned to panic. Men fought to outdistance their neighbors.

A shell burst upon a roof-top in an adjoining square.

Women fainted and were trampled. Hoarse shouts of anger mingled with screams of terror, and then into the midst of it from Margaretha Street rode a man on horseback. Behind him were a score of officers. A trumpeter raised his instrument to his lips, and above the din of the fleeing multitude rose the sharp, triple call that announces the coming of the king. The mob halted and turned.

Looking down upon them from his saddle was Leopold of Lutha. His palm was raised for silence and there was a smile upon his lips. Quite suddenly, and as by a miracle, fear left them.

They made a line for him and his staff to ride through. One of the officers turned in his saddle to address a civilian friend in an automobile.

"His majesty is riding to the firing line," he said and he raised his voice that many might hear. Quickly the word passed from mouth to mouth, and as Barney Custer, of Beatrice, passed along Margaretha Street he was followed by a mad din of cheering that drowned the booming of the distant cannon and the bursting of the shells above the city.

The balance of the day the pseudo-king rode back and forth along his lines. Three of his staff were killed and two horses were shot from beneath him, but from the moment that he appeared the Luthanian line ceased to waver or fall back. The advanced trenches that they had abandoned to the Austrians they took again at the point of the bayonet. Charge after charge they repulsed, and all the time there hovered above the enemy Lutha's sole aeroplane, watching, watching, ever watching for the coming of the allies. Somewhere to the northeast the Serbians were advancing toward Lustadt. Would they come in time?

It was five o'clock in the morning of the second day, and though the Luthanian line still held, Barney Custer knew that it could not hold for long. The Austrian artillery fire, which had been rather wild the preceding day, had now become of deadly accuracy. Each bursting shell filled some part of the trenches with dead and wounded, and though their places were taken by fresh men from the reserve, there would soon be no reserve left to call upon.

At his left, in the rear, the American had massed the bulk of his reserves, and at the foot of the heights north of the city and just below the forts the major portion of the cavalry was drawn up in the shelter of a little ravine. Barney's eyes were fixed upon the soaring aeroplane.

In his hand was his watch. He would wait another fifteen minutes, and if by then the signal had not come that the Serbians were approaching, he would strike the blow that he had decided upon. From time to time he glanced at his watch.

The fifteen minutes had almost elapsed when there fluttered from the tiny monoplane a paper parachute. It dropped for several hundred feet before it spread to the air pressure and floated more gently toward the earth and a moment later there burst from its basket a puff of white smoke. Two more parachutes followed the first and two more puffs of smoke. Then the machine darted rapidly off toward the northeast.

Barney turned to Prince von der Tann with a smile. "They are none too soon," he said.

The old prince bowed in acquiescence. He had been very happy for two days. Lutha might be defeated now, but she could never be subdued. She had a king at last—a real king. Gott! How he had changed. It reminded Prince von der Tann of the day he had ridden beside the impostor two years before in the battle with the forces of Peter of Blentz. Many times he had caught himself scrutinizing the face of the monarch, searching for some proof that after all he was not Leopold.

"Direct the commanders of forts three and four to concentrate their fire on the enemy's guns directly north of Fort No. 3," Barney directed an aide. "Simultaneously let the cavalry and Colonel Kazov's infantry make a determined assault on the Austrian trenches."

Then he turned his horse toward the left of his line, where, a little to the rear, lay the fresh troops that he had been holding in readiness against this very moment. As he galloped across the plain, his staff at his heels, shrapnel burst about them. Von der Tann spurred to his side.

"Sire," he cried, "it is unnecessary that you take such grave risks. Your staff is ready and willing to perform such service that you may be preserved to your people and your throne."

"I believe the men fight better when they think their king is watching them," said the American simply.

"I know it, sire," replied Von der Tann, "but even so, Lutha could ill afford to lose you now. I thank God, your majesty, that I have lived to see this day—to see the last of the Rubinroths upholding the glorious traditions of the Rubinroth blood."

Barney led the reserves slowly through the wood to the rear of the extreme left of his line. The attack upon the Austrian right center appeared to be meeting with much greater success than the American dared to hope for. Already, through his glasses, he could see indications that the enemy was concentrating a larger force at this point to repulse the vicious assaults of the Luthanians. To do this they must be drawing from their reserves back of other portions of their line.

It was what Barney had desired. The three bombs from the aeroplane had told him that the Serbians had been sighted three miles away. Already they were engaging the Austrians. He could hear the rattle of rifles and quick-firers and the roar of cannon far to the northeast. And now he gave the word to the commander of the reserve.

At a rapid trot the men moved forward behind the extreme left end of the Luthanian left wing. They were almost upon the Austrians before they emerged from the shelter of the wood, and then with hoarse shouts and leveled bayonets they charged the enemy's position. The fight there was the bloodiest of the two long days. Back and forth the tide of battle surged. In the thick of it rode the false king encouraging his men to greater effort. Slowly at last they bore the Austrians from their trenches. Back and back they bore them until retreat became a rout. The Austrian right was crumpled back upon its center!

Here the enemy made a determined stand; but just before dark a great shouting arose from the heights to their left, where the bulk of their artillery was stationed. Both the Luthanian and Austrian troops engaged in the plain saw Austrian infantry and artillery running down the slopes in disorderly rout. Upon their heads came a cheering line of soldiers firing as they ran, and above them waved the battleflag of Serbia.

A mighty shout rose from the Luthanian ranks—an answering groan from the throats of the Austrians. Hemmed in between the two lines of allies, the Austrians were helpless. Their artillery was captured, retreat cut off. There was but a single alternative to massacre—the white flag.

A few regiments between Lustadt and Blentz, but nearer the latter town, escaped back into Austria, the balance Barney arranged with the Serbian minister to have taken back to Serbia as prisoners of war. The Luthanian army corps that the American had promised the Serbs was to be utilized along the Austrian frontier to prevent the passage of Austrian troops into Serbia through Lutha.

The return to Lustadt after the battle was made through cheering troops and along streets choked with joy-mad citizenry. The name of the soldier-king was upon every tongue. Men went wild with enthusiasm as the tall figure rode slowly through the crowd toward the palace.

Von der Tann, grim and martial, found his lids damp with the moisture of a great happiness. Even now with all the proofs of reality about him, it seemed impossible that this scene could be aught but the ephemeral vapors of a dream—that Leopold of Lutha, the coward, the craven, could have become in a single day the heroic figure that had loomed so large upon the battlefield of Lustadt—the simple, modest gentleman who received the plaudits of his subjects with bowed head and humble mien.

As Barney Custer rode up Margaretha Street toward the royal palace of the kings of Lutha, a dust-covered horseman in the uniform of an officer of the Horse Guards entered Lustadt from the south. It was the young aide of Prince von der Tann's staff, who had been sent to Blentz nearly a week earlier with a message for the king, and who had been captured and held by the Austrians.

During the battle before Lustadt all the Austrian troops had been withdrawn from Blentz and hurried to the front. It was then that the aide had been transferred to the castle, from which he had escaped early that morning. To reach Lustadt he had been compelled to circle the Austrian position, coming to Lustadt from the south.

Once within the city he rode straight to the palace, flung himself from his jaded mount, and entered the left wing of the building—the wing in which the private apartments of the chancellor were located.

Here he inquired for the Princess Emma, learning with evident relief that she was there. A moment later, white with dust, his face streamed with sweat, he was ushered into her presence.

"Your highness," he blurted, "the king's commands have been disregarded—the American is to be shot tomorrow. I have just escaped from Blentz. Peter is furious. He realizes that whether the Austrians win or lose, his standing with the king is gone forever.

"In a fit of rage he has ordered that Mr. Custer be sacrificed to his desire for revenge, in the hope that it will insure for him the favor of the Austrians. Something must be done at once if he is to be saved."

For a moment the girl swayed as though about to fall. The young officer stepped quickly to support her, but before he reached her side she had regained complete mastery of herself. From the street without there rose the blare of trumpets and the cheering of the populace.

Through senses numb with the cold of anguish the meaning of the tumult slowly filtered to her brain—the king had come. He was returning from the battlefield, covered with honors and flushed with glory—the man who was to be her husband; but there was no rejoicing in the heart of the Princess Emma.

Instead, there was a dull ache and impotent rebellion at the injustice of the thing—that Leopold should be reaping these great rewards, while he who had made it possible for him to be a king at all was to die on the morrow because of what he had done to place the Rubinroth upon his throne.

"Perhaps Lieutenant Butzow might find a way," suggested the officer. "He or your father; they are both fond of Mr. Custer."

"Yes," said the girl dully, "see Lieutenant Butzow—he would do the most."

149

The officer bowed and hastened from the apartment in search of Butzow. The girl approached the window and stood there for a long time, looking out at the surging multitude that pressed around the palace gates, filling Margaretha Street with a solid mass of happy faces.

They cheered the king, the chancellor, the army; but most often they cheered the king. From a despised monarch Leopold had risen in a single bound to the position of a national idol.

Repeatedly he was called to the balcony over the grand entrance that the people might feast their eyes on him. The princess wondered how long it was before she herself would be forced to offer her congratulations and, perchance, suffer his caresses. She shivered and cringed at the thought, and then there came a knock upon the door, and in answer to her permission it opened, and the king stood upon the threshold alone.

At a glance the man took in the pain and sorrow mirrored upon the girl's face. He stepped quickly across the room toward her.

"What is it?" he asked. "What is the matter?"

For a moment he had forgotten the part that he had been playing—forgot that the Princess Emma was ignorant of his identity. He had come to her to share with her the happiness of the hour—the glory of the victorious arms of Lutha. For a time he had almost forgotten that he was not the king, and now he was forgetting that he was not Barney Custer to the girl who stood before him with misery and hopelessness writ so large upon her countenance.

For a brief instant the girl did not reply. She was weighing the problematical value of an attempt to enlist the king in the cause of the American. Leopold had shown a spark of magnanimity when he had written a pardon for Mr. Custer; might he not rise again above his petty jealousy and save the American's life? It was a forlorn hope to the woman who knew the true Leopold so well; but it was a hope.

"What is the matter?" the king repeated.

"I have just received word that Prince Peter has ignored your commands, sire," replied the girl, "and that Mr. Custer is to be shot tomorrow."

Barney's eyes went wide with incredulity. Here was a pretty pass, indeed! The princess came close to him and seized his arm.

"You promised, sire," she said, "that he would not be harmed—you gave your royal word. You can save him. You have an army at your command. Do not forget that he once saved you."

The note of appeal in her voice and the sorrow in her eyes gave Barney Custer a twinge of compunction. The necessity for longer concealing his identity in so far as the salvation of Lutha was concerned seemed past; but the American had intended to carry the deception to the end.

He had given the matter much thought, but he could find no grounds for belief that Emma von der Tann would be any happier in the knowledge that her future husband had had nothing to do with the victory of his army. If she was doomed to a life at his side, why not

150

permit her the grain of comfort that she might derive from the memory of her husband's achievements upon the battlefield of Lustadt? Why rob her of that little?

But now, face to face with her, and with the evidence of her suffering so plain before him, Barney's intentions wavered. Like most fighting men, he was tender in his dealings with women. And now the last straw came in the form of a single tiny tear that trickled down the girl's cheek. He seized the hand that lay upon his arm.

"Your highness," he said, "do not grieve for the American. He is not worth it. He has deceived you. He is not at Blentz."

The girl drew her hand from his and straightened to her full height.

"What do you mean, sire?" she exclaimed. "Mr. Custer would not deceive me even if he had an opportunity—which he has not had. But if he is not at Blentz, where is he?"

Barney bowed his head and looked at the floor.

"He is here, your highness, asking your forgiveness," he said.

There was a puzzled expression upon the girl's face as she looked at the man before her. She did not understand. Why should she? Barney drew a diamond ring from his little finger and held it out to her.

"You gave it to me to cut a hole in the window of the garage where I stole the automobile," he said. "I forgot to return it. Now do you know who I am?"

Emma von der Tann's eyes showed her incredulity; then, act by act, she recalled all that this man had said and done since they had escaped from Blentz that had been so unlike the king she knew.

"When did you assume the king's identity?" she asked.

Barney told her all that had transpired in the king's apartments at Blentz before she had been conducted to the king's presence.

"And Leopold is there now?" she asked.

"He is there," replied Barney, "and he is to be shot in the morning."

"Gott!" exclaimed the girl. "What are we to do?"

"There is but one thing to do," replied the American, "and that is for Butzow and me to ride to Blentz as fast as horses will carry us and rescue the king."

"And then?" asked the girl, a shadow crossing her face.

"And then Barney Custer will have to beat it for the boundary," he replied with a sorry smile.

She came quite close to him, laying her hands upon his shoulders.

"I cannot give you up now," she said simply. "I have tried to be loyal to Leopold and the promise that my father made his king when I was only a little girl; but since I thought that you were to be shot, I have wished a thousand times that I had gone with you to America two years ago. Take me with you now, Barney. We can send Lieutenant Butzow to rescue the king, and before he has returned we can be safe across the Serbian frontier."

The American shook his head.

"I got the king into this mess and I must get him out," he said. "He may deserve to be shot, but it is up to me to prevent it, if I can. And there is your father to consider. If Butzow rides to Blentz and rescues the king, it may be difficult to get him back to Lustadt without the truth of his identity and mine becoming known. With me there, the change can be effected easily, and not even Butzow need know what has happened.

"If the people should guess that it was not Leopold who won the battle of Lustadt there might be the devil to pay, and your father would go down along with the throne. No, I must stay until Leopold is safe in Lustadt. But there is a hope for us. I may be able to wrest from Leopold his sanction of our marriage. I shall not hesitate to use threats to get it, and I rather imagine that he will be in such a terror-stricken condition that he will assent to any terms for his release from Blentz. If he gives me such a paper, Emma, will you marry me?"

Perhaps there never had been a stranger proposal than this; but to neither did it seem strange. For two years each had known the love of the other. The girl's betrothal to the king had prevented an avowal of their love while Barney posed in his own identity. Now they merely accepted the conditions that had existed for two years as though a matter of fact which had been often discussed between them.

"Of course I'll marry you," said the princess. "Why in the world would I want you to take me to America otherwise?"

As Barney Custer took her in his arms he was happier than he had ever before been in all his life, and so, too, was the Princess Emma von der Tann.

XII

LEOPOLD WAITS FOR DAWN

After the American had shoved him through the secret doorway into the tower room of the castle of Blentz, Leopold had stood for several minutes waiting for the next command from his captor. Presently, hearing no sound other than that of his own breathing, the king ventured to speak. He asked the American what he purposed doing with him next.

There was no reply. For another minute the king listened intently; then he raised his hands and removed the bandage from his eyes. He looked about him. The room was vacant except for himself. He recognized it as the one in which he had spent ten years of his life as a prisoner. He shuddered. What had become of the American? He approached the door and listened. Beyond the panels he could hear the two soldiers on guard there conversing. He called to them.

"What do you want?" shouted one of the men through the closed door.

"I want Prince Peter!" yelled the king. "Send him at once!"

The soldiers laughed.

"He wants Prince Peter," they mocked. "Wouldn't you rather have us send the king to you?" they asked.

"I am the king!" yelled Leopold. "I am the king! Open the door, pigs, or it will go hard with you! I shall have you both shot in the morning if you do not open the door and fetch Prince Peter."

"Ah!" exclaimed one of the soldiers. "Then there will be three of us shot together."

Leopold went white. He had not connected the sentence of the American with himself; but now, quite vividly, he realized what it might mean to him if he failed before dawn to convince someone that he was not the American. Peter would not be awake at so early an hour, and if he had no better success with others than he was having with these soldiers, it was possible that he might be led out and shot before his identity was discovered. The thing was preposterous. The king's knees became suddenly quite weak. They shook, and his legs gave beneath his weight so that he had to lean against the back of a chair to keep from falling.

Once more he turned to the soldiers. This time he pleaded with them, begging them to carry word to Prince Peter that a terrible mistake had been made, and that it was the king and not the American who was confined in the death chamber. But the soldiers only laughed at him, and finally threatened to come in and beat him if he again interrupted their conversation.

It was a white and shaken prisoner that the officer of the guard found when he entered the room at dawn. The man before him, his face streaked with tears of terror and self-pity, fell upon his knees before him, beseeching him to carry word to Peter of Blentz, that he was the king. The officer drew away with a gesture of disgust.

"I might well believe from your actions that you are Leopold," he said; "for, by Heaven, you do not act as I have always imagined the American would act in the face of danger. He has a reputation for bravery that would suffer could his admirers see him now."

"But I am not the American," pleaded the king. "I tell you that the American came to my apartments last night, overpowered me, forced me to change clothing with him, and then led me back here."

A sudden inspiration came to the king with the memory of all that had transpired during that humiliating encounter with the American.

"I signed a pardon for him!" he cried. "He forced me to do so. If you think I am the American, you cannot kill me now, for there is a pardon signed by the king, and an order for the American's immediate release. Where is it? Do not tell me that Prince Peter did not receive it."

"He received it," replied the officer, "and I am here to acquaint you with the fact, but Prince Peter said nothing about your release. All he told me was that you were not to be shot this morning," and the man emphasized the last two words.

Leopold of Lutha spent two awful days a prisoner at Blentz, not knowing at what moment Prince Peter might see fit to carry out the verdict of the Austrian court martial. He could convince no one that he was the king. Peter would not even grant him an audience. Upon the evening of the third day, word came that the Austrians had been defeated before Lustadt, and those that were not prisoners were retreating through Blentz toward the Austrian frontier.

The news filtered to Leopold's prison room through the servant who brought him his scant and rough fare. The king was utterly disheartened before this word reached him. For the moment he seemed to see a ray of hope, for, since the impostor had been victorious, he would be in a position to force Peter of Blentz to give up the true king.

There was the chance that the American, flushed with success and power, might elect to hold the crown he had seized. Who would guess the transfer that had been effected, or, guessing, would dare voice his suspicions in the face of the power and popularity that Leopold knew such a victory as the impostor had won must have given him in the hearts and minds of the people of Lutha? Still, there was a bare possibility that the American would be as good as his word, and return the crown as he had promised. Though he hated to admit it, the king had every reason to believe that the impostor was a man of honor, whose bare word was as good as another's bond.

He was commencing, under this line of reasoning, to achieve a certain hopeful content when the door to his prison opened and Peter of Blentz, black and scowling, entered. At his elbow was Captain Ernst Maenck.

"Leopold has defeated the Austrians," announced the former. "Until you returned to Lutha he considered the Austrians his best friends. I do not know how you could have reached or influenced him. It is to learn how you accomplished it that I am here. The fact that he signed your pardon indicates that his attitude toward you changed suddenly—almost within an hour. There is something at the bottom of it all, and that something I must know."

"I am Leopold!" cried the king. "Don't you recognize me, Prince Peter? Look at me! Maenck must know me. It was I who wrote and signed the American's pardon—at the point of the American's revolver. He forced me to exchange clothing with him, and then he brought me here to this room and left me."

The two men looked at the speaker and smiled.

"You bank too strongly, my friend," said Peter of Blentz, "upon your resemblance to the king of Lutha. I will admit that it is strong, but not so strong as to convince me of the truth of so improbable a story. How in the world could the American have brought you through the castle, from one end to the other, unseen? There was a guard before the king's door and another before this. No, Herr Custer, you will have to concoct a more plausible tale."

"No," and Peter of Blentz scowled savagely, as though to impress upon his listener the importance of his next utterance, "there were more than you and the king involved in his sudden departure from Blentz and in his hasty change of policy toward Austria. To be quite candid, it seems to me that it may be necessary to my future welfare—vitally necessary, I may say—to know precisely how all this occurred, and just what influence you have over Leopold of Lutha. Who was it that acted as the go-between in the king's negotiations with you, or rather, yours with the king? And what argument did you bring to bear to force Leopold to the action he took?"

"I have told you all that I know about the matter," whined the king. "The American appeared suddenly in my apartment. When he brought me here he first blindfolded me. I have no idea by what route we traveled through the castle, and unless your guards outside this door were bribed they can tell you more about how we got in here than I can—provided we entered through that doorway," and the king pointed to the door which had just opened to admit his two visitors.

"Oh, pshaw!" exclaimed Maenck. "There is but one door to this room—if the king came in here at all, he came through that door."

"Enough!" cried Peter of Blentz. "I shall not be trifled with longer. I shall give you until tomorrow morning to make a full explanation of the truth and to form some plan whereby you may utilize once more whatever influence you had over Leopold to the end that he grant to myself and my associates his royal assurance that our lives and property will be safe in Lutha."

"But I tell you it is impossible," wailed the king.

"I think not," sneered Prince Peter, "especially when I tell you that if you do not accede to my wishes the order of the Austrian military court that sentenced you to death at Burgova will be carried out in the morning."

With his final words the two men turned and left the room. Behind them, upon the floor, inarticulate with terror, knelt Leopold of Lutha, his hands outstretched in supplication.

The long night wore its weary way to dawn at last. The sleepless man, alternately tossing upon his bed and pacing the floor, looked fearfully from time to time at the window through which the lightening of the sky would proclaim the coming day and his last hour on earth. His windows faced the west. At the foot of the hill beneath the castle nestled the village of Blentz, once more enveloped in peaceful silence since the Austrians were gone.

An unmistakable lessening of the darkness in the east had just announced the proximity of day, when the king heard a clatter of horses' hoofs upon the road before the castle. The sound ceased at the gates and a loud voice broke out upon the stillness of the dying night demanding entrance "in the name of the king."

New hope burst aflame in the breast of the condemned man. The impostor had not forsaken him. Leopold ran to the window, leaning far out. He heard the voices of the sentries in the barbican as they conversed with the newcomers. Then silence came, broken only by the rapid footsteps of a soldier hastening from the gate to the castle. His hobnail shoes pounding upon the cobbles of the courtyard echoed among the angles of the lofty walls. When he had entered the castle the silence became oppressive. For five minutes there was no sound other than the pawing of the horses outside the barbican and the subdued conversation of their riders.

Presently the soldier emerged from the castle. With him was an officer. The two went to the barbican. Again there was a parley between the horsemen and the guard. Leopold could hear the officer demanding terms. He would lower the drawbridge and admit them upon conditions.

One of these the king overheard—it concerned an assurance of full pardon for Peter of Blentz and the garrison; and again Leopold heard the officer addressing someone as "your majesty."

Ah, the impostor was there in person. Ach, Gott! How Leopold of Lutha hated him, and yet, in the hands of this American lay not only his throne but his very life as well.

Evidently the negotiations proved unsuccessful for after a time the party wheeled their horses from the gate and rode back toward Blentz. As the sound of the iron-shod hoofs diminished in the distance, with them diminished the hopes of the king.

When they ceased entirely his hopes were at an end, to be supplanted by renewed terror at the turning of the knob of his prison door as it swung open to admit Maenck and a squad of soldiers.

"Come!" ordered the captain. "The king has refused to intercede in your behalf. When he returns with his army he will find your body at the foot of the west wall in the courtyard."

With an ear-piercing shriek that rang through the grim old castle, Leopold of Lutha flung his arms above his head and lunged forward upon his face. Roughly the soldiers seized the unconscious man and dragged him from the room.

Along the corridor they hauled him and down the winding stairs within the north tower to the narrow slit of a door that opened upon the courtyard. To the foot of the west wall they brought him, tossing him brutally to the stone flagging. Here one of the soldiers brought a flagon of water and dashed it in the face of the king. The cold douche returned Leopold to a consciousness of the nearness of his impending fate.

He saw the little squad of soldiers before him. He saw the cold, gray wall behind, and, above, the cold, gray sky of early dawn. The dismal men leaning upon their shadowy guns seemed unearthly specters in the weird light of the hour that is neither God's day nor devil's night. With difficulty two of them dragged Leopold to his feet.

Then the dismal men formed in line before him at the opposite side of the courtyard. Maenck stood to the left of them. He was giving commands. They fell upon the doomed man's ears with all the cruelty of physical blows. Tears coursed down his white cheeks. With incoherent mumblings he begged for his life. Leopold, King of Lutha, trembling in the face of death!

XIII

THE TWO KINGS

Twenty troopers had ridden with Lieutenant Butzow and the false king from Lustadt to Blentz. During the long, hard ride there had been little or no conversation between the American and his friend, for Butzow was still unsuspicious of the true identity of the man who posed as the ruler of Lutha. The lieutenant was all anxiety to reach Blentz and rescue the American he thought imprisoned there and in danger of being shot.

At the gate they were refused admittance unless the king would accept conditions. Barney refused—there was another way to gain entrance to Blentz that not even the master of Blentz knew. Butzow urged him to accede to anything to save the life of the American. He recalled all that the latter had done in the service of Lutha and Leopold. Barney leaned close to the other's ear.

"If they have not already shot him," he whispered, "we shall save the prisoner yet. Let them think that we give up and are returning to Lustadt. Then follow me."

Slowly the little cavalcade rode down from the castle of Blentz toward the village. Just out of sight of the grim pile where the road wound down into a ravine Barney turned his horse's head up the narrow defile. In single file Butzow and the troopers followed until the rank undergrowth precluded farther advance. Here the American directed that they dismount, and, leaving the horses in charge of three troopers, set out once more with the balance of the company on foot.

It was with difficulty that the men forced their way through the bushes, but they had not gone far when their leader stopped before a sheer wall of earth and stone, covered with densely growing shrubbery. Here he groped in the dim light, feeling his way with his hands before him, while at his heels came his followers. At last he separated a wall of bushes and disappeared within the aperture his hands had made. One by one his men followed, finding themselves in inky darkness, but upon a smooth stone floor and with stone walls close upon either hand. Those who lifted their hands above their heads discovered an arched stone ceiling close above them.

Along this buried corridor the "king" led them, for though he had never traversed it himself the Princess Emma had, and from her he had received minute directions. Occasionally he struck a match, and presently in the fitful glare of one of these he and those directly behind him saw the foot of a ladder that disappeared in the Stygian darkness above.

"Follow me up this, very quietly," he said to those behind him. "Up to the third landing."

They did as he bid them. At the third landing Barney felt for the latch he knew was there— he was on familiar ground now. Finding it he pushed open the door it held in place, and through a tiny crack surveyed the room beyond. It was vacant. The American threw the door wide and stepped within. Directly behind him was Butzow, his eyes wide in wonderment. After him filed the troopers until seventeen of them stood behind their lieutenant and the "king."

Through the window overlooking the courtyard came a piteous wailing. Barney ran to the casement and looked out. Butzow was at his side.

"Himmel!" ejaculated the Luthanian. "They are about to shoot him. Quick, your majesty," and without waiting to see if he were followed the lieutenant raced for the door of the apartment. Close behind him came the American and the seventeen.

It took but a moment to reach the stairway down which the rescuers tumbled pell-mell.

Maenck was giving his commands to the firing squad with fiendish deliberation and delay. He seemed to enjoy dragging out the agony that the condemned man suffered. But it was this very cruelty that caused Maenck's undoing and saved the life of Leopold of Lutha. Just before he gave the word to fire Maenck paused and laughed aloud at the pitiable figure trembling and whining against the stone wall before him, and during that pause a commotion arose at the tower doorway behind the firing squad.

Maenck turned to discover the cause of the interruption, and as he turned he saw the figure of the king leaping toward him with leveled revolver. At the king's back a company of troopers of the Royal Horse Guard was pouring into the courtyard.

Maenck snatched his own revolver from his hip and fired point-blank at the "king." The firing squad had turned at the sound of assault from the rear. Some of them discharged their pieces at the advancing troopers. Butzow gave a command and seventeen carbines poured their deadly hail into the ranks of the Blentz retainers. At Maenck's shot the "king" staggered and fell to the pavement.

Maenck leaped across his prostrate form, yelling to his men "Shoot the American." Then he was lost to Barney's sight in the hand-to-hand scrimmage that was taking place. The American tried to regain his feet, but the shock of the wound in his breast had apparently paralyzed him for the moment. A Blentz soldier was running toward the prisoner standing open-mouthed against the wall. The fellow's rifle was raised to his hip—his intention was only too obvious.

Barney drew himself painfully and slowly to one elbow. The man was rapidly nearing the true Leopold. In another moment he would shoot. The American raised his revolver and, taking careful aim, fired. The soldier shrieked, covered his face with his hands, spun around once, and dropped at the king's feet.

The troopers under Butzow were forcing the men of Blentz toward the far end of the courtyard. Two of the Blentz faction were standing a little apart, backing slowly away and at the same time deliberately firing at the king. Barney seemed the only one who noticed them. Once again he raised his revolver and fired. One of the men sat down suddenly, looked vacantly about him, and then rolled over upon his side. The other fired once more at the king and the same instant Barney fired at the soldier. Soldier and king—would-be assassin and his victim—fell simultaneously. Barney grimaced. The wound in his breast was painful. He had done his best to save the king. It was no fault of his that he had failed. It was a long way to Beatrice. He wondered if Emma von der Tann would be on the station platform, awaiting him—then he swooned.

Butzow and his seventeen had it all their own way in the courtyard and castle of Blentz. After the first resistance the soldiery of Peter fled to the guardroom. Butzow followed them, and there they laid down their arms. Then the lieutenant returned to the courtyard to look for the king and Barney Custer. He found them both, and both were wounded. He had them carried to the royal apartments in the north tower. When Barney regained consciousness he found the scowling portrait of the Blentz princess frowning down upon him. He lay upon a great bed where the soldiers, thinking him king, had placed him. Opposite him, against the farther wall, the real king lay upon a cot. Butzow was working over him.

"Not so bad, after all, Barney," the lieutenant was saying. "Only a flesh wound in the calf of the leg."

The king made no reply. He was afraid to declare his identity. First he must learn the intentions of the impostor. He only closed his eyes wearily. Presently he asked a question.

"Is he badly wounded?" and he indicated the figure upon the great bed.

Butzow turned and crossed to where the American lay. He saw that the latter's eyes were open and that he was conscious.

"How does your majesty feel?" he asked. There was more respect in his tone than ever before. One of the Blentz soldiers had told him how the "king," after being wounded by Maenck, had raised himself upon his elbow and saved the prisoner's life by shooting three of his assailants.

"I thought I was done for," answered Barney Custer, "but I rather guess the bullet struck only a glancing blow. It couldn't have entered my lungs, for I neither cough nor spit blood. To tell you the truth, I feel surprisingly fit. How's the prisoner?"

"Only a flesh wound in the calf of his left leg, sire," replied Butzow.

"I am glad," was Barney's only comment. He didn't want to be king of Lutha; but he had foreseen that with the death of the king his imposture might be forced upon him for life.

After Butzow and one of the troopers had washed and dressed the wounds of both men Barney asked them to leave the room.

"I wish to sleep," he said. "If I require you I will ring."

Saluting, the two backed from the apartment. Just as they were passing through the doorway the American called out to Butzow.

"You have Peter of Blentz and Maenck in custody?" he asked.

"I regret having to report to your majesty," replied the officer, "that both must have escaped. A thorough search of the entire castle has failed to reveal them."

Barney scowled. He had hoped to place these two conspirators once and for all where they would never again threaten the peace of the throne of Lutha—in hell. For a moment he lay in thought. Then he addressed the officer again.

"Leave your force here," he said, "to guard us. Ride, yourself, to Lustadt and inform Prince von der Tann that it is the king's desire that every effort be made to capture these two men. Have them brought to Lustadt immediately they are apprehended. Bring them dead or alive."

Again Butzow saluted and prepared to leave the room.

"Wait," said Barney. "Convey our greetings to the Princess von der Tann, and inform her that my wound is of small importance, as is also that of the—Mr. Custer. You may go, lieutenant."

When they were alone Barney turned toward the king. The other lay upon his side glaring at the American. When he caught the latter's eyes upon him he spoke.

159

"What do you intend doing with me?" he said. "Are you going to keep your word and return my identity?"

"I have promised," replied Barney, "and what I promise I always perform."

"Then exchange clothing with me at once," cried the king, half rising from his cot.

"Not so fast, my friend," rejoined the American. "There are a few trifling details to be arranged before we resume our proper personalities."

"Do you realize that you should be hanged for what you have done?" snarled the king. "You assaulted me, stole my clothing, left me here to be shot by Peter, and sat upon my throne in Lustadt while I lay a prisoner condemned to death."

"And do you realize," replied Barney, "that by so doing I saved your foolish little throne for you; that I drove the invaders from your dominions; that I have unmasked your enemies, and that I have once again proven to you that the Prince von der Tann is your best friend and most loyal supporter?"

"You laid your plebeian hands upon me," cried the king, raising his voice. "You humiliated me, and you shall suffer for it."

Barney Custer eyed the king for a long moment before he spoke again. It was difficult to believe that the man was so devoid of gratitude, and so blind as not to see that even the rough treatment that he had received at the American's hands was as nothing by comparison with the service that the American had done him. Apparently Leopold had already forgotten that three times Barney Custer had saved his life in the courtyard below. From the man's demeanor, now that his life was no longer at stake, Barney caught an inkling of what his attitude might be when once again he was returned to the despotic power of his kingship.

"It is futile to reason with you," he said. "There is only one way to handle such as you. At present I hold the power to coerce you, and I shall continue to hold that power until I am safely out of your two-by-four kingdom. If you do as I say you shall have your throne back again. If you refuse, why by Heaven you shall never have it. I'll stay king of Lutha myself."

"What are your terms?" asked the king.

"That Prince Peter of Blentz, Captain Ernst Maenck, and old Von Coblich be tried, convicted, and hanged for high treason," replied the American.

"That is easy," said the king. "I should do so anyway immediately I resumed my throne. Now get up and give me my clothes. Take this cot and I will take the bed. None will know of the exchange."

"Again you are too fast," answered Barney. "There is another condition."

"Well?"

"You must promise upon your royal honor that Ludwig, Prince von der Tann, remain chancellor of Lutha during your life or his."

"Very well," assented the king. "I promise," and again he half rose from his cot.

160

"Hold on a minute," admonished the American; "there is yet one more condition of which I have not made mention."

"What, another?" exclaimed Leopold testily. "How much do you want for returning to me what you have stolen?"

"So far I have asked for nothing for myself," replied Barney. "Now I am coming to that part of the agreement. The Princess Emma von der Tann is betrothed to you. She does not love you. She has honored me with her affection, but she will not wed until she has been formally released from her promise to wed Leopold of Lutha. The king must sign such a release and also a sanction of her marriage to Barney Custer, of Beatrice. Do you understand what I want?"

The king went livid. He came to his feet beside the cot. For the moment, his wound was forgotten. He tottered toward the impostor.

"You scoundrel!" he screamed. "You scoundrel! You have stolen my identity and my throne and now you wish to steal the woman who loves me."

"Don't get excited, Leo," warned the American, "and don't talk so loud. The Princess doesn't love you, and you know it as well as I. She will never marry you. If you want your dinky throne back you'll have to do as I desire; that is, sign the release and the sanction.

"Now let's don't have any heroics about it. You have the proposition. Now I am going to sleep. In the meantime you may think it over. If the papers are not ready when it comes time for us to leave, and from the way I feel now I rather think I shall be ready to mount a horse by morning, I shall ride back to Lustadt as king of Lutha, and I shall marry her highness into the bargain, and you may go hang!

"How the devil you will earn a living with that king job taken away from you I don't know. You're a long way from New York, and in the present state of carnage in Europe I rather doubt that there are many headwaiters jobs open this side of the American metropolis, and I can't for the moment think of anything else at which you would shine—with all due respect to some excellent headwaiters I have known."

For some time the king remained silent. He was thinking. He realized that it lay in the power of the American to do precisely what he had threatened to do. No one would doubt his identity. Even Peter of Blentz had not recognized the real king despite Leopold's repeated and hysterical claims.

Lieutenant Butzow, the American's best friend, had no more suspected the exchange of identities. Von der Tann, too, must have been deceived. Everyone had been deceived. There was no hope that the people, who really saw so little of their king, would guess the deception that was being played upon them. Leopold groaned. Barney opened his eyes and turned toward him.

"What's the matter?" he asked.

"I will sign the release and the sanction of her highness' marriage to you," said the king.

"Good!" exclaimed the American. "You will then go at once to Brosnov as originally planned. I will return to Lustadt and get her highness, and we will immediately leave Lutha via Brosnov. There you and I will effect a change of raiment, and you will ride back to Lustadt with the small guard that accompanies her highness and me to the frontier."

"Why do you not remain in Lustadt?" asked the king. "You could as well be married there as elsewhere."

"Because I don't trust your majesty," replied the American. "It must be done precisely as I say or not at all. Are you agreeable?"

The king assented with a grumpy nod.

"Then get up and write as I dictate," said Barney. Leopold of Lutha did as he was bid. The result was two short, crisply worded documents. At the bottom of each was the signature of Leopold of Lutha. Barney took the two papers and carefully tucked them beneath his pillow.

"Now let's sleep," he said. "It is getting late and we both need the rest. In the morning we have long rides ahead of us. Good night."

The king did not respond. In a short time Barney was fast asleep. The light still burned.

XIV

"THE KING'S WILL IS LAW"

The Blentz princess frowned down upon the king and impostor impartially from her great gilt frame. It must have been close to midnight that the painting moved—just a fraction of an inch. Then it remained motionless for a time. Again it moved. This time it revealed a narrow crack at its edge. In the crack an eye shone.

One of the sleepers moved. He opened his eyes. Stealthily he raised himself on his elbow and gazed at the other across the apartment. He listened intently. The regular breathing of the sleeper proclaimed the soundness of his slumber. Gingerly the man placed one foot upon the floor. The eye glued to the crack at the edge of the great, gilt frame of the Blentz princess remained fastened upon him. He let his other foot slip to the floor beside the first. Carefully he raised himself until he stood erect upon the floor. Then, on tiptoe he started across the room.

The eye in the dark followed him. The man reached the side of the sleeper. Bending over he listened intently to the other's breathing. Satisfied that slumber was profound he stepped quickly to a wardrobe in which a soldier had hung the clothing of both the king and the American. He took down the uniform of the former, casting from time to time apprehensive glances toward the sleeper. The latter did not stir, and the other passed to the little dressing-room adjoining.

A few minutes later he reentered the apartment fully clothed and wearing the accouterments of Leopold of Lutha. In his hand was a drawn sword. Silently and swiftly he crossed to the

162

side of the sleeping man. The eye at the crack beside the gilded frame pressed closer to the aperture. The sword was raised above the body of the slumberer—its point hovered above his heart. The face of the man who wielded it was hard with firm resolve.

His muscles tensed to drive home the blade, but something held his hand. His face paled. His shoulders contracted with a little shudder, and he turned toward the door of the apartment, almost running across the floor in his anxiety to escape. The eye in the dark maintained its unblinking vigilance.

With his hand upon the knob a sudden thought stayed the fugitive's flight. He glanced quickly back at the sleeper—he had not moved. Then the man who wore the uniform of the king of Lutha recrossed the apartment to the bed, reached beneath one of the pillows and withdrew two neatly folded official-looking documents. These he placed in the breastpocket of his uniform. A moment later he was walking down the spiral stairway to the main floor of the castle.

In the guardroom the troopers of the Royal Horse who were not on guard were stretched in slumber. Only a corporal remained awake. As the man entered the guardroom the corporal glanced up, and as his eyes fell upon the newcomer, he sprang to his feet, saluting.

"Turn out the guard!" he cried. "Turn out the guard for his majesty, the king!"

The sleeping soldiers, but half awake, scrambled to their feet, their muscles reacting to the command that their brains but half perceived. They snatched their guns from the racks and formed a line behind the corporal. The king raised his fingers to the vizor of his helmet in acknowledgment of their salute.

"Saddle up quietly, corporal," he said. "We shall ride to Lustadt tonight."

The non-commissioned officer saluted. "And an extra horse for Herr Custer?" he said.

The king shook his head. "The man died of his wound about an hour ago," he said. "While you are saddling up I shall arrange with some of the Blentz servants for his burial—now hurry!"

The corporal marched his troopers from the guardroom toward the stables. The man in the king's clothes touched a bell which was obviously a servant call. He waited impatiently a reply to his summons, tapping his finger-tips against the sword-scabbard that was belted to his side. At last a sleepy-eyed man responded—a man who had grown gray in the service of Peter of Blentz. At sight of the king he opened his eyes in astonishment, pulled his foretop, and bowed uneasily.

"Come closer," whispered the king. The man did so, and the king spoke in his ear earnestly, but in scarce audible tones. The eyes of the listener narrowed to mere slits—of avarice and cunning, cruelly cold and calculating. The speaker searched through the pockets of the king's clothes that covered him. At last he withdrew a roll of bills. The amount must have been a large one, but he did not stop to count it. He held the money under the eyes of the servant. The fellow's claw-like fingers reached for the tempting wealth. He nodded his head affirmatively.

"You may trust me, sire," he whispered.

The king slipped the money into the other's palm. "And as much more," he said, "when I receive proof that my wishes have been fulfilled."

"Thank you, sire," said the servant.

The king looked steadily into the other's face before he spoke again.

"And if you fail me," he said, "may God have mercy on your soul." Then he wheeled and left the guardroom, walking out into the courtyard where the soldiers were busy saddling their mounts.

A few minutes later the party clattered over the drawbridge and down the road toward Blentz and Lustadt. From a window of the apartments of Peter of Blentz a man watched them depart. When they passed across a strip of moonlit road, and he had counted them, he smiled with relief.

A moment later he entered a panel beside the huge fireplace in the west wall and disappeared. There he struck a match, found a candle and lighted it. Walking a few steps he came to a figure sleeping upon a pile of clothing. He stooped and shook the sleeper by the shoulder.

"Wake up!" he cried in a subdued voice. "Wake up, Prince Peter; I have good news for you."

The other opened his eyes, stretched, and at last sat up.

"What is it, Maenck?" he asked querulously.

"Great news, my prince," replied the other.

"While you have been sleeping many things have transpired within the walls of your castle. The king's troopers have departed; but that is a small matter compared with the other. Here, behind the portrait of your great-grandmother, I have listened and watched all night. I opened the secret door a fraction of an inch—just enough to permit me to look into the apartment where the king and the American lay wounded. They had been talking as I opened the door, but after that they ceased—the king falling asleep at once—the American feigning slumber. For a long time I watched, but nothing happened until near midnight. Then the American arose and donned the king's clothes.

"He approached Leopold with drawn sword, but when he would have thrust it through the heart of the sleeping man his nerve failed him. Then he stole some papers from the room and left. Just now he has ridden out toward Lustadt with the men of the Royal Horse who captured the castle yesterday."

Before Maenck was half-way through his narrative, Peter of Blentz was wide awake and all attention. His eyes glowed with suddenly aroused interest.

"Somewhere in this, prince," concluded Maenck, "there must lie the seed of fortune for you and me."

Peter nodded. "Yes," he mused, "there must."

For a time both men were buried in thought. Suddenly Maenck snapped his fingers. "I have it!" he cried. He bent toward Prince Peter's ear and whispered his plan. When he was done the Blentz prince grasped his hand.

"Just the thing, Maenck!" he cried. "Just the thing. Leopold will never again listen to idle gossip directed against our loyalty. If I know him—and who should know him better—he will heap honors upon you, my Maenck; and as for me, he will at least forgive me and take me back into his confidence. Lose no time now, my friend. We are free now to go and come, since the king's soldiers have been withdrawn."

In the garden back of the castle an old man was busy digging a hole. It was a long, narrow hole, and, when it was completed, nearly four feet deep. It looked like a grave. When he had finished the old man hobbled to a shed that leaned against the south wall. Here were boards, tools, and a bench. It was the castle workshop. The old man selected a number of rough pine boards. These he measured and sawed, fitted and nailed, working all the balance of the night. By dawn, he had a long, narrow box, just a trifle smaller than the hole he had dug in the garden. The box resembled a crude coffin. When it was quite finished, including a cover, he dragged it out into the garden and set it upon two boards that spanned the hole, so that it rested precisely over the excavation.

All these precautions methodically made, he returned to the castle. In a little storeroom he searched for and found an ax. With his thumb he felt of the edge—for an ax it was marvelously sharp. The old fellow grinned and shook his head, as one who appreciates in anticipation the consummation of a good joke. Then he crept noiselessly through the castle's corridors and up the spiral stairway in the north tower. In one hand was the sharp ax.

The moment Lieutenant Butzow had reached Lustadt he had gone directly to Prince von der Tann; but the moment his message had been delivered to the chancellor he sought out the chancellor's daughter, to tell her all that had occurred at Blentz.

"I saw but little of Mr. Custer," he said. "He was very quiet. I think all that he has been through has unnerved him. He was slightly wounded in the left leg. The king was wounded in the breast. His majesty conducted himself in a most valiant and generous manner. Wounded, he lay upon his stomach in the courtyard of the castle and defended Mr. Custer, who was, of course, unarmed. The king shot three of Prince Peter's soldiers who were attempting to assassinate Mr. Custer."

Emma von der Tann smiled. It was evident that Lieutenant Butzow had not discovered the deception that had been practiced upon him in common with all Lutha—she being the only exception. It seemed incredible that this good friend of the American had not seen in the heroism of the man who wore the king's clothes the attributes and ear-marks of Barney Custer. She glowed with pride at the narration of his heroism, though she suffered with him because of his wound.

It was not yet noon when the detachment of the Royal Horse arrived in Lustadt from Blentz. At their head rode one whom all upon the streets of the capital greeted enthusiastically as king. The party rode directly to the royal palace, and the king retired immediately to his apartments. A half hour later an officer of the king's household knocked upon the door of the Princess Emma von der Tann's boudoir. In accord with her summons he entered, saluted respectfully, and handed her a note.

165

It was written upon the personal stationary of Leopold of Lutha. The girl read and reread it. For some time she could not seem to grasp the enormity of the thing that had overwhelmed her—the daring of the action that the message explained. The note was short and to the point, and was signed only with initials.

DEAREST EMMA:

The king died of his wounds just before midnight. I shall keep the throne. There is no other way. None knows and none must ever know the truth. Your father alone may suspect; but if we are married at once our alliance will cement him and his faction to us. Send word by the bearer that you agree with the wisdom of my plan, and that we may be wed at once—this afternoon, in fact.

The people may wonder for a few days at the strange haste, but my answer shall be that I am going to the front with my troops. The son and many of the high officials of the Kaiser have already established the precedent, marrying hurriedly upon the eve of their departure for the front.

With every assurance of my undying love, believe me,

Yours,
B. C.

The girl walked slowly across the room to her writing table. The officer stood in respectful silence awaiting the answer that the king had told him to bring. The princess sat down before the carved bit of furniture. Mechanically she drew a piece of note paper from a drawer. Many times she dipped her pen in the ink before she could determine what reply to send. Ages of ingrained royalistic principles were shocked and shattered by the enormity of the thing the man she loved had asked of her, and yet cold reason told her that it was the only way.

Lutha would be lost should the truth be known—that the king was dead, for there was no heir of closer blood connection with the royal house than Prince Peter of Blentz, whose great-grandmother had been a Rubinroth princess. Slowly, at last, she wrote as follows:

SIRE:

The king's will is law.

EMMA

That was all. Placing the note in an envelope she sealed it and handed it to the officer, who bowed and left the room.

A half hour later officers of the Royal Horse were riding through the streets of Lustadt. Some announced to the people upon the streets the coming marriage of the king and princess. Others rode to the houses of the nobility with the king's command that they be present at the ceremony in the old cathedral at four o'clock that afternoon.

Never had there been such bustling about the royal palace or in the palaces of the nobles of Lutha. The buzz and hum of excited conversation filled the whole town. That the choice of the king met the approval of his subjects was more than evident. Upon every lip was praise

166

and love of the Princess Emma von der Tann. The future of Lutha seemed assured with a king who could fight joined in marriage to a daughter of the warrior line of Von der Tann.

The princess was busy up to the last minute. She had not seen her future husband since his return from Blentz, for he, too, had been busy. Twice he had sent word to her, but on both occasions had regretted that he could not come personally because of the pressure of state matters and the preparations for the ceremony that was to take place in the cathedral in so short a time.

At last the hour arrived. The cathedral was filled to overflowing. After the custom of Lutha, the bride had walked alone up the broad center aisle to the foot of the chancel. Guardsmen lining the way on either hand stood rigidly at salute until she stopped at the end of the soft, rose-strewn carpet and turned to await the coming of the king.

Presently the doors at the opposite end of the cathedral opened. There was a fanfare of trumpets, and up the center aisle toward the waiting girl walked the royal groom. It seemed ages to the princess since she had seen her lover. Her eyes devoured him as he approached her. She noticed that he limped, and wondered; but for a moment the fact carried no special suggestion to her brain.

The people had risen as the king entered. Again, the pieces of the guardsmen had snapped to present; but silence, intense and utter, reigned over the vast assembly. The only movement was the measured stride of the king as he advanced to claim his bride.

At the head of each line of guardsmen, nearest the chancel and upon either side of the bridal party, the ranks were formed of commissioned officers. Butzow was among them. He, too, out of the corner of his eye watched the advancing figure. Suddenly he noted the limp, and gave a little involuntary gasp. He looked at the Princess Emma, and saw her eyes suddenly widen with consternation.

Slowly at first, and then in a sudden tidal wave of memory, Butzow's story of the fight in the courtyard at Blentz came back to her.

"I saw but little of Mr. Custer," he had said. "He was slightly wounded in the left leg. The king was wounded in the breast." But Lieutenant Butzow had not known the true identity of either.

The real Leopold it was who had been wounded in the left leg, and the man who was approaching her up the broad cathedral aisle was limping noticeably—and favoring his left leg. The man to whom she was to be married was not Barney Custer—he was Leopold of Lutha!

A hundred mad schemes rioted through her brain. The wedding must not go on! But how was she to avert it? The king was within a few paces of her now. There was a smile upon his lips, and in that smile she saw the final confirmation of her fears. When Leopold of Lutha smiled his upper lip curved just a trifle into a shadow of a sneer. It was a trivial characteristic that Barney Custer did not share in common with the king.

Half mad with terror, the girl seized upon the only subterfuge which seemed at all likely to succeed. It would, at least, give her a slight reprieve—a little time in which to think, and possibly find an avenue from her predicament.

She staggered forward a step, clapped her two hands above her heart, and reeled as though to fall. Butzow, who had been watching her narrowly, sprang forward and caught her in his arms, where she lay limp with closed eyes as though in a dead faint. The king ran forward. The people craned their necks. A sudden burst of exclamations rose throughout the cathedral, and then Lieutenant Butzow, shouldering his way past the chancel, carried the Princess Emma to a little anteroom off the east transept. Behind him walked the king, the bishop, and Prince Ludwig.

XV

MAENCK BLUNDERS

After a hurried breakfast Peter of Blentz and Captain Ernst Maenck left the castle of Blentz. Prince Peter rode north toward the frontier, Austria, and safety, Captain Maenck rode south toward Lustadt. Neither knew that general orders had been issued to soldiery and gendarmerie of Lutha to capture them dead or alive. So Prince Peter rode carelessly; but Captain Maenck, because of the nature of his business and the proximity of enemies about Lustadt, proceeded with circumspection.

Prince Peter was arrested at Tafelberg, and, though he stormed and raged and threatened, he was immediately packed off under heavy guard back toward Lustadt.

Captain Ernst Maenck was more fortunate. He reached the capital of Lutha in safety, though he had to hide on several occasions from detachments of troops moving toward the north. Once within the city he rode rapidly to the house of a friend. Here he learned that which set him into a fine state of excitement and profanity. The king and the Princess Emma von der Tann were to be wed that very afternoon! It lacked but half an hour to four o'clock.

Maenck grabbed his cap and dashed from the house before his astonished friend could ask a single question. He hurried straight toward the cathedral. The king had just arrived, and entered when Maenck came up, breathless. The guard at the doorway did not recognize him. If they had they would have arrested him. Instead they contented themselves with refusing him admission, and when he insisted they threatened him with arrest.

To be arrested now would be to ruin his fine plan, so he turned and walked away. At the first cross street he turned up the side of the cathedral. The grounds were walled up on this side, and he sought in vain for entrance. At the rear he discovered a limousine standing in the alley where its chauffeur had left it after depositing his passengers at the front door of the cathedral. The top of the limousine was but a foot or two below the top of the wall.

Maenck clambered to the hood of the machine, and from there to the top. A moment later he dropped to the earth inside the cathedral grounds. Before him were many windows. Most of them were too high for him to reach, and the others that he tried at first were securely fastened. Passing around the end of the building, he at last discovered one that was open—it led into the east transept.

Maenck crawled through. He was within the building that held the man he sought. He found himself in a small room—evidently a dressing-room. There were two doors leading from it. He approached one and listened. He heard the tones of subdued conversation beyond.

Very cautiously he opened the door a crack. He could not believe the good fortune that was revealed before him. On a couch lay the Princess Emma von der Tann. Beside her her father. At the door was Lieutenant Butzow. The bishop and a doctor were talking at the head of the couch. Pacing up and down the room, resplendent in the marriage robes of a king of Lutha, was the man he sought.

Maenck drew his revolver. He broke the barrel, and saw that there was a good cartridge in each chamber of the cylinder. He closed it quietly. Then he threw open the door, stepped into the room, took deliberate aim, and fired.

The old man with the ax moved cautiously along the corridor upon the second floor of the Castle of Blentz until he came to a certain door. Gently he turned the knob and pushed the door inward. Holding the ax behind his back, he entered. In his pocket was a great roll of money, and there was to be an equal amount waiting him at Lustadt when his mission had been fulfilled.

Once within the room, he looked quickly about him. Upon a great bed lay the figure of a man asleep. His face was turned toward the opposite wall away from the side of the bed nearer the menacing figure of the old servant. On tiptoe the man with the ax approached. The neck of his victim lay uncovered before him. He swung the ax behind him. A single blow, as mighty as his ancient muscles could deliver, would suffice.

Barney Custer opened his eyes. Directly opposite him upon the wall was a dark-toned photogravure of a hunting scene. It tilted slightly forward upon its wire support. As Barney's eyes opened it chanced that they were directed straight upon the shiny glass of the picture. The light from the window struck the glass in such a way as to transform it into a mirror. The American's eyes were glued with horror upon the reflection that he saw there—an old man swinging a huge ax down upon his head.

It is an open question as to which of the two was the most surprised at the cat-like swiftness of the movement that carried Barney Custer out of that bed and landed him in temporary safety upon the opposite side.

With a snarl the old man ran around the foot of the bed to corner his prey between the bed and the wall. He was swinging the ax as though to hurl it. So close was he that Barney guessed it would be difficult for him to miss his mark. The least he could expect would be a frightful wound. To have attempted to escape would have necessitated turning his back to his adversary, inviting instant death. To grapple with a man thus armed appeared an equally hopeless alternative.

Shoulder-high beside him hung the photogravure that had already saved his life once. Why not again? He snatched it from its hangings, lifted it above his head in both hands, and hurled it at the head of the old man. The glass shattered full upon the ancient's crown, the man's head went through the picture, and the frame settled over his shoulders. At the same instant Barney Custer leaped across the bed, seized a light chair, and turned to face his foe upon more even terms.

The old man did not pause to remove the frame from about his neck. Blood trickled down his forehead and cheeks from deep gashes that the broken glass had made. Now he was in a berserker rage.

As he charged again he uttered a peculiar whistling noise from between his set teeth. To the American it sounded like the hissing of a snake, and as he would have met a snake he met the venomous attack of the old man.

When the short battle was over the Blentz servitor lay unconscious upon the floor, while above him leaned the American, uninjured, ripping long strips from a sheet torn from the bed, twisting them into rope-like strands and, with them, binding the wrists and ankles of his defeated foe. Finally he stuffed a gag between the toothless gums.

Running to the wardrobe, he discovered that the king's uniform was gone. That, with the witness of the empty bed, told him the whole story. The American smiled. "More nerve than I gave him credit for," he mused, as he walked back to his bed and reached under the pillow for the two papers he had forced the king to sign. They, too, were gone. Slowly Barney Custer realized his plight, as there filtered through his mind a suggestion of the possibilities of the trick that had been played upon him.

Why should Leopold wish these papers? Of course, he might merely have taken them that he might destroy them; but something told Barney Custer that such was not the case. And something, too, told him whither the king had ridden and what he would do there when he arrived.

He ran back to the wardrobe. In it hung the peasant attire that he had stolen from the line of the careless house frau, and later wished upon his majesty the king. Barney grinned as he recalled the royal disgust with which Leopold had fingered the soiled garments. He scarce blamed him. Looking further toward the back of the wardrobe, the American discovered other clothing.

He dragged it all out upon the floor. There was an old shooting jacket, several pairs of trousers and breeches, and a hunting coat. In a drawer at the bottom of the wardrobe he found many old shoes, puttees, and boots.

From this miscellany he selected riding breeches, a pair of boots, and the red hunting coat as the only articles that fitted his rather large frame. Hastily he dressed, and, taking the ax the old man had brought to the room as the only weapon available, he walked boldly into the corridor, down the spiral stairway and into the guardroom.

Barney Custer was prepared to fight. He was desperate. He could have slunk from the Castle of Blentz as he had entered it—through the secret passageway to the ravine; but to attempt to reach Lustadt on foot was not at all compatible with the urgent haste that he felt necessary. He must have a horse, and a horse he would have if he had to fight his way through a Blentz army.

But there were no armed retainers left at Blentz. The guardroom was vacant; but there were arms there and ammunition. Barney commandeered a sword and a revolver, then he walked into the courtyard and crossed to the stables. The way took him by the garden. In it he saw a coffin-like box resting upon planks above a grave-like excavation. Barney investigated. The box was empty. Once again he grinned. "It is not always wise," he mused, "to count your corpses before they're dead. What a lot of work the old man might have spared himself if he'd only caught his cadaver first—or at least tried to."

Passing on by his own grave, he came to the stables. A groom was currying a strong, clean-limbed hunter haltered in the doorway. The man looked up as Barney approached him. A puzzled expression entered the fellow's eyes. He was a young man—a stupid-looking lout. It was evident that he half recognized the face of the newcomer as one he had seen before. Barney nodded to him.

"Never mind finishing," he said. "I am in a hurry. You may saddle him at once." The voice was authoritative—it brooked no demur. The groom touched his forehead, dropped the currycomb and brush, and turned back into the stable to fetch saddle and bridle.

Five minutes later Barney was riding toward the gate. The portcullis was raised—the drawbridge spanned the moat—no guard was there to bar his way. The sunlight flooded the green valley, stretching lazily below him in the soft warmth of a mellow autumn morning. Behind him he had left the brooding shadows of the grim old fortress—the cold, cruel, depressing stronghold of intrigue, treason, and sudden death.

He threw back his shoulders and filled his lungs with the sweet, pure air of freedom. He was a new man. The wound in his breast was forgotten. Lightly he touched his spurs to the hunter's sides. Tossing his head and curveting, the animal broke into a long, easy trot. Where the road dipped into the ravine and down through the village to the valley the rider drew his restless mount into a walk; but, once in the valley, he let him out. Barney took the short road to Lustadt. It would cut ten miles off the distance that the main wagonroad covered, and it was a good road for a horseman. It should bring him to Lustadt by one o'clock or a little after. The road wound through the hills to the east of the main highway, and was scarcely more than a trail where it crossed the Ru River upon a narrow bridge that spanned the deep mountain gorge that walls the Ru for ten miles through the hills.

When Barney reached the river his hopes sank. The bridge was gone—dynamited by the Austrians in their retreat. The nearest bridge was at the crossing of the main highway over ten miles to the southwest. There, too, the river might be forded even if the Austrians had destroyed that bridge also; but here or elsewhere in the hills there could be no fording—the banks of the Ru were perpendicular cliffs.

The misfortune would add nearly twenty miles to his journey—he could not now hope to reach Lustadt before late in the afternoon. Turning his horse back along the trail he had come, he retraced his way until he reached a narrow bridle path that led toward the southwest. The trail was rough and indistinct, yet he pushed forward, even more rapidly than safety might have suggested. The noble beast beneath him was all loyalty and ambition.

"Take it easy, old boy," whispered Barney into the slim, pointed ears that moved ceaselessly backward and forward, "you'll get your chance when we strike the highway, never fear."

And he did.

So unexpected had been Maenck's entrance into the room in the east transept, so sudden his attack, that it was all over before a hand could be raised to stay him. At the report of his revolver the king sank to the floor. At almost the same instant Lieutenant Butzow whipped a revolver from beneath his tunic and fired at the assassin. Maenck staggered forward and stumbled across the body of the king. Butzow was upon him instantly, wresting the revolver

171

from his fingers. Prince Ludwig ran to the king's side and, kneeling there, raised Leopold's head in his arms. The bishop and the doctor bent over the limp form. The Princess Emma stood a little apart. She had leaped from the couch where she had been lying. Her eyes were wide in horror. Her palms pressed to her cheeks.

It was upon this scene that a hatless, dust-covered man in a red hunting coat burst through the door that had admitted Maenck. The man had seen and recognized the conspirator as he climbed to the top of the limousine and dropped within the cathedral grounds, and he had followed close upon his heels.

No one seemed to note his entrance. All ears were turned toward the doctor, who was speaking.

"The king is dead," he said.

Maenck raised himself upon an elbow. He spoke feebly.

"You fools," he cried. "That man was not the king. I saw him steal the king's clothes at Blentz and I followed him here. He is the American—the impostor." Then his eyes, circling the faces about him to note the results of his announcements, fell upon the face of the man in the red hunting coat. Amazement and wonder were in his face. Slowly he raised his finger and pointed.

"There is the king," he said.

Every eye turned in the direction he indicated. Exclamations of surprise and incredulity burst from every lip. The old chancellor looked from the man in the red hunting coat to the still form of the man upon the floor in the blood-spattered marriage garments of a king of Lutha. He let the king's head gently down upon the carpet, and then he rose to his feet and faced the man in the red hunting coat.

"Who are you?" he demanded.

Before Barney could speak Lieutenant Butzow spoke.

"He is the king, your highness," he said. "I rode with him to Blentz to free Mr. Custer. Both were wounded in the courtyard in the fight that took place there. I helped to dress their wounds. The king was wounded in the breast—Mr. Custer in the left leg."

Prince von der Tann looked puzzled. Again he turned his eyes questioningly toward the newcomer.

"Is this the truth?" he asked.

Barney looked toward the Princess Emma. In her eyes he could read the relief that the sight of him alive had brought her. Since she had recognized the king she had believed that Barney was dead. The temptation was great—he dreaded losing her, and he feared he would lose her when her father learned the truth of the deception that had been practiced upon him. He might lose even more—men had lost their heads for tampering with the affairs of kings.

"Well?" persisted the chancellor.

172

"Lieutenant Butzow is partially correct—he honestly believes that he is entirely so," replied the American. "He did ride with me from Lustadt to Blentz to save the man who lies dead here at your feet. The lieutenant thought that he was riding with his king, just as your highness thought that he was riding with his king during the battle of Lustadt. You were both wrong—you were riding with Mr. Bernard Custer, of Beatrice. I am he. I have no apologies to make. What I did I would do again. I did it for Lutha and for the woman I love. She knows and the king knew that I intended restoring his identity to him with no one the wiser for the interchange that had taken place. The king upset my plans by stealing back his identity while I slept, with the result that you see before you upon the floor. He has died as he had lived—futilely."

As he spoke the Princess Emma had crossed the room toward him. Now she stood at his side, her hand in his. Tense silence reigned in the apartment. The old chancellor stood with bowed head, buried in thought. All eyes were upon him except those of the doctor, who had turned his attention from the dead king to the wounded assassin. Butzow stood looking at Barney Custer in open relief and admiration. He had been trying to vindicate his friend in his own mind ever since he had discovered, as he believed, that Barney had tricked Leopold after the latter had saved his life at Blentz and ridden to Lustadt in the king's guise. Now that he knew the whole truth he realized how stupid he had been not to guess that the man who had led the victorious Luthanian army before Lustadt could not have been the cowardly Leopold.

Presently the chancellor broke the silence.

"You say that Leopold of Lutha lived futilely. You are right; but when you say that he has died futilely, you are, I believe, wrong. Living, he gave us a poor weakling. Dying, he leaves the throne to a brave man, in whose veins flows the blood of the Rubinroths, hereditary rulers of Lutha.

"You are the only rightful successor to the throne of Lutha," he argued, "other than Peter of Blentz. Your mother's marriage to a foreigner did not bar the succession of her offspring. Aside from the fact that Peter of Blentz is out of the question, is the more important fact that your line is closer to the throne than his. He knew it, and this knowledge was the real basis of his hatred of you."

As the old chancellor ceased speaking he drew his sword and raised it on high above his head.

"The king is dead," he said. "Long live the king!"

XVI

KING OF LUTHA

Barney Custer, of Beatrice, had no desire to be king of Lutha. He lost no time in saying so. All that he wanted of Lutha was the girl he had found there, as his father before him had found the girl of his choice. Von der Tann pleaded with him.

"Twice have I fought under you, sire," he urged. "Twice, and only twice since the old king died, have I felt that the future of Lutha was safe in the hands of her ruler, and both these

173

times it was you who sat upon the throne. Do not desert us now. Let me live to see Lutha once more happy, with a true Rubinroth upon the throne and my daughter at his side."

Butzow added his pleas to those of the old chancellor. The American hesitated.

"Let us leave it to the representatives of the people and to the house of nobles," he suggested.

The chancellor of Lutha explained the situation to both houses. Their reply was unanimous. He carried it to the American, who awaited the decision of Lutha in the royal apartments of the palace. With him was the Princess Emma von der Tann.

"The people of Lutha will have no other king, sire," said the old man.

Barney turned toward the girl.

"There is no other way, my lord king," she said with grave dignity. "With her blood your mother bequeathed you a duty which you may not shirk. It is not for you or for me to choose. God chose for you when you were born."

Barney Custer took her hand in his and raised it to his lips.

"Let the King of Lutha," he said, "be the first to salute Lutha's queen."

And so Barney Custer, of Beatrice, was crowned King of Lutha, and Emma became his queen. Maenck died of his wound on the floor of the little room in the east transept of the cathedral of Lustadt beside the body of the king he had slain. Prince Peter of Blentz was tried by the highest court of Lutha on the charge of treason; he was found guilty and hanged. Von Coblich committed suicide on the eve of his arrest. Lieutenant Otto Butzow was ennobled and given the confiscated estates of the Blentz prince. He became a general in the army of Lutha, and was sent to the front in command of the army corps that guarded the northern frontier of the little kingdom.

Note from the Editor

Odin's Library Classics strives to bring you unedited and unabridged works of classical literature. As such this is the complete and unabridged version of the original English text. The English language has evolved since the writing and some of the words appear in their original form, or at least the most commonly used form at the time. This is done to protect the original intent of the author. If at any time you are unsure of the meaning of a word, please do your research on the etymology of that word. It is important to preserve the history of the English language.

Taylor Anderson

Made in the USA
Columbia, SC
14 December 2020